THE UNTIDY PILGRIM

D0862668

A Deep South Book

OTHER BOOKS BY EUGENE WALTER

FICTION
Jennie the Watercress Girl
Love You Good, See You Later
The Likes of Which
The Byzantine Riddle

POETRY
Monkey Poems
Shapes of the River
The Pokeweed Alphabet
The Pack Rat
Lizard Fever

COOKBOOKS
American Cooking: Southern Style
Delectable Dishes from Termite Hall
Hints and Pinches

The

UNTIDY PILGRIM

Eugene Walter

With an Introduction
by Katherine Clark

THE UNIVERSITY OF ALABAMA PRESS
Tuscaloosa and London

Introduction copyright © 2001
The University of Alabama Press
Tuscaloosa, Alabama 35487-0380
All rights reserved
Manufactured in the United States of America

The four phrases which serve as subtitles for the four sections of this
novel are drawn from poems in *The Ego and the Centaur* by Jean Garrigue,
and are used by permission of the author and the publisher,
New Directions, 333 Sixth Avenue, New York 14, N.Y.

The lines beginning ". . . our wandering psalms" are from a poem, "This
Day Is Not Like That Day," by the same author. Grateful acknowledgment is
made to Miss Garrigue, and to the editor of *Botteghe Oscure,*
in which biannual the poem originally appeared.

The other two verse fragments are from the *Hesperides* of Robert Herrick.

1 3 5 7 9 8 6 4 2
02 04 06 08 09 07 05 03 01

∞

The paper on which this book is printed meets the minimum requirements
of American National Standard for Information Science–Permanence of
Paper for Printed Library Materials, ANSI Z39.48-1984.

Library of Congress Cataloging-in-Publication Data

Walter, Eugene, 1921–
The untidy pilgrim / Eugene Walter ; with an
introduction by Katherine Clark.
p. cm. — (Deep South Books)
ISBN 0-8173-1143-2 (pbk. : alk. paper)
1. Mobile (Ala.)—Fiction. 2. Law students—Fiction.
3. Young men—Fiction. I. Title.
PS3573.A47228 U5 2001
813'.54—dc21
2001027909

British Library Cataloguing-in-Publication Data available

CONTENTS

THE UNTIDY PILGRIM

INTRODUCTION

Mobile Madness

Eugene Walter loved to say about his beloved hometown of Mobile that it was "not North America; it was North Haiti." He also loved that ancient concept of the "salt line," which delineates the coastal region of the Southern states. For Eugene, the salt line defined the south of the South, what he liked to call a "separate kingdom," a different world, a different people, a different culture, and a different ethos from the rest of the South.

Eugene Walter's first novel, *The Untidy Pilgrim,* is about a young man from a small central Alabama town who moves south of the salt line, to Mobile, in order to begin making his way in the world and achieve the American dream of success through hard work. But as soon as this unnamed untidy pilgrim arrives in Mobile, he realizes that—although he is still in Alabama—he has entered a separate physical kingdom of banana trees and palm trees, subtropical heat and humidity, old houses and lacy wrought-iron balconies. It does not take him long to realize also that this separate physical kingdom brings with it a separate state of mind: a different mental, emotional, and spiritual kingdom as well.

The novel traces what happens to this young man once he enters this "kingdom of monkeys, the land of clowns," and "sweet lunacy's county seat." Our pilgrim/narrator begins his story by quoting an old saying about Mobile, that "you were never the same after living there." Ostensibly, the purpose of his narrative is to explain how this "kingdom of monkeys" brought about a revolutionary change in himself and his life.

Like many small-town Alabama pilgrims, our pilgrim comes to Mobile (the Big City), to get started on what would seem to be his career path. During the day he works at a bank while at night he studies law. Obviously he is a hard-working, studious, get-ahead young man, because his cousin Lola—with whose family he boards—

objects strenuously to the way he closets himself with his books every night. "'Don't you ever just *play*?'" she complains. "'Don't you ever give yourself an evening off?'" Greatly irritated by the disturbances and interruptions Lola brings in her wake, our pilgrim soon finds other lodgings where he can study in peace. Or so he thinks.

Despite the best intentions of this conscientious young man determined to "make it" in the big city, his career path and life plan prove unworkable in Mobile. As soon as he arrives in this lush, tropical city, our pilgrim begins to encounter the erratic, the erotic, the eccentric, and the exotic. These forces immediately begin to undermine and subvert his straight and narrow life ambitions. In the land of clowns and the kingdom of monkeys—in the town that can claim the oldest Mardi Gras in America—there is no Puritan work ethic. The only ruling forces in this separate kingdom are those of chaos, craziness, and caprice, which his landlady, Miss Fiffy, calls "the Three-Eyed Goddess." These are forces not of rule but of misrule, and these are the forces which overtake our pilgrim, seduce him away from the beaten career path, and set him on what he calls his "zigzag course" through life.

The purveyors of these forces of misrule are the Mobilians themselves, whom our pilgrim calls "monkeys." Anyone who knew Eugene knew that the monkey was his favorite animal, and it was not hard to figure out why. Like Eugene, the monkey is a creature of subtropical climates, noted for its high-jinks and high spirits. These are the qualities Eugene celebrates in his *Monkey Poems,* and these are the qualities exemplified by the Mobilians in his novel.

The first "monkey" encountered is Lola, who complains of her young male cousin's studiousness and is forever trying to make him her companion in fun and games. Her constant flirting, along with her outrageous ploys to attract his attention—"clacking to the bathroom in her old pink wrapper that didn't hide one thing she had"— at first only annoy and anger our pilgrim, so much so that he seeks another place to live.

Lola is an airhead, a flirt, a bit of a husband-hunter, a typical "Southern girl" without a thought in her head except for things like her "Dark Chrysanthemum" lipstick, but our pilgrim has a lot to learn from her fun-loving, carefree, happy-go-lucky approach to life. Most importantly, he learns to be amused, not annoyed, by the comic spectacle she presents, not even if, but especially if, it interrupts his daily grind. Learning how to "laugh out loud" is perhaps "the moral" of our pilgrim's story, as he hints at the beginning.

The "monkey" who makes the most significant contribution to our pilgrim's life is Miss Fiffy, his landlady. She is the quintessential batty old lady, living alone downtown with her servants in a somewhat gone-to-seed three-story mansion "with high iron porches painted white." Former Queen of Mardi Gras, Miss Fiffy is the reigning queen of all chaos, craziness, and caprice in the novel. At age seventy-plus, Miss Fiffy still has "sweet anarchy in her soul." Everything around her is in anarchy as well. "Her hair was like a hurricane, for all the dozen combs like a flotilla of storm-threatened fishing boats." Instead of having a garden, she has what she calls a "private jungle," in which her weeds are as precious as her "fancy" flowers.

Shortly after he moves in, our pilgrim offers to fix Miss Fiffy's third step, which "was wobbly and clanged like a firebell when you stepped there." Much to his surprise, Miss Fiffy adamantly refuses this favor, and cites as one of her reasons a "delight in disorder." This delight in a carefully preserved and cultivated disorder—like that in Miss Fiffy's "private jungle"—is probably the greatest lesson our pilgrim learns from his wonderfully batty landlady.

It is Philene, Miss Fiffy's beautiful, hot-blooded niece, with hair as "black as India ink," who succeeds where Lola had not, in seducing our pilgrim away from work and then in literally seducing him. When he agrees to play "hooky" for a day from his job, Philene takes him to the studio of the painter Kosta Reynolds, yet another Mobile "monkey" who has a tremendous effect on our pilgrim. Described as "a little pixie man, about two thousand years old," his studio is filled with "big statues of naked gods and goddesses cavorting like the illustrations in Bulfinch at home, pictures everywhere, odds and ends of arms, legs, and torsos in plaster, pieces of dingy curtain material, and bunches of dead flowers." Most of these pictures are nude portraits of beautiful male and female models, Philene among them. Our pilgrim is greatly aroused.

Soon after this meeting, our pilgrim encounters for the first time in years his cousin Perrin, whom he calls "the original Electric Monkey"—"a creature too apt, too clever, and too handsome to be any good at all in the workaday world." Uncle Acis and his new bride, Ada Mary Stewart, along with all the servants—Fern, Tony, Etta Mae, and Modena—complete this circle of monkeys. From them, our pilgrim knows he has contracted "Mobile madness."

This particular form of "madness" represents a rejection of the American norm—the workaday world and the drudges or drones who live there. At first, our pilgrim tries to approach Mobile as if it were the workaday world, and gives every indication of trying to become just another drudge, so he can "make it" in this world. He quickly realizes that Mobile is another world altogether. Its inhabitants are monkeys, not drones, and they succeed in making a monkey out of him as well. Thus the novel celebrates the insularity as well as the eccentricity of Mobile, which is cut off from the American mainstream, and therefore cut off from the ordinary world where the Puritan work ethic is the ruling force and people keep their bank jobs and do go on to become lawyers.

Our narrator's untidy pilgrimage eventually leads him to a house party at Bayou Clair (Bayou La Batre), where there is art (Kosta Reynolds), music (Ada), literature (Acis), cooking (Miss Fiffy and company), nature, and love. There is everything that makes life worth living, in Eugene Walter's estimation. What's missing is that American angst over what you are going to "do" and what you are going to make of your life. Here there is no soul-searching or browbeating over career, profession, jobs, or making a living. Human existence is founded on the notion that life is, as Miss Fiffy says, *"excellent."* What is important is the living and enjoying of this *"excellent"* life. Our pilgrim learns to rejoice "in sheer delight of drawing mortal breath," as Eugene says in one of his *Monkey Poems*. In many ways, the novel as a whole is an echo of perhaps the most famous lines from *Monkey Poems:* "O, I am monstrous proud/This life to live, this joy to laugh out loud."

The novel does not mean to suggest, however, that the Mobile world it applauds is some kind of Arcadia. It is not. It has death, treachery, lost love; it has pain, grief, and suffering. There are wonderful possibilities that do not work out, like the long-ago engagement between Miss Fiffy and Kosta Reynolds. This is not a world of total laissez-faire or Anything Goes, either. There are bad monkeys, like Philene and Perrin, as well as good ones, and the mischief and monkeyshines of these bad monkeys are often destructive and pain-

[4]

ful to others. Perrin and Philene detract more than they contribute to the general happiness of the monkey kingdom.

Most importantly, perhaps, this is not an idle world where labor is unnecessary. As in any other fallen world, labor is essential. What distinguishes the Mobile world, however, is that its labor is directed not toward making a living, but rather toward the making of life itself. What labor there is goes into cooking, gardening, painting—the enjoyment of life. As Eugene himself always said, "Fun is worth any amount of preparation." In this world, what the untidy pilgrim learns to work at is not work but fun.

Contemporary readers and reviewers were quick to recognize and appreciate the fact that *The Untidy Pilgrim* portrayed a very different South, a "separate kingdom," from the one usually found in Southern literature. "To readers under the impression that the Deep South of the United States is one large Faulknerian sanctuary or a land populated by Capote freaks and McCullers cripples, *The Untidy Pilgrim* should come as both a pleasure and a surprise," said one of the early reviews. "It is a relief to discover he pictures the old Southern aristocracy as a cosmopolitan, intelligent people rather than a decadent, unmoral tribe," says another reviewer. "There is no nostalgia here for some fabulous Old South, no sentimentalizing about moonlight through honeysuckle vines. The people here are modern, full-blooded," says yet another. "With nary a Confederate flag-waving nor a mint julep sipped 'neath the magnolias, here's a story about the deep South, as up-to-date as tomorrow," writes another. A British reviewer was most relieved to find that "dumb oxen, poor white trash, sadism in the sun and the rest of the paraphernalia are not in the purview" of the novel. The judges for the 1954 Lippincott Fiction Contest, Jacques Barzun, Diana Trilling, and Bernard DeVoto, were equally impressed; they chose *The Untidy Pilgrim* to be the winner of that year's Lippincott Prize.

Eugene himself told me that in his first attempt at novel writing, he did try to fit into the Southern literary tradition and write what he called a "gloom-doom" novel. It was about a man from a small Baptist town who killed his wife, saying, "Think how many years you kept me here when I could have been in New Orleans." But, Eugene told me, "Murder is not my thing. I'm triple Sagittarius

[5]

with a healthy liver; I couldn't do gloom and doom. It just ain't in me." He disposed of the novel in the "circular file" on the floor.

Instead of trying to fit in, *The Untidy Pilgrim* thumbs its nose at the "gloom-doom" tradition by being a deliberately comic Southern novel. Thus, there is no burden of Southern history, no problem of Southern identity in Eugene's novel. The Southern gothic and grotesque are not to be found here either. Indeed, at one point in the novel, these strains in Southern literature are explicitly satirized. A mysterious Brother John closeted in one of Fiffy's upstairs rooms is not an "ancient invalid brother," or an imbecile relative, or a clandestine lover, or an illegitimate child. It is Miss Fiffy's beloved old cat. The difference between Eugene's novel and many other works in the Southern literary canon is, as Eugene told one interviewer, "the difference between driving another nail in the coffin—it's all over—and let's have another drink: we're not dead yet."

Although the novel is not autobiographical, no one exemplified the notion of the untidy pilgrim and his untidy pilgrimage better than the author himself, Eugene Walter. Born in downtown Mobile in 1921, Eugene set out on his own "zigzag course" after serving as an air force cryptographer in the Aleutian Islands for three years during World War II. When he left Mobile and headed to New York, Eugene had no definite plans for his life. "I just blunder ahead successfully," Eugene used to say.

In New York, Eugene "blundered" into the artistic community of Greenwich Village. There he won prizes for set design for Off-Broadway theatre productions; gave parties for Dylan Thomas and Anaïs Nin; met Peggy Guggenheim and Andy Warhol, among many famous others. In Paris, he "blundered" into a group of young men from Harvard who were trying to launch a new literary magazine that became the *Paris Review*. Eugene was one of its founding contributors, and he also "blundered" into a position as editorial assistant to Princess Marguerite Caetani, the publisher of *Botteghe Oscure*. She eventually persuaded him to move to Rome, the headquarters of her magazine, and there he stumbled into the golden age of Italian cinema, including a role in Fellini's masterpiece, *8 1/2*.

Eugene's myriad accomplishments during the thirty years of his pilgrimage outside the South show just how much can happen when one's main ambition is to live life to the fullest. In the course of his seventy-six years, Eugene was so many things—set designer, actor, editor, marionetteer, translator, scriptwriter, and librettist, to name a few. He always identified himself as either a writer or a poet, however, and undoubtedly, his greatest achievements are in this line. In addition to the prize-winning *Untidy Pilgrim,* his most important works are *Monkey Poems,* a collection of verse that won a Sewanee-Rockefeller fellowship prize; the best-selling *American Cooking: Southern Style,* compiled for the Time-Life "Foods of the World" series; and the short story "Troubadour," which appeared in the first issue of the *Paris Review,* won an O. Henry citation, and was dramatized as a radio play. But the fact that Eugene could work with glee and expertise in so many different fields of artistic endeavor made him the extraordinary writer and person that he was.

For those of us who knew Eugene, it was the person who meant the most to us. Because he did personify the themes of *The Untidy Pilgrim,* his companionship was a joy and a treasure to all of his friends. Obviously this was the case in Europe as well, where Eugene became renowned as a host, especially in Rome. At the same time he was editing *Botteghe Oscure* and appearing in over one hundred Italian films, he was entertaining the likes of Judy Garland, Leontyne Price, and Isak Dinesen, among many other luminaries and celebrities who enjoyed his hospitality. The writer Muriel Spark said that in Rome, Eugene "held the nearest thing to a salon," and that "all roads led to him."

By virtue of both his writing and his remarkable life, Eugene Walter deserves to be better known at home, in Alabama and in America in general. When asked by an interviewer for *Negative Capability* why he was never listed in any of the reference books on Southern writers, Eugene replied: "They lost me during the three decades I lived in Paris and Rome, I reckon. I don't mind. It makes me 'unofficial.' Mine has been an 'unofficial' education, an 'unofficial' life, and I write 'unofficial' publications."

Unofficial the untidy pilgrim should remain, but unknown—no. For this reason, we are all indebted to The University of Alabama Press for bringing back Eugene Walter's prize-winning Alabama classic.

—Katherine Clark

[7]

FOR TOTTY AND KATE

Old images beset the scoundrel eye

An eye that dwells long upon a star must be refreshed with lesser beauties and strengthened with greens and looking-glasses . . .
—Jeremy Taylor, *Discourse of Friendship*, 1657

Why, sir, I should rather have a mouse's ear wrought in gold than any encyclopaedia you might care to mention!
—Harriet Guimauve, *Letters*, 1887

The human heart's a most untidy pilgrim.
—Dr. S. Willoughby, *Vues d'optiques*, 1926

Down in Mobile they're all crazy, because the Gulf Coast is the kingdom of monkeys, the land of clowns, ghosts and musicians, and Mobile is sweet lunacy's county seat. I can tell you that's the truth. I know. You used to say you were never the same after living there, and I reckon I'm not either. Few years there done fixed me up. Which is what I want to tell you about. People have been saying of me, "Hasn't he changed?" and "My, he is certainly different," and the thing is, they're right, I *have* changed, but it's not some change you can point at with your finger and say lookathere, see-what-I-mean. It's more subtle than that, and it occurred in strange degrees and lapses, quick and slow, long and short, noted and unheeded. I suppose it might be considered a change from country boy to somewhat citified boy, if you honestly believe in those distinctions. I don't, myself, especially after a glimpse of New York. Some people would say I've become civilized, others would say I've gone to hell with myself. What is civilized, I ask you, and as far as that goes, what is going to hell?

But then I have a lot of questions to ask. Almost as many questions to ask as I have tales to tell. But I'll only ask one for now, that can't be answered, because it's only a manner of speaking. Which is, how can places so close be as different as my home and Mobile County. I mean, *different*. Hell, you know I love the Gulf Coast. My home, in Persepolis, is only five hours on the bus north of Mobile, but Mobile is coastal, that's the gag, I guess, and the people by consequence are more pleasure-loving and Frenchified. It's a city of clubs and parties, I can tell you, and a city of cats I mean the talking kind.

[11]

And they do talk, they do make the King's English work for its living there. Make it jump through hoops as well. Stand on its ear, dance a jig. Southern talk! It's a toss-up whether they rank the pleasures of the table or the pleasures of the bed first, but it's a concrete certainty that talk follows close after. Right along with likker and gardening. Folks down in Mobile are like folks all over the South: mighty mean if you rub them the wrong way, but real civil and accommodating if you rub them right.

It's a pleasant trip down on the bus, though the prettiest part of the county thereabouts is hid from highway and railroad. Everything worth seeing, like the ruined hotel at Palaprat Springs, and the oak trees at D'Olive Landing, is set off the road closer to the River. But you do see fine cowcumber magnolias in one place; I saw them in full bloom. (My Uncle Acis is nutty over that particular tree, next to sweet olive.) And it's always fun to pass Hollis' Happytime Café, above Camden, where the Negro in the white coat rings a bell to tell the world that dinner is always being served there. If the weather's good, and he's in a good humor, he sings, or shouts out rhymes, like he was when we stopped there. He was calling out:

> "Get it! Get it!
> Chicken inside,
> Baked or fried,
> Greens on the side!
> Yassuh, folks, come on in!"

I was brimming over with that "goin' some place" feeling; the same sensation you can have when you read the first part of *Robinson Crusoe*, where he's setting out to seek his fortune, you remember. Looking back, I realize it was a truer feeling than I could guess at the time. Because it was the commencement of a lot of voyaging for me, and I don't mean only in Geography. Anyway Mobile is certainly a kind of island: they have banana trees and palm trees there in a profusion and lushness they never attain in Persepolis. So going down there from home was like going to some foreign place for me, a picture postcard world come true, with the sun setting (very pink and runny) in the South, over some well-known Sight to See.

I have to tell you I'd never been alone to any sizable city before. We used to drive up, my family and me, to Chicago or like that for vacation in the summertime, and once I went to Lake Cunahoochee with my older brother Tobey, but apart from running up to Auburn and back for school I'd never been out sojourneying alone, and I got a sizable kick out of stepping from that bus in downtown Mobile into the hustlebustle of five-o'clock traffic and a littered bus station jumping with sluts, sailors, drunks; and gentle country folk going to homes in Fairhope, Silver Hill, Bay Minette and so forth.

Pop had written our cousins the Morelands telling them I was coming, and asking could I stay with them till I found a room of my own. They said yes, I could have Son's room while he away in school in New York City—you remember *him!* He writes poetry. He won a swimming meet in Baldwin County three summers ago, but he writes poetry. The two don't go together. That's what I mean crazy, and that's what I mean you can't isolate it. Mrs. Moreland—Cousin Annie—is a sweet dopey woman who always looks as if she expects the plaster to fall, she looks up to the ceiling every third word; while Mr. Moreland—Cousin Charlie—is a deep one, says about two words a week, makes money hand over fist in real estate. They have these two children roughly my age: Son (I hate that boy!) and this talking-machine daughter Lola.

I had not seen any of this crew since we children were eleven-ish and twelve-ish: so much can happen in the years just after, but those are the sort of knobbly-kneed, cowlick, first-cigarette years when you've ceased to exist as a child, but nobody yet notices you as grown up. My memories of spats with these cousins didn't lead me into any hi-jinks of enthusiasm for this visit, but I was moderately pleased to see that

[13]

Lola was sort of good-looking, and was happy that Son was away.

Pop had gotten me a job, too—it's an easy thing to do when every tenth person in the county is your cousin, and most of them in solid politics, or the lumber or real estate business: all of them pious on Sunday, at ease on Saturday, and out for blood the other five days of the week. Not that I, you understand, am a divinity student, but all I mean is, it's a real comedy to come as an outsider from a place like Persepolis and see those boys cutting each other's throats with the most angelic expressions. As for those men's luncheon clubs, like the Progressive, the County Boosters, the Keep Smiling, etc., where those congenial villains gather to clap each other on the back—there's a fraternal spirit of boyish bounce and humor there that I find somewhat, at the least, grisly. Don't get me wrong. I went there already knowing how to swim in stormy seas: who to drink with, who only to smile at, and of whom to say "He means well, *but*—" All I'm saying is I didn't particularly enjoy that world. Now I know to laugh out loud where then I knew only to manage a sickly grin. Maybe learning to laugh out loud is one of the big differences I'm going to tell you about, and maybe it's the moral of my story. We'll see.

I moved in with the Morelands, and shoved Son's old Shakespeare books out of the way to make room for my lawbooks. Took down his pictures, too; he had these modern art things that look as good upside down: "Fish Eyes in a Whirlwind," stuff like that.

My room was upstairs in the back, with a little porch over the dining alcove, looked out into the tops of some camphor and chinaberry trees. Very cool and pleasant. Next to me was the bath and on the other side was Laura's room, my cousin; they call her Lola but Laura is really her name. She had just finished a couple of years at some junior college upstate, and was spending a year at home before going to the University. Lola's not what you'd call a problem child, but no one with two eyes would describe her as a nun either.

[14]

Well after supper every evening and it was still light to read I'd be sitting in my window with my books and papers I had to bring home from the office, and every time, like clockwork, here comes Lola *clack clack* in those damnable house shoes some women *will* wear, that have hard bangy little heels but nothing not even a strap to hold that shoe to the foot, so what can they do but *slop slop* through the house. You always expect a whiny voice to go with it, and it often does. I've heard Lola clopping downstairs sound like a string of penny firecrackers going off, honest to Christ Jesus. *Bang, bang, bang.*

Several times every evening I'd be treated to the spectacle of Miss Priss clacking to the bathroom in her old pink wrapper that didn't hide one thing she had. She'd come in my room as free as if Son were there. She'd make me feel how soft her hair was after she washed it. I think she washed it ten times a day. Crazy. "Feel! Just feel it!" she'd say. There's a natural barrier between brother and sister, but not between cousins. I suppose Lola wanted me to grab her wrist and throw her across the bed, but I never would oblige. Boy, I knew how she'd scream. I knew she wanted a fright, not a loving.

She came in one night, trailing a cloud of perfume would suffocate a horse, her hair shiny. "Well!" she says. "I don't think you've changed a bit since you were a child. Remember when we all used to be at Uncle Acis' for the summer, and how you were always skulking off somewheres by yourself? I see you're the same now. Don't you ever just *play?*"

"Go get your Rook cards, and some Cokes, and we'll play now," I answered.

"You're hopeless," she said. "Rook!"

"What would you suggest?" I said sarcastically, closing my book.

"What I meant was, don't you ever give yourself an evening off? Like going to a movie, for example?"

"Sometimes."

[15]

"I'd die in two days, cooped up with those lawbooks. How can you stand it?"

"It's easier to stand than the sound of the pony express going up and down this hall day and night."

"Stuck-up, stuck-up, stuck-up!" she cried, and kicked over a pile of books near the door, and ran out slamming it. Then from outside she uttered an awful oath, which she couldn't have learned from Son, he's too damn pure; I guess she learned it from a sorority sister.

Sometimes she came to use the pier-glass in my room (her room only had enough mirrors for a Crazy House at the fair) saying the light was better or something, anything for an excuse. She'd stand two inches away from that mirror, pulling her eyebrows and crying out like it was killing her, and keeping her eyes on me to see if I was taking it all in, her act. Sometimes she curled her eyelashes with a regular little instrument of torture she had. Anything to give me a show. She might as well have slept with me, too, she spent so much time in my room. Like Grampa used to tell Aunt Lily, coquetry is one thing, and provocation is another. . . .

So you can see I was ripe to leave that house and locate on my own, where I could slam the door and have peace and quiet. There's the difference between immediate family and cousins again: with my family I'd have slammed the hinges off that door in two minutes flat, but with cousins you have to be polite, even with a half-naked tease romping in your room. I'm not nearly as anti-social as I sound, but it's a theory that runs in my family about the august privilege of each individual human creature over ten years old to have a place where he can go and slam the door after him. My Grampa, who was a lawyer in Persepolis, had lots of these same ideas and I guess I take after him. When he knew he was dying he locked himself in his room to keep the doctors and clergy from getting at him, and died in perfect peace and quiet. My father and brother had to put a ladder against the side of the house to unlock his door from the inside.

Obviously this family strain hadn't reached Lola, she didn't

[16]

like to be alone, she liked attention; more, she *needed* it. I'd have ended despising her, save for two things made me realize what a child she was, what a silly fool, and you can't help but love somebody as dumb and harmless as I finally knew her to be.

Her birthday was in the first month I was there, and Mr. Moreland gave her a little fur piece he brought from New York for her: some nasty beady-eyed stone martens to wear around the neck, biting their tails knowingly. I went in her room to steal back a little stool she was always stealing from me and here was Lola, big as life and twice as natural, dressed in her birthday suit, not another stitch, with those beasts around her neck, studying herself in the mirror, holding her hair on top of her head. I took in this sight (I can see it clearly still) and escaped before she knew I was there.

Not long after I found her one afternoon, when I came home from the office, crying big juicy tears over *Heidi* which she was reading. She was sitting on the floor of the upstairs back porch, her feet filthy-dirty from going barefoot; she had eaten a lemon and peelings were in a neat little pile by her, and she was bawling over that book. Now, I don't know what was in it made her cry, since when I was in school Pleasure Books were divided up, and girls and boys didn't read the same things. I was reading *Kidnapped* when the girls were all in *Heidi,* and will probably go to my grave without reading *Heidi.* But crying she was, so I gave her my handkerchief and said, "Blow your silly nose and act your age," but I was thinking oh, you silly adorable fool, if you aren't the bird-brained wonder, then I don't know who is.

"People will think," I grinned at her, "that there's another Ada Mary Stewart in the world." She managed to smile at this. Ada Mary Stewart is Pollock Stewart's daughter at Belle Fontaine; all you have to do is look at her twice and she'll burst into tears. She's fat and has a very sad nature.

"I guess Ada Mary would sure enough enjoy this book," said Lola, grinning herself now. "I oughta send it to her, if

[17]

she hasn't read it. It's good for a gallon, I reckon. But she probably only reads Edgar Allan Poe."

"That girl could cry over the Montgomery Ward catalogue."

"I'd like to know what it takes to make you cry," said Lola, fixing me with a look. "And I'd do it, if I knew how."

"Nothing you could do," I chided, " 'ud make me cry."

"We'll see, we'll just see," she answered.

Afterwards, in my room, I tried to think when and where I'd cried, and for what, and best I could do was remember a Saturday afternoon a thousand years ago, when Grampa took me to a movie about a forest fire in Michigan, and I cried with terror when the hero and his girl had to escape by canoe over some waterfalls. It was very thrilling, and canoes have made me nervous ever since. I keep expecting the rapids. I never cry at funerals, only clam up.

I had been to see some pretty crummy rooms in boarding houses, and some rather nice rooms, bosom-of-the-family sort of things in old houses, and none of them suited me, I had this obsession about the kind of place I wanted to live in. Time was drawing close to Son's arrival, though he kept changing it, and I was damned if I'd share a room with him, though of course I was in his room as only a temporary guest from the beginning.

So happily one of the boys at the office, Hastings Martin, did you know him at Citadel? well he told me he'd heard from his cousin Phyllis Porfirio (who gets to at least six parties a week, therefore she should certainly know) that there was this old lady had a big house just north of St. Anthony Street, lived alone in it, was very pleasant, and might be willing to take in a single young man. I took down the address, and left for lunch at ten-thirty in the morning. I was pretty anxious to get away from my cousins by then, and was getting desperate, so I flew across town.

Just north of the downtown business district of Mobile are some shady streets bypassed in the town's westward growth.

Many of them are still shaded by the fine stands of live oak, and are comprised of handsome town houses built between the 1840's and the 1880's. The best-looking are the oldest, built of rosyred brick, and ornamented with fanciful iron lace galleries and balconies; with fences of this same crazy curlycue work enclosing the gardens.

So I was pleased to find that the address I had been given was an imposing three-storied house with high iron porches painted white, and a side wing hid in wisteria vines and crepe myrtle trees, dense and jungly. On the fancy gate (a lyre and fool's bauble twined with grapevines) was a polished brass plate engraved *FIFIELD* in shaded letters. When I pushed the gate it gave a little *scree-eek* on its iron hinges, and afterward closed behind me like doom. Going up the perforated iron steps I jumped, for when I stepped on the third step it was wobbly and clanged like a firebell when you stepped there. I could see some bolts were missing which should have held it to the underframe.

I rang the bell, then I heard one of the inside folding shutters move, and knew someone was looking me over. That's an awful feeling when you can't see who's watching you. Finally I heard a bolt slide and the door opened enough for one of those aristocratic old brown Negro women to say, "Miss Fiffy she ain' expecting nobody." My grandfather used to say, "Take black, let brown be." But he lived in cotton country, and here in Mobile they go in for proud browns.

I explained my business and she said, "Wait" and closed the door and bolted it again, right in my face, leaving me to stare at the tile porch floor. Everything was scrubbed and trim, not a leaf on the porch, and the brass knob and handle were polished to that blond look of brass that's kept polished, which made me think, well, this is a clean place, anyway, though I wondered why they didn't fix that step. There was an iron chair down at the end of the porch and next to it a huge lead flower-pot shaped like a swan, on a stand, full of a big clump of bracken fern. Nothing else. All the shutters, which were the inside kind, were closed, showing their scumbly paint to the street.

Then the door opened, the woman said, "Miss Fiffy say please to come in." So I followed her into the dark hall, blind as a bat after the sunlight outside, then into the first door which opened into the tremendous double-parlor, like a ballroom, though you'd never dance there, what with sofas, a shiny piano, chairs and tables, lots of china doodads and bunches of flowers. The room had high ceilings with fancy-work of plaster, dusty white and dingy gold, from which hung bronze chandeliers all over dangling with crystals. This room took up the whole side of the house, and had looking-glasses at the long ends which reflected each other and made it seem endless and submerged, for the mirrors were old and watery. I thought no one was there, it was so quiet and shady, though not dark, when here came this voice it seemed out of a bunch of cornflowers blue as ink.

"You like my pretty room."

I heard the servant's feet moving out of the room, and the door closing. I went into the back part and there in a low chair by the window, amidst a mess of books and papers and magazines was this ancient lady in a faded dress, with the wildest white hair you ever saw escaping from combs and hairpins, and lying in ducktail curls on the nape of her neck.

"How do you do?" she said, "I'm Miss Nonie Fifield."

I told her my name and where I was from.

"That makes you kin to the Morelands and Mr. Lakeland d'Aurevilly," she said.

"Yes'm, that's right," I replied, gazing about me.

"I haven't been to Persepolis since the last season of the Hotel at Palaprat Springs, you probably know it's all of forty-five years."

"Yes'm."

"But I remember your grandfather very well. He was very gallant."

"Yes'm, I think he was."

[20]

"Oh, and of course your cousin—no, your uncle—your Uncle Acis. He's a dear friend of mine."

"He's a fine person. But I tell you why I came calling on you. I'm told you might be led to consider renting a room out to a single young man?"

"You were told right. I hope you understand that I don't run a rooming house," she went on. "But I should be happy to have one young man here. I know there are lots of rooming houses, and worse, in this part of town, but this is not one of them, though I understand there is vast profit to be made in a rooming house, and even more to be made in the worse, but I rest content, ah yes. I have a room upstairs over the dining-room which I've been considering renting out to some nice person like you. You may have noticed the little balcony on the side, overlooking my private jungle?"

"Yes'm, I did."

"That's the room. We'll go see it tereckly. But we'll have some ice-tea first." And she picked up a little bell out the window-sill and rang the be-Jesus out of it, and here comes the servant in a door I hadn't even noticed.

"Whatchu have, Miss Fiffy?"

"Bring us some ice-tea and a box of Nabiscos, please, Fern."

When she had gone for the tea, we went on talking of this and that, finding out who we knew in common, or who was kin to who we knew in common, and who we knew lived in places we'd been in common, and all such. More than any other people of the world, the Southerners have that where-do-you-come-from, and where-have-you-been sense for the proper introduction of conversation.

I was studying Miss Fifield's eyes this while, which were both beautiful and peculiar. First, they were the eyes of a young girl, I mean they were perfectly clear, the color which was greenbluegray seemed to lie deep under the clear pupils. The whites were fresh, not at all an old woman's eyes. However, the lids were droopy, and the eyes were set in bony sockets, so only when she was surprised or busy emphasizing something and opened them wide, and even then only if she

[21]

faced the light a certain way, could you see the pupils were full of glints, like skinny stretched-out freckles, of golden yellow. Like as if she had laugh-lines *in* her eyes, as well as alongside. When she looked at you full, you could feel her scrutiny. Then, too, she had this cute way of cutting her eyes around at you, with the face still pointing away. I've seen young spaniels cut their eyes around like that when they're playing mischief with you.

Fern brought us ice-tea and a box of Nabiscos, and Miss Fifield snatched that box open and had eaten a clutch of them before you could say Jack Robinson. Then she passed them to me.

"I love Nabiscos, don't you? First of all I like them 'cause I like sugar-wafers, but second I like them 'cause they've never changed that *good* red-and-white-and-gold box. I hate things change their labels when you used to them. That's why I like Louis Sherry chocolates, that's a fine box with violets; I have hundreds of them in this house, every button and spool I own for fifty years has been kept in a Louis Sherry tin box."

And not on your clothes that's a natural fact I was thinking seeing the safety-pin holding her belt together. But she was rambling on, while we tinkled our ice-tea glasses with the long-handled spoons.

"Lemon?" she asked, not caring whether I took it or not, since she'd started her song. "And Crayolas, what a tacky box, but what would you do if they changed it?" Then you know what, she held up a box of Crayolas—yes, a regular school-child's box of Crayolas—out of that window-sill. There was *everything* in that window-sill but bluejays and money. What she used Crayolas for I don't know or care to, but when she held them up it reminded me of Cartright's windows in Persepolis in September when they drag out those artificial autumn leaves that must have come out the Ark they so dirty by now, and they hang those leaves and a dozen or so Redbird tablets on thin wires like they are floating in space, while the floor is solid with the Crayolas and blackboard erasers, and pencilboxes with those pocket sharpeners that

[22]

work once, then give up the ghost. Well, thinking of Cartright's fly-blown shopwindows and that awful September feeling of school again didn't make me cry over Redbird tablets. Why, I wouldn't give you a hot copper cent for enough Redbird tablets to pave Mobile County—but here's this batty however sweet old lady just carrying on over her Nabiscos like they had been invented by her own true love. How do you explain it?

"They took the windmills off Old Dutch Cleanser," she said sadly. "I don't find it nearly so effective now." This chilled my bones to think it mattered to her, and I started thinking of possible changes of subject, while on she went.

"My little grandniece Philine used to think that the Dutch woman on Old Dutch Cleanser had something to do with Sweet Peas because her head looks like a Sweet Pea in that silly bonnet. I've thought so, myself, since she pointed it out. I don't know what though."

You don't know what! I thought, and I'm absolutely certain I don't.

"Do you live here alone, Miss Fifield?" I ventured.

At this she paused, with her eyes wandering out the window, then cut them back to me, and said lightful, "Oh, Fern and her husband Tony live in the back. They're my family. Fern's son Ben lives in New Orleans, he comes to visit us sometimes, and once in a while Philine stays with me, then I have friends who visit. But let's us go up now and see if this room will suit."

So she pulled herself up and hopped out into the hall with a surprising speed, me following; then as we started up the steps Fern appeared carrying a tray with a cutglass pitcher of milk and something in a napkin. She followed us up the stairs, to go into a room in the front over the parlor; Miss Fifield's I supposed. We went on into this big old bedroom with a grand bed, a marble-top dresser, a chifforobe with a mirror, and two other mirrors beside—over the mantel and on the door leading to a private bath. Minute I peeked in the room I knew it was for me, and said so, and all the time

I was trying the mattress she kept wanting me to look at this and that pretty useless thing in the room—"This is from Italy" and "This is from France," she kept saying, as though it mattered to me; all I could think was how late I was and still had to eat lunch, I can't live off Nabiscos no matter how much gold is on the box. So we agreed on terms, she seemed pleased with me, I was certainly pleased with her for I saw she lived in Cloud-Cuckoo and would surely leave me alone; then to conclude I told her I thought it was very nice of her to open her house to strangers in the housing shortage. You know what she said? I'll tell you: it gave me something to think about for that day.

"Tra-la-la! my dear young man! You're not *strangers*. And you must understand why I decided to rent out this room. I've lived in this house all my life without outsiders, but as I grow older I sleep less and read more and all night I hear the floors and walls snapping and creaking as they do at night. Atmospheric conditions: it sounds as though there were people in the house. So I said to myself since it *sounds* that way, why shouldn't it *be* that way: some nice young man. I like young women, but I like young men more. Just like I hate sniveling children, but I hate weak coffee more. Oh, I don't want you to think my house is haunted; not that there weren't some darling people lived here who'd be welcome to haunt it if they chose: and I rather cherish the idea of finding them all together in the parlor some night, with candles lit and glasses clinking. I seldom give parties any more, but why shouldn't they?"

All I said was, "Well, yes'm, I have to go now. 'Bye."

I chose a morning when Lola was going swimming at the Country Club pool as a good morning to move, and Mrs. Moreland (bobbing her head and mumbling even when outside, maybe she thought the sky was going to fall, too; Chicken Licken all over) and their cook Etta Mae insisted on helping tote my things out to the taxicab, and waved goodbye like I was going off on an ocean cruise, after ex-

[24]

tracting promises for Sunday dinner and one thing and another.

"It's a Gawd's blessing," said Etta Mae, puffing from my suitcase, "that somebody likes to stuff their gut like you does is going to live with a good cook like Miss Fifield's Fern."

"Oh, Oh!" bobbed Cousin Annie. "It's a pretty new ten dollar bill for you if you can write down the *exact* formula for her black-eye-pea cakes."

"Get the same price for our form-ulas." Etta Mae laughed. "And be careful how you aggravate you weight. You don't wanta be apple-plexed before you was thirty."

"Remember you can always have Son's room when Son's in New York," said Cousin Annie. In my head I answered you can have Son in school or out, dead or alive. Then aloud, I replied, "Thank you, Cousin Annie, I'll remember." And added to myself, no, thanks but no-thanks, I'm loose now and want to stay that way. Just a thing let loose.

First thing I did when I had gotten all my things up the stairs into my room at Miss Fifield's was to take some of her treasures and cache them on the top shelf of the closet: like a tortoise-shell box from Naples, some beat-up candlesticks, and so forth. Then I put my clothes away. While I was busy here came Tony with a glass of wine on a tray.

"Miss Vivvy say drink this, welcome to the house."

"Thank you, Tony."

I came to know Fern and Tony very well, for I saw them both every morning at breakfast (the only meal I took regularly at Miss Fifield's table) which I ate on the latticed back porch. I never saw Miss Fiffy (I soon called her that, everybody did, down to the grocery boy) unless I made a point of searching her out in her parlor, her dining-room, or her yard. But there were always traces of her, for she'd bring flowers out the yard into my room while I was at work, fresh ones every day. She grew fancy things in beds edged with bricks, but the yard was crowded with things that seeded themselves and came up every year, like four-o'clocks, digitalis, phlox and larkspur. She was hipped on cornflowers, had little vases of them all over the house, and sometimes she'd be tying up bundles of them to send to her neighbors. "It's this blue, this real *blue* blue," she'd explain happily to me. She was a great one for weeds, too; she'd take a handful of Johnson grass, nut grass and wishing grass and make a regular bouquet in a teacup. Can you imagine?

Sometimes, leaving the house of a morning, I'd catch a sight of her rooting around in her yard, and a sight she was. She'd have on this sunhat that seemed to have been hit by a Mack truck when young, and under it her hair was like a storm at sea. She wore regular ditch-digger's gloves with fringed cuffs and JOLLY BOY STANDARD printed on them, always diamond earbobs in her pierced ears. She'd wave and I'd wave back and perhaps I wouldn't see her again till next morning. Sometimes, if Fern made something special she'd send me up some, like almond cookies or blackberry sherbet.

Fern and Tony were both studies, I can tell you. They were both brown aristocratic personages, politeness itself without being servile. Tony was rather quiet and thoughtful, while Fern, though dignified, on occasion showed a crazy and talkative sense of humor. She and Miss Fiffy were always laughing together over something. There was a stupid-looking mottled gray-and-white kitten hanging around the back porch; Fern fed it, it didn't really belong to anybody, just adopted the place. It was a big joke between Fern and Fiffy about this cat, they pretended it had been sent by Miss Elissa Moylan (*the* gossip) to spy out their business: they called the cat Elissa, and there was an involved secondary stage of foolishness where they pretended to be confused as to which Elissa (cat or woman) the other was talking about.

"Pore Elissa got cobwebs in her whiskers this mawning," Fern might say.

"Well!" Fiffy would answer. "What d'you expect if she's gonna stick her nose just about everyplace?" And those two fools would laugh, how they'd laugh. The final joke, of course, is that they had their own highly efficient grapevine system. It was probably better than Miss Moylan's, who distrusts servants and has none, for Fern knew all the cooks around, and saw plenty more at early market. Unlike Miss Moylan (who took malicious delight in others' misfortunes: her telephone conversations commenced at daybreak and went on till noon) Miss Fiffy and Fern were always most concerned with news of comings and goings.

"Mr. Buster Bradford is going to Make a Trip to N'Aw-luns, I'm told."

"Miz Bradford going?" asked Miss Fiffy.

"No, she's not going a-tall."

"That means we can expect her for a visit, oh dear."

"No, she is going later to Make a Visit to her sister in La Grange."

"Well, that will leave old Mr. Will Bristol alone in the house."

"No, 'cause Miz Bradford's Ella has got to sleep there for three nights till Mr. Bradford come home."

"And we, we will put the diphtheria sign on our front door."

"Yes, and the Hannaberry fambly is going to Make a Trip to Sea Island, Georgia, to be gone some time."

"*Look!*" cried Miss Fiffy. "Look at Elissa dress up her ears at that!"

"Oh no-count animal!" laughed Fern. "So busy paying us mind you is got cobwebs in your milk."

But if I didn't see much of Miss Fiffy, I'd often hear her, playing her piano in the parlor, she played fast old-timy pieces, same as my mother, though she didn't falter like Mother did, who didn't ever keep her music up, and always regretted it. She wanted me to take piano but I balked. I never could see a boy playing music, unless in a band or like that. But Miss Fiffy played those skimming songs where she'd run up and down the piano like greased eels, having herself a real romp. I got where I liked to hear it; it's nice to hear music in the house, I mean like a piano or violin,

[27]

even a flute being played right in the house but without you having to squinch in a chair and concentrate on it.

One afternoon I came home from work, it had been a perfect day and now the four-o'clocks were strong, even more than usual. It was a real crazy waltz I heard, I think, but I wouldn't swear. Anyway when I came in the front door, I stopped to listen, then sidled into the front half of the parlor, thinking to pass the time of day with her when she finished tinkling. But she knew I was there, and stopped and cocked her bright eyes at me and said, "I studied piano in Paris" and picked up the phrase of music where she'd dropped it and went frisking on. I never knew how for sure to react with her, seemed she was always handing me hummingbird eggs. But I had to say something so I said it. I had grown sick of that clanging front step.

"Miss Fiffy?"

"Hmmmm?" she said, without missing a lick. Tinkle-tinkle-tum-te-tum.

"You know what?"

"What?"

"I can fix that step in front that makes such a racket. I can get those stubby-headed short bolts from McGowin-Lyons and fix that step for you in a jiffy." She left off playing, and turned to me, wide-eyed.

"Oh, no, that's my doorbell! That step is my doorbell."

"Ma'am?" I gasped.

She laughed. "I see you don't understand me at all. My *real* doorbell. What I mean is, I can tell when somebody's coming up the steps, and stop playing or hide or whatever before they even get to the doorbell. That clanging step drowns out the sound of my piano and also warns me who's coming. I can tell my regulars by their steps on that iron. I know yours now. Oh, no, I don't want it fixed. Tony could have fixed it years ago if I did. That step has saved me unnumbered hours of backbiting with Elissa Moylan, and more hours of symptom recital with Fresh-Air Charlie. Oh, and besides, delight in disorder, you know."

[28]

"Oo-ee, Miz Moylan!" came Fern's voice, as she passed through the room. "She could steal sweetness out a ginger cake without touching the crust." Then they looked at each other and laughed. They were more like two batty sisters than mistress and servant.

"I was just takin' these up to John," said Fern, presenting the tray for inspection.

"Oh, he'll love them!" cried Miss Fiffy.

John?—John?—I thought. But my mind was so busy leap-frogging over what she'd already just said, that I didn't have presence of mind to ask right away, and then in a flash I remembered how many times I'd seen Fern carrying that little tray upstairs. Why, there's someone else in this house I thought and yet she never mentions him. John . . . her brother, maybe her child? My Uncle Acis, who hates Mobile, and never leaves the farm if he can help it, save for Mardi Gras, used to say that every nice family in Mobile had some-body locked upstairs in a back bedroom. But he was robbed of his wallet in the old Southern Hotel, and never got over it. He was drunk. Does John ever come downstairs I won-dered.

I didn't know many people in town, and didn't get around much because of having such a siege of work to be done at night, so the only dates I had were with my snippy cousin Lola. She was kind of fun when I could pick her up for an evening and afterwards dump her off at home again, didn't have to put up with her running around half-naked, flaunt-ing herself.

One Sunday afternoon, late, after we had eaten at Lola's house, then gone to the first show at the Saenger, we came back to Miss Fiffy's for late afternoon coffee, by invitation. Lola was popping to meet her, since she'd heard so much about her, it seems. Well, Lola is incorrigible. Because she'd come by any number of wild stories about Miss Fiffy's youth, and apparently there were plenty to tell—seems Miss Fiffy had been all indicated truly by the word *belle*—Lola had gotten herself up in a regular movie-star outfit, all black, and had on a lot of lipstick, and was talking that party-talk of hers; it's a scream when she thinks she's English, because she has that high whiny voice some Southern girls have, and a drawl you could stretch from here to Orlando Beach. Lola, knowing Miss F. had lived in Europe, and been Queen of the Mardi Gras, and I don't know what-all else, was determined to be hot stuff. I'd been cautioned against calling her Lola, it was her name Laura like christened or pop a gusset, that Sunday. Well, Miss Fiffy was done up for the encounter, too, with shell and silver combs holding her tempest in place, and she had moved from her magpie corner in back to a velours chair in front with a table by, for cups and things. No sooner had I introduced "My cousin, Laura Moreland" (Miss Fiffy stared at her real hard, then rearranged her combs for something to do while the sight sank in) than Fern came with the coffee pot and said delightedly, "Little Miss Lolo Moreland! How's Son?"

Lola was vexed, but she answered politely: "Oh, he's fine, thank you. He's in New York, coming home soon."

"Laura is all in black, like a Parisienne," said Miss Fiffy, handing round the cups of coffee, and starting off the sugar.

"Mama doesn't like my wearing black. She says I'm much too young."

"Oh, rumbun. Girls with good color should always have a little black thing to show off their complexions."

"I'm glad you think so."

"What do you think, Pensive?" demanded Miss Fiffy of me. I wasn't Pensive though; my name was Busy: I had my mouth full of Fern's fresh-baked goodies, and I wasn't studying them.

"Oh," said I. "I never notice especially what girls wear, except I like bright colors. I get annoyed at pink." I was thinking Lola could deck herself any way she liked, she'd never please me like the sight of her prissing in front of her mirror with nothing on but her old animal skins. Even if she is rather thin, she has a mighty cute fanny.

[30]

"I believe you took your schooling in Europe, Miss Fifield," says Lola, stirring daintily.

"No, schooling took me in Europe," she replied, "or rather *to* Europe. But I never took *to* schooling *in* Europe. There was too much else to see and do. Dumbness brought me home. Papa wanted me to stay and have a year in Italy as he had done as a young man, but you know I got homesick for Mobile, and all my friends, mostly dead now however."

"Were you there long?"

"Oh yes, five years altogether. Mostly England and France. Most of all, Paris. I had a glimpse of Italy, but I was impatient for home. I do wish I had learned some Italian, for Dante and Aretino, you know."

"I plan," said Lola, elegantly, "to have a year in Switzerland." Liar, thought I, your daddy would blister your silly hide if he heard you say that, and your mother would have one cool tissy, I daresay. She'd make the plaster *really* fall. But Lola was frothing on.

"Most girls seem to prefer New York after junior college, but not me. I definitely plan Switzerland."

"I hope you won't regret it. The Swiss are hopelessly dull; their scenery has stunned them permanently. What will you study?"

"Well, I want to be a mannequin."

"Oh dear, Switzerland is rather the last place for that. Now if you were interested in watch-repairing, or rock-gardens . . ."

"Lola wants to model furs," said I absently, and Lola gave me a questioning look.

"My ambition was to be a bareback rider," said Miss Fiffy. "When I was very young, Papa took me to see a wonderful Italian woman in tutu and white tights, who stood on the back of a galloping dapple gray. For me it was the last word. She was with the circus came to Frascati Park the day after Oscar Wilde spoke there. After an evening with him, I wanted to adopt classical draperies and play the lyre, then

[31]

I saw her and knew it was spangles and sawdust for me. Maybe your ambition will change as readily."

Lola made nothing out of this, but she kept on swimming. "How did you find Paris?" she asked, being Lady Audley at the high high tea.

"With the blessed assistance of Mr. Baedeker," answered Fiff, with a perfectly straight face. Lola hadn't the remotest idea of what a Baedeker was; I wouldn't have if there hadn't been some in our attic at home, old red guides of Paris and Vienna. So on they chattered, I was happy to drink my coffee and eat the almond cookies and little spiced doughnuts. Miss Fiffy kept staring at Lola's cup, even after she'd replenished it. Or rather it turned out not to be Lola's cup, but her little finger crooked in the air, with real shrimp-picker elegance. So you know what that crazy old lady did? She slyly grabbed one of those doughnuts, I'll never forget it long as I live, and reached over and stuck it on Lola's little finger.

"Ho-ho!" she hooted, "Trapped that pinkie!"

Now can you beat that? Fern saved the day though by coming in, asking Miss Fiffy to come with her a minute. Lola just looked at that swollen finger-ring, and then removed it in a single gulp. Then she put down her cup and whispered, "That nasty old bitch!"

"Baby!" I exclaimed.

"Something obscene 'bout the way she did that."

"Pfttttt," I said. "She was tickled at your giving yourself airs."

"Giving myself airs?"

"Don't know what else you call it, and don't get on your high-ass horse with me. I'll spank you right here."

"Oh," she groaned. "You're mean as you can be. I'll be so glad when Perrin comes home. He's the only person I can talk to."

"You mean that you can twist around your little finger."

"If you only knew, hardhead," she answered, glaring. "There are a good many are happy to be twisted around my

[32]

little finger. Thank God, they're not many like you in this world—or this old lunatic here."

So she sulked, and put on fresh lipstick; after a minute Miss Fiffy returned, all smiles, carrying a mangy velvet box, and said to Lola: "Here some pretties to go with your black." Lola looked doubtful for a minute, then lit up when she saw what it was: a pair of fine jet eardrops. So she ran squealing to the mirror and treated us to a Cecil B. De Mille production called *Putting on the Earrings*. All it lacked was fireworks. Afterwards, she was ashamed at having been so angry with the old lady, and kissed her when she said goodbye. But on the street, she said, "That lady is nutty as a fruitcake; it's just the house for you, stuck-up," but I only laughed and pinched her hard.

September was unbearably hot. Stifling. Not a soul on the streets, the shops might as well have closed, and the only soul I saw in the bank on this particular day was Miss Elissa Moylan telling the history of the world to Eddie Backenberger, who was too polite to escape. I left the office at four to run home for bathing trunks and a towel and the fellows from the office picked me up for a dip at Spring Hill Lake; after, we ate cold supper at Carlton Wister's house out there. Even after the sun went down it was scorching. We sat on Carlton's lawn, sipping gin-and-tonic, and watching big old blue clouds piling up for rain, full of forked lightning and faint thunder.

Everybody was too whipped by the heat to talk much, so I got home early and stretched out on the bed fully dressed and fell dead to sleep without meaning to. I must have slept for hours, tired in the way that heat will tire you, and guess I would have slept till morning, but a terrific crash of thunder woke me and brought me bolt upright. It was black night and pouring down rain.

I jumped up to shut the side windows because it was blowing in; it must have been raining a good thirty minutes, I reckon. It was a cloudburst, with a lot of wild tossing wind

[33]

in the treetops, and a great roar of rushing water down the gutterpipes and rumbling out into the stone drains on the ground. It sounded hollow and subterraneous, because from my window I could hear at least four drainpipes. Too, I could hear water falling with flat loud splashes from the eaves in places where the gutters were stopped up with oak leaves. There was thunder roaming around the heavens, and the small thunder those big raindrops make on magnolia and leathery oak leaves. I could hear people called from deep sleep to close windows, quiet fretful babies and scared animals. Through the black tangle of Miss Fiffy's "private jungle" I would see a yellow square light up, then disappear, then another here and there, people I didn't know in houses across the way. The asphalt street was a shining black river with water almost over the curb, what I could glimpse of it through the wisteria vines.

I stood on the balcony outside the alcove of my room, even though the roof leaked, and the wind sent spray across me. The rain tasted good when I licked my lips. And smelt better. I could feel the world relaxing after the hottest day. That cool smell of dirt that *needed* rainwater, and the smell of rotting oak leaves, and sweetness of Grand Duke jessamines.

As I stood there I realized that some sounds came from this house where I stood. I listened, with a kind of nervous excitement. From my balcony, in the wing, I could see into the upstairs hall window to the door of Fiffy's room in the front. Suddenly a light cut across the hall from her door, which had opened. The cry was faint but audible, almost not human, I've heard hounds whimper in their sleep like that, and babies. I can't describe it.

It gave me the creeps and I hugged myself. Then I saw Miss Fiffy in a yellow kimono with long sleeves stride across the room to fetch something, and stride back. I could hear her making comforting sounds, but the only words I could make out were "Poor darling baby!" and all over again I began wondering about John. I decided he wasn't an ancient

[34]

invalid brother, but an infant, then considering Miss Fiffy's age I decided that wasn't possible, unless he was some kind of idiot who could be thirty years old and still a baby. I've seen them like that.

Is it her brother, I asked myself, her lover, her child? Then it came to me that Fern and Tony both called him John, never Mr. John. This led me to suppose that either he was a child, or had been at some time a child in their care. Which led me to the moron theory again. I had the feeling I had heard his cry before, maybe in my sleep, but I couldn't remember, and just then Miss Fiffy passed her door and saw that I was on the balcony watching the storm, which she could easily do, even through the vines hanging down, for I wore my white linens still, and my bedlamp was on, shining through the french windows on to me.

She came into the hall, to the window, and through the little space that was open—leaning down to it with her hair falling about her, it was long—she cried out above the roar of wind and water.

"Isn't it a wonderful storm?" she shrilled. "And oh, how we needed it! It scared poor Brother John. I had to fix hot milk for him."

Brother John, brother . . . ran through my head.

All I could think of to say was, "I know the farmers will be happy."

"Wonderful, wonderful!" she cried. "It'll bring heaven only knows what up from the bottom of the Bay. And the causeway is certainly flooded. A storm like this makes me wish I had nerve enough to spell my name with four F's— Fififfield!"

"Why-ud you do a thing like that?" asked I, laughing in spite of myself.

"Sake of Caprice, who else? Caprice, the Three-Eyed Goddess. She has one eye in her navel; it gives her a total view. She's not to be argued with, now is she?"

"Guess not," I answered.

Laughing merrily amidst the storm, she nodded goodnight

and disappeared. On that I went inside myself, and undressed and brushed my teeth, and got into bed, but not to sleep. She had said the thunder would bring things up from the bottom of the Bay, like bodies and old tires, I guess; but her words had brought things up from the bottom of my mind. I lay there under a single sheet, on two big pillows in the rainy dark and unleashed my mind. And off it went. Why, I asked the storm, would anyone want to spell their name with four F's when two F's is the correct way? And what connection does that have with the cloudburst, in spite of this goddess Caprice? Besides look how many names she has already: Miss Fiffy to most, but she's really Miss Fifield, Tony makes it into Miss Vivvy, she's Miss Nonie Fifield, she's Miss Ninetta Susan Fifield, and in all the yellowed clipping scrapbooks downstairs of when she was Queen of the Mardi Gras it's "the beautiful Queen Ninetta." That's plenty names and here she wants to make up another.

Why they all have more names than one, I thought. Lola was christened Laura, Tony calls Fern "Fernee" and she calls him "Tow" and they are Mr. and Mrs. Somebody, even if you don't know it. First names alone are kinder, and colored people are kind, that's really why they are known by first names alone I guess. Just think, I was suckled at the breast of a black nurse, and she raised me till I was ten years old, and I never knew what her last name was. I'm glad now I don't because what last name could ever fit with "Jordana"? Thinking of Jordana living now on her farm outside Persepolis, I realized I missed being home, and how much I'd changed in the short time I'd been in Mobile.

I don't think a person ought to let their mind go roaming up and down around useless questions *or* answers. Like I don't think people should look at themselves too much in mirrors. I think you should be able to close up your mind like a box or a book and not be troubled. That's real mental discipline. Uncle Acis has a book called *How to Concentrate*, but I've never seen one called *How to Unconcentrate*. There

[36]

was a lady at Cypress Turn went raving just mulling over quilt patterns. She got obsessed.

Boy, you are homesick, I told myself. It could have been that, but there was more in the back of my mind, misty. You are in a foreign country, I told myself, even if Persepolis *is* only five hours away by bus. This is the Coast, remember those damn palm trees, and bananas; where you find them you find monkeys, and you are sure enough in the kingdom of monkeys. Look at Lola. Look at old Fiff.

I thought of home, and my mind ranged through all the rooms there, and I heard all the people there—my pop, my mother, my little sister Sara, my brother Tobey, Aunt Lily, the servants, the dogs. I smelt the smells of hot summer there, and thought of winter mornings, but there was no sensation could be conjured to satisfy whatever I was lacking, the thing I was so busy aching for. Lying in the dark, listening to the rain, I thought again for no reason, of Robinson Crusoe on his island. You need a Friday, I told myself, to unbutton your mind with. And you are, you are on an island. You're on the Island of Monkeys, and have got to learn Monkey talk.

I remember my grampa saying once he was homesick, and when Lily raised her eyebrows and said, "Homesick for what? You're home," he smiled and said, "Homesick for some place I've never been."

"How can that be?"

"It can very easily be. 'Cause I am."

"Don't judge others by yourself. Where are you homesick for?"

"For Zuolagaland."

"My God, where's that?"

"I dunno."

"How you know its name, if you can't locate it?"

" 'Cause I made up that name in my own head, to be the name of the place I'm homesick for."

"You Grampa," warned Lily. "Tuscaloosa is gonna be your new address."

[37]

"Ladies that are pregnant," sighed Grampa, "get themselves in a frenzy for things like fresh strawberries out of season, and everybody takes it for granted. But nobody understands that men have moments in their life when they're hungry in their minds for places they've never been."

Lily shrugged. She was unmarried.

"Besides," mused Grampa, "I think I must have eaten a page from the Atlas when I was very small. Otherwise I can't explain why I have always been agitated in my blood with a love of far places."

By then Lily was real sent with the whole idea, and burst out laughing. "What you need to do is start a stamp collection," she said. But Grampa didn't honor that with an answer. Ever after, till the day he died, about once a week at breakfast Lily would say, "Well, Gramp, what's the latest from Zuolagaland?" and he'd make up some silly answer like "The buttonhook crop is failing for want of rain," or "They've put down the revolt of the elevator operators," and when Mama would be hurrying us through our dawdling Saturday breakfast to start fixing for her club luncheon in the house that day he would answer Lily's question with: "This week, in Zuolagaland, they're shooting all ladies who belong to clubs, even if they're mothers."

So, you see, after I assured myself it wasn't home I was homesick for, I decided it must be Grampa's Zuolagaland. You're going to say all I needed was a girl in my arms, but it wasn't that kind of need: no mistaking that. It was a yearning for that place in an unknown latitude (is it island or continent?) where you can set down on smooth rock and say, "Here I am." There was every reason, actually, for me to be happy: in this fine house, in a big bed inside listening to the outside rain.

I could have gotten brain fever I thought so much that night. I lay there thinking till the rain had stopped and the only sound was the trees and eaves dripping interminably. It was as if that thunderclap had waked me to the storm and to something else I couldn't name.

[38]

Well, the weather had turned. It was certainly not cool yet, it was still hot, but it turned rainy. Rained almost every day, a kind of bored steady downfall that makes everything soggy underfoot, everything inside damp to the touch, makes window frames stick. Miss Fiffy spent this whole time with her books, rubbing down the leather ones with some kind of stinky white polish, stopping to admire the sheen, then re-arranging them back on the shelves after sprinkling borax to discourage roaches. Old houses on the Gulf Coast have cockroaches big as your hand, with long antennae. Go in the kitchen quietly some night then turn on the light suddenly, and see what a cotillion you've surprised at its height.

One afternoon I came home dripping and while I was shaking my umbrella at the front door, she called from back there for me to come have coffee with her, so I sloshed down the hall, and joined her in her library.

It was a square room back of the double-parlor, built right in the corner of the house, and with a corner fireplace. After the two windows and the shelves there was only room for two small chairs, and a children's tea-table, much scarred. Everything was a little musty, and the paper was peeling from the marbled fileboxes (like lawyers have) that were heaped higgledy-piggledy on the shelves amongst the heaps of old leather books, gilt-edged, brightly traced and starred with gold on their spines. There were pictures of her papa, a mustachioed dark gentleman with the devil sitting in his eyes (I think he wrote several books, among other things) and an old globe of the world with Oceania smashed in and waterstained.

"I'm sitting here counting over my gilt-edged securities," said she, as I entered.

While we were drinking our coffee, she talked about those books; they really were as precious to her as solid gold, I guess she'd read them all more than once. Some were her papa's, some were hers. She said again she wished she could read Italian. Well, I thought, here's a lady would like to be batty in three languages; she spoke in French, I knew, since

I'd heard her parley-vooing on the telephone. Yes sir, talking French over the telephone!

"I'll put Daisy Miller next to Tristram Shandy," she mused, putting some smallish volumes back on the shelf. Why, she's giving them places like at a dinner party, I realized. Then she read to me out of a poetry book. I've never for one minute gone in for that "Through my lips wake up the trumpet's prophecy, o wild wild wind!" stuff (though I well remember having to hear my sister Sara in her memory work: nobody can ever know how I loathe Wynken, Blynken and Nod, those nips). Sometimes in winter, my mama reads to us out of the *Golden Treasury* of a Sunday evening: I never listen to the words, only the sound of her voice singsonging in the air, weaving and fainting. But Miss Fiffy read me out of two little fat books that were a set, both written by this one man in the olden time.

> *"But if that Golden Age would come again,*
> *And Charles here rule as he before did reign;*
> *If smooth and unperplext the seasons were,*
> *As when the sweet Maria lived here;*
> *I should delight to have my curls half drown'd*
> *In Tyrian dews, and head with roses crown'd,*
> *And once more yet (ere I am laid out dead)*
> *Knock at a star with my exalted head."*

That's the one she liked most, they were short poems mostly about getting drunk, and picking flowers, and women's lips and bosoms. Some poems in those little fat books were only two lines long, and were mean sayings about people this poetry-writer had known, and I swear I've seen the same kind of things chalked on the sidewalk outside Tutwiler High in Persepolis.

I sat there drinking coffee and staring past her wild head into the back yard, and her voice strumming the air gave me a funny feeling of being in the long-time-ago. I only once had that feeling, that was when Uncle Acis was telling about

[40]

Cypress Turn in the old days when there were only ten families there, and one general store. He told about the time it snowed and stayed on the ground, which it doesn't usually do, even in that part of Alabama, and the New Year's callings. They had this big bonfire at Turnbull's, as was their custom, and Miss Lulie Stewart, who is now older than God, caught her dress on fire and had to be rolled on the snow to be put out. I mean, I had that feeling that way back there wasn't maybe as different from us now today as you'd think, when you look at the pictures in say *Harper's Weekly* for 1870, or the *Illustrated London News* for 1850, both of which are in our attic. I mean, I had the feeling that we weren't *separated* from a long-time-ago but were continued from it, like another chapter of a story. Can you see how this crazy Fiffy reading her old jingles could give me my first lesson in continuity? Anyway, it did.

Another thing. During that rainy spell, I came home one day and she was letter-writing in her chair by that magpie-nest window of hers. She heard me, and called out, "Come in here, I want to read you something delightful I just wrote." Pleased with herself.

I sallied in, keeping my cool distance, for it seemed she just wanted to crowd my head with things I didn't have time to think about.

"Listen," she said. "I'm making categories. I'm writing this letter to my brother-in-law, a witty man, God love him, with time to write long letters. I'm making categories of fours. These are the things that should be evenly divided over a happy life." She beat the letter with her middle finger. "The four elements, of course, are my point of departure. None of this has anything to do at all with the reason of my letter, which is to confirm that Philine will be met at the train. My niece; she's coming over from New Orleans for a visit."

Do Jesus! I thought. Here comes her mongoloid niece from New Orleans to add to the pleasures of our happy home. Brother John, Philine, Fern, Tony, Miss Fiffy and yours truly. Fine company for a rainy weekend.

"Anyway," she went on, "you'll probably like her, I think, and it would be nice if you ate with us, whenever you feel like it, while she's here. You can let me know when you *can't* make it, otherwise Fern will set for three. Well, the four elements. Earth, air, fire, and water. Then—"

Four elements is right, I thought. Earth is Fern and Tony 'cause they're earth-colored, air is Miss Fiffy 'cause that's what's in her skull, fire is Miss Philine who is this ten-year-old imbecile child who undoubtedly plays with matches, and water is me 'cause I'm going to flow out of this house in the morning and not flow back till midnight during her visit.

"—I make my category of the four elements of happiness as Love (in its greatest sense), then Art (all of it), then Physicality (what you'd call Sex), then Creole Cookery (which has connections with all the other three, and which no human is immune to). My four categories under Love are: Love that breaks the heart, and Love that mends it; Love that is permanent (like of the color blue and the place where you were born) and Love that is transient (like falling desperately in love with a face you see from a train, but forgetting it). Under Art is: Art that exists in itself, and Art that is *summoned*, like ballets or music; Art that reveals, and Art that disguises. Under Physicality I list that which comforts and that which intoxicates, that which numbs, and that which sharpens the senses. Under Creole Cookery, I give away *no* information. When I die Philine will get all recipe books, including my dissertation on the difference between one large onion and two small ones."

Then I guess she'd have subdivided four to infinity but she looked up and it was too quick for me to change my baffled expression and put on a smile. I reckon I was frowning. For she put down her letter, cocked her eyes in that way she has, and said, "That's all for now. Thus endeth the first lesson. Go dry your hair." So I did, wondering if Brother John had to hear acrostics in the small hours.

[42]

The following week the rain stopped, and Tuesday turned out a perfect day: hot clear sun, but a breeze from the Bay, and the first ineffable hint of fall in the air. It was now clearing up, October soon to commence. Miss Fiffy had cosmos, poppies, and some last ragged Liliputians. I was mad, because the fellows at the office teased me about being in love, for they had caught me staring across the roofs to the River, far over the Bay, not once but several times. First of all, it *was* the kind of day you stared. You could see the cliffs at Montrose it was so clear, and I kept wishing all day that I was on a white banana boat, steaming in or out the Bay. But, too, I had been turning Fiff's nonsense over in my mind. It was the first time I'd ever heard a lady say the word *sex* without supplying it with invisible quotation marks in the air.

When I pushed open the iron gate marked *FIFIELD*, I looked up from my fog and stood dead-still, for there on the porch, down by that lead swan full of bracken fern, was the prettiest girl I ever saw. Actually, now, I know she's not the prettiest girl I ever saw, but she always seemed to be. She's not really beautiful, if you study her cool and straight-faced (which nobody can) but it's the fact she makes you think she's so pretty.

First thing I noticed was her smooth calves and tiny waist. Her hair was black as India ink, but shiny, as though Tony had waxed it when he waxed that piano inside. It was fairly short compared with Lola's (who has a Zulu growth) and curled up at the ends. She was wearing a yellow linen dress, with short sleeves, and a bunch of thin fine silver-wire bracelets all on one wrist. I've always been very partial to black-haired girls in yellow linen dresses.

She was standing perfectly still looking at something, maybe a bird, in the tallowberry tree. She made me think of Living Pictures in the seventh grade, seeing her framed by the iron pillars and rail. (Who can forget fat Ada Mary Stewart as "Simplicity"—God, how appropriate, I thought at the time.) But I knew at a glance this living picture was

[43]

nowise like those sappy things we had in Picture Studies. I knew this was, though indeed a picture, sure enough a study, and then some.

She heard my step and turned. She took my breath away. She had those big black eyes and heavy black eyebrows, not too heavy, but I guess she didn't pull them out like Lola or the other girls. She had a honey tan, full lips, and a mole on her chin. She didn't have on any make-up except this real red lipstick I could have eaten off then and there.

But what got me she didn't do a thing when she saw me. Just looked, and smiled a very small smile. Didn't move, didn't bat a lash, just looked. When I reached her, she said in this cute voice, lower than Lola's, and a little Yankee-sounding (they have a special accent in New Orleans)—"I'm Philine." Just like that, very calmly. "I'm Philine." I saw then that there were tiny freckles on her nose and cheeks and that her eyes were brown, not black. Those thick lashes made them darker. But what impressed me was this kind of poise that wasn't at all biggety, just simply calm.

So I introduced myself and we talked a little about nothing. She had arrived that day, didn't know for how long, but she did plan to run over to Romar on the Gulf, some friends had a place there. She liked it best this time of year. She loved Mobile but of course New Orleans was the only place, it was her home. Though Mobile was her second home, because of Aunt Netta and because her grandmother, Netta's sister, had lived there for years.

"How can Miss Fifield be your aunt and still be your grandmother's sister?"

"Oh, I guess she's really greataunt, but Aunt Netta is everybody's contemporary."

"Oh, I see," I said, though I didn't. As if conjured by our words Miss Fiffy came and cracked a blind and peeked out.

"Philine, why don't you take Brother John his tray. You haven't seen him, and you know he'll be pleased. Better wash up for supper, young man." Then she disappeared.

[44]

"Why can't John come get it?" I asked jokingly, but wanting to know.

"You know he's too old. Haven't you seen him?"

"No, haven't had the pleasure."

She threw back her head and laughed lightly. Her black hair made all slitheries around her ears when she did. I didn't see the joke. Maybe it really was so funny that somebody would like to meet this toothless old moron brother they had caged upstairs. I don't know.

As I washed up, I stared at my face in the mirror and thought the big joke right now is how different Philine is from how you pictured her. Thinking of her I had this nervous tingle in the middle of my body, just like I had the moment I had to walk up for my diploma. God, how different she is from Lola, I thought; why, if it had been Lola visiting *her* aunt, and meeting a boy who lived in the house, Lola would have carried on. She would never just have turned around and said I'm Lola, no, she'd have shot off fireworks and ended by singing "Dixie."

You won't believe it, and I didn't believe it of myself, but I felt shy about going down to supper. I'd never eaten formal supper with Miss Fiffy, though we had eaten together plenty of times on the back porch. But to be honest, it was Philine I felt shy about. As I stood there in that dim stairwell, slowly descending, dragging one hand along the mahogany rail it came over me suddenly that *John was Philine's child,* and what she'd said was faking to throw me off. I made up the whole history: Philine had left the child with her loony aunt and had gone gallivanting off to Paris, to let the atmosphere clear. *But who was the father?* Why, some sweet-talking painter or piano-player or poetry-writer in New Orleans, I'd no doubt. Some fool like Son, who'd get a girl with child, then wonder how in hell it happened. Then go off versifying. Butterfly-brain. I couldn't blame Philine somehow. I knew at a glance her blood was hot, and I knew it took something different from six months of winter to cool her off.

[45]

All this was bucking around in my head when I ambled into the dining-room. Philine was already at table, reading a letter to herself. Miss Fiffy came in, I held her chair, then sat and glanced across at Philine. She looked up and smiled at me, again without saying anything.

Damn your eyes, I thought. Oh damn damn damn damn your sweet sweet eyes! (Was there ever a girl who was a tract against clothes, like Philine? Were there ever two objects like her small high breasts, save maybe on a rosestone peach tree?)

Fern had made a shrimp salad, baked a red snapper; afterwards we ate lemon Bavarian for dessert. Miss Fiffy chattered on so, she was so pleased to have company, that neither that girl nor I said more than mumble-jumble the whole meal.

Fern brought the coffee and I passed the sugarbowl across to Philine and just then her foot touched mine and I tensed my whole body without meaning to. She raised her eyebrows, smiled, and put the toe of her shoe over my toe and pressed lightly.

"Hello!" she said in her fantastical way.

"Hello what?" asked Miss Fiffy.

"We're playing footsy." Philine laughed.

"Oh?" the old lady said doubtfully, looking from one to the other of us, like a clever parrot. Then she said, "What, am I suddenly fallen from chatelaine to chaperone? For shame, Miss Philine, not in the house twenty-four hours and you flirt with this young man! Well, coquette, you're not to corrupt this young man, or you'll answer to me."

Philine made a silly face, and said, "Excuse me, Madam Chairman, I stand corrected." Then I really had to laugh for they were like two children playing a game. After I laughed I suddenly felt *good*. Have you ever felt good all of a sudden? I thought how lucky I was to be there. I mean, in spite of everything, at that moment I was *glad*. I wouldn't have cared if Philine had a nursery full of idiot children upstairs. I wouldn't have cared.

[46]

Afterwards we sat under the pecan tree in the back yard. It was more like spring than fall, and the leaves hadn't even thought of shedding. Philine and Miss Fiffy kept up this cat's-cradle conversation about Uncle Whosis and Cousin Whatsis and Aunt Sowhat in New Orleans and Violet Parish, and wasn't it a mess about poor Alletta Wendelken in Natchez (she married again before her decree was final, thus making a bigamist of herself, the skinniest girl in the state of Mississippi) and Lakeland d'Aurevilly—my cousin who looks like the grasshopper refused by the ant, he's ancient and tiny; he was the first man to cross the United States of America entirely by canoe (he's ninety-four and one-half years old now)—has decided to write a book about Evangeline and the Acadians (he must not have heard of Henry *Wadsworth* Longfellow); AND one must remember to inquire just what it is keeps Acis so occupied down there at Bayou Clair, there have been stories going round . . . on they went, and I was perfectly happy to hear them rambling on, making sounds of delight, of woe, of pity, of horror, then back to laughing again.

All night I dreamed of Philine. I never dream a great deal, and usually can't remember my dreams; but these connected dreams were vivid in my memory next morning. The strangest was where Philine came into my room and undressed and turned into Lola. In another part, strangely, Philine and I were walking together in Persepolis. We were going along the old road that leads across Shattuck's property to the Ilevert branch of the Alabama River. In this dream Philine had picked a brief spray of yellow jessamine, and was holding it in her teeth while she talked, turning it round and round, her face framed by those black locks.

But always in the dream her eyes were the same, looking right at me, right to me, right through me, saying in effect, "Take me." Lola in the dream was like Lola in life, like I had seen her that time before the mirror. I suppose that most girls would be pretty amazed if they learned some of the cavortings and carryings-on they do in boys' night-thoughts.

That old hellishness in the blood has refused virgins the right to be virgins, at least in dreams. Next morning I was so grouchy from having slept so fitfully, and sipping my second cup of coffee and loathing the idea of going to the office when here came Philine onto the back porch in a white housecoat, her hair tousled.

"Mawning, mawning," she said to Fern and me.

"How you like your eggs this morning, Miss Philine?"

"Scrambled. But I want some coffee right this minute, please, Fern."

"Said than done," mumbled Fern, and came back with it in a second.

"What good square hands you have," observed Philine, letting her hand roam over the back of mine, where it rested on the *Register.* "Do you play the piano?"

"No."

"You should, with hands like that."

"Do you play?"

"A little. Aunt Netta was my first teacher."

"I guess she's a good one."

"Oh, sure. What do you do?"

"I work at Hartley and Craven's office, you know that."

"Of course I know *that,* but I mean what do you *do?* What are you *really* interested in?"

"Enjoying life."

"That's what I'm getting at. How do you enjoy life?"

"There's lotta ways."

"Doubtless. Oh, doubtless. Do you make chewing-gum murals or rob graves? One never knows," she sighed, "with these Alabama boys."

I raised my eyebrows. "Neither. I guess I rather like to perform autopsies on clocks and motors." That wasn't what I was thinking, though, studying her deep-plunging neck-line.

"Somehow," she said, "that's not the manner I expected. But it'll do. Are you interested in art?"

"Honey, if you're an artist, I'm interested in art."

[48]

She laughed and started to eat the eggs Fern had brought.

"I got news for you, I *am* an artist. *Un peu. Un petit peu.* Until just lately I suppose I ranked as a dabbler, nothing more."

"Is that bad?" I frowned. *Dabble* was a word I associated with going down to the river on Saturday afternoons to do nothing special, just be there.

"It's according to your tone of voice when you say it, I guess."

"I don't know a thing about art; why don't you teach me?" I said, thinking I'd like to teach her some things, too, or maybe she already knew as well as me.

"The first lesson," she smiled wickedly, "would necessitate your playing hooky from work today. Are you game?"

Damn if that's not the oompteenth time in a space of days I've heard *first lesson:* I'm starting school over again, thought I. Then I considered all the reasons for not to take off from work, but my mind had made itself up when Philine smiled, and there was nothing to do but go telephone that I wasn't coming to the office that day. Which I did. When I came back to the table she was stretching luxuriously. "I'll be ready in two shakes of a lamb's tail, *mon enfant,*" she said, and sidled inside.

Strolling along under the oak trees on North Conception Street, freckled by the bright sunlight sifting through the leaves, while Philine was holding my arm and saying something now and again in that Lazy River voice of hers, I was happy enough to sing. We turned into St. Anthony Street, then went south on Joachim; it was a perfect breezy day, and the streets smelled of coffee roasting. Zuolagaland (island or continent?) sank slowly into a blue placid sea.

"We are going to call on one of the charmingest creatures in this town," said Philine.

"Who might that be?" I asked.

"An old man named Kosta Reynolds; he's a painter. He

[49]

used to be Court painter to one of the Balkan Courts, before the first World War."

"What am I going to say to him?" I inquired, being a little uneasy.

"Don't have to say anything—all you do is say *Mmmmm* once or twice very knowingly, and mumble something with the word *chiaroscuro* in it."

"What's that?" I asked.

"It's an Italian word that means hodge-podge of light and dark, you know—contrasty. If you use that word people will think you are the cat's pajamas, and know all about painting."

"Say it again."

"*Chiaroscuro*. Like this, kee-ar-oss-koo-ro. Try it."

"Karrus-kurrus."

"Good enough! Don't forget."

"Okay."

We came to a stairway door on the noisiest part of Conti Street, and started a four flights' climb through the high whitewashed halls. Behind the paneled doorways could be heard the drone and occasional whine of electric fans. When we reached the top, we pulled a braided cord, and after a minute a little pixie man, about two thousand years old, with bright eyes, came and opened in reply.

"Philine, Philine!" he cried rapturously.

He kissed her cheeks, then patted her arms and kept on patting them.

"And who is this young man?" he said, with a sharp glance my way.

So we were introduced, then he led us through a wide hall hung with lithographs and things to a huge room that ran the entire length of the building. It had been whitewashed once, but not recently. The windows either end were open, which was a blessing, since the panes were so begrimed you couldn't see through them. There were big statues of naked gods and goddesses cavorting like the illustrations in Bulfinch at home, pictures everywhere, odds and ends of arms, legs, and torsos in plaster, pieces of dingy curtain material, and bunches of dead flowers. There were two little fireplaces lost in the shuffle, over one of them a life-size painting of a fat man in a kind of hussar uniform, the sort that has that eternal dangling sleeve on the shoulder, braided and fussed up like the senior class operetta. Near the windows at the back were some wicker chairs and sofas in a little clearing; there he led us.

"You've heard of my tragedy?" he moaned to Philine.

"What tragedy?"

"Baudauer's dead."

"Oh, no, no!" she exclaimed, then softly, "What a shame, I'm so sorry."

"I haven't painted since, I'm so bereft. He was fifteen years. I had him the whole time."

"Poor Baudauer. When did it happen?"

"About two months ago. Old age they said. He was sick the night before he came back from the country—I had had to go to Atlanta to hang an exhibition. I rushed him to Dr. Pratt's in a taxi; just before he died he opened his eyes and looked at me, and twitched his tail. I broke down afterwards, and they brought me home. I took to my bed, thinking I might die of sorrow. Usually it's the other way round. The pet dies of sorrow for the master."

"I can't believe he's gone." Then turning to me, Philine added, "It's Mr. Kosta's lovely poodle. Where's his portrait, Kosta?"

"I'll get it." Then he went skitting off to another room, returning with a huge canvas which he propped up in a chair. It was an oil of a big brown poodle with eyes hidden under raggedy eyebrows. But that old man had painted two little specks of light in the eyes that made you see the deviltry of that dog, almost human. While we studied it, he disappeared and brought a big folder of drawings which he spread on the floor—all of the dog: sleeping, eating, sitting on a sofa, looking out the window, one in a hat with a plume.

"Oh, that sweet animal," said Philine, glancing again.

[51]

through all the drawings and making little cooing sounds of sympathy. So I looked at them all politely; I love dogs, too, but I couldn't get into the gloom-fest with them 'cause I didn't know Baudauer. So while they were telling each other all of this animal's smart tricks, I went on safari through the room.

It reminded me of two things: our attic, and Lily's gift and greeting-card shop in Persepolis. I mean, there was *more* than you could look at, even if your eyes went in different directions. I started on the big paintings, since they were the biggest. Some looked to me like the Gulf Coast and some were wild mountainous scenery like used to be made up into jigsaw puzzles. They were pleasant pictures, full of sunlight and bright skies. None of your "Fish Eyes in a Whirlwind" like Son likes. Then there were small oils, painted in a kind of unfinished manner, though I guess that was intentional, of Hindu youths in brilliant turbans, some in uniforms, some in plain white jackets. Then unexpectedly I found a portrait of Philine, just smaller than life. It was her expression, but with a difference. Deviltry again.

I studied this for a while, wondering how it could be so like, and yet have this other quality. All the time, Mr. Kosta Reynolds was chitterchattering on.

"We buried poor Baudauer in the country. I thought I'd do a small statue, 'Pan Grieving,' or something, to mark the grave."

"But how lovely."

"I hope so."

All the time I couldn't take my eyes off the portrait of Philine: the eyes were like I knew them, but when you looked long enough you saw that the painter had made the mouth *mean*. I left though to poke through the piles of unframed canvases stacked in the corners. They all bored me, I never could get excited about views of the States Docks, or glimpses of ruined factories and all that kind of thing. Gimme good-looking people, or a dinner table with fruit and wine bottles tumbling over each other—or best of all a good landscape you can climb into and live there for hours at a time. My grampa liked Franz Hals and Salvator Rosa, also those luscious Dutch still lives, with the careful dewdrops on the careful roses, and the conspicuous ladybugs on the leaves.

There was a table covered in aged baize and a big ratty-looking portfolio lying on it, with chewed-up corners. Hmmm, I thought, Baudauer must have been left alone here, and bored, at some point. I flipped it open idly, and saw something to send my eyebrows up up up, disappearing into my hairline. It was Philine in her birthday suit. Buck. Stark. Nary a stitch. Not once, but a dozen times, a whole series of careful drawings of the girl, one or two with wisps of drapery about her, but mostly without. No mistaking who it was: the face and its expressions were too explicit to leave any doubt whatever. So, I thought, she can be found running around this establishment like September Morn on the right occasions. I must say I wondered at the ability of a man of Kosta Reynolds' age to make such sexy drawings. Having such a model, I guess he simply rose to the occasion, so to speak. You'd think by now though that all the fires were banked. But you never can tell. All the other hundred or so drawings were naked young men, every detail in place, save some of a beautiful Negro girl.

I studied the portrait of Philine a while longer. Mr. Kosta was saying, "But I am a worshiper of youth," and I thought this is no news to me, Kosta boy, after those drawings. Then I heard Philine laugh, and it was like she pulled a string, for I went trotting back to them.

"Been gallery-going, huh?" demanded Mr. Kosta, eying me.

"Yes," I said, shy before his disrobing gaze.

"Like what you saw?"

"Yes. Oh, sure I did, very much."

"For example?"

"Oh, everything, I guess."

"Phooey, that's politeness. What'd you *like?*"

"Well, I like the picture of children by the river, and Philine's portrait."

"Ah," said Philine.

"I guess you like that portfolio of drawings, too, eh?"

I stammered something and he laughed at me.

"I know what pleases young men," he said cockily. "Come here, I'll show you something you don't see every day of the week."

Philine smiled knowingly. "Might as well go see it." I followed him out the studio to a tiny room opening off the hall. By the small amount of light penetrating the grimy window, I saw it was a kind of storeroom, which must be his model's dressing-room, too. He lifted a soiled smock and revealed a statue: about two feet high, three foot long. It was two creatures from the Mythology: half goat and half human, both male, both supine, engaged in a sport I wouldn't want to have to describe to my mother or sister.

"Ever see anything like that?" asked Mr. Kosta, his bright eyes intent on my face.

"No," I said honestly.

"It's one of Rodin's lesser known works. This is the sketch; the bronze I believe is in England. Those English have a taste and a half for the wilder aspects of classical reference, but only when by impeccable artists, you understand. I adore the English. Look, ain't this-here cute?" He pointed delightedly at a specific detail. Nasty old hellion, I thought, I can see where your ideas lie, but I had to laugh. Older than time itself, and still going strong.

"You come back and see me sometime, alone." He winked. "I'll show you lotta things."

I bet you will, I thought. So then we rejoined Philine, and he served us coffee he made himself in a strange European coffee gadget, all polished metal and dinky-doos, and we talked. He forgot about Baudauer in a hurry it seemed to me, for no sooner did he put the pictures of his late lamented animal away than he was full of spirits and kept us laughing the rest of the visit.

Seems he had given Philine all sorts of addresses in Paris of cafés and this and that and the other that he'd known there, and although she obviously hadn't been to half of them, he kept on asking about Paris. He scarcely noticed me, save to fill my cup now and again.

That old man had been everywhere, and we laughed going over the Alps with him, and we roared in a storm on the Indian Ocean. It was after lunch time before leaving even entered our minds, and we left hurriedly as the Cathedral's deep bronze voice orated its leisured *bongs* over the sound of traffic. Mr. Kosta stood at the top of the stairs waving, and looking like a cockatoo with that white topknot bobbing.

"Don't forget," he said to me, "you're coming to see me."

"Karrus-kurrus!" I replied, playing the fool.

After supper that night (we helped Miss Fiffy in her garden in the afternoon and came in for supper ravenous) when I had finished getting up my laundry bundle, and had written to my folks, I was lying on my bed puffing smoke up to the ceiling and thinking of what a fine day it had been, and how I hated work; not that it wasn't pleasant in the office and the job interesting—but that it was the fact of getting up the same time every day, going through the same street to the same building, saying "Good morning" to people I didn't give a damn about, day after day after day.

I was deep in revery, when there came a tap at my door, and Philine came in without waiting for an answer. She was fresh from her bath, in her housecoat.

"Come here," she said, and glided out the room.

I followed onto the upstairs back porch. She was standing by the banister pointing. Over the top of the pecan trees, was rising a great yellow moon. The sky was very light, not a cloud or a star could be seen, only the moon big as a washtub and pulling the eye irresistibly. We didn't say anything. We sat in the rickety chairs there, and lit cigarettes. There was the sound of crickets, and now and again you'd hear voices or a door closing somewhere in the neighborhood. Faintly radios in other houses were chattering, or sounding music. Night on the Gulf Coast is very beautiful and has a special character that diminishes further north you go.

I studied Philine. Could her mouth make itself go mean like the mouth in Kosta Reynolds' picture of her? I decided perhaps it could, and hoped I'd never see it. Blackheaded women all have a set of expressions that are noticeable chiefly because framed in black. I guess what the artist saw was an example.

"Night's nice, isn't it?" drawled Philine, huskily.

"Yes," I softly answered.

We sat there staring at the moon for who knows how long. There simply wasn't anything to say, being bathed in that unbelievable wash of pale light. We heard Fern and Tony come back from the movies, and heard the radios silenced in the houses around. Then, by degrees, we found ourselves in each other's arms: it just happened, as natural as moons rising or leaves falling. When we'd reached a certain pitch, we broke away from each other, regarding each other fixedly. After the briefest of instants she led me into her room, where, by the light of the moon inundating the chamber, we fell into bed.

I suppose in all one's life there are maybe two or three, at most, events that arrange themselves so aptly, so unhurriedly, and so unreservedly, without any effort: I suppose that's why everything after, between Philine and me, was like an echo dying away, and we never were so much to each other again.

I originally learned the natural facts of life from a good-natured country girl name Ruby Lee Jimson, as I suppose did all the other boys my age and in the same class at Tutwiler High. Under the railroad viaduct, near Perkinson's Creek, is a pleasant mossy bank, secluded, high enough ground to be moderately free of mosquitoes, supplied sometimes—if the wind is right—with a whiff of honeysuckle or sweet-pepper from the woods beyond, and by common assent widely skirted by late strollers after about eight at night.

Here, under the burry golden stars of summer, Miss Ruby

Lee Jimson distributes a largesse of amorous favors which has earned her a place in the filling-station and all-night-café folklore of Sophia County. Wherever the boys congregate, her name is sure to come up, already a name seen down Fame's wistful vista, and spoken with reverent familiarity. "Ole Ruby," they say, and wink, but it's that cap-in-hand tone reserved for "Stonewall" and "Dizzy." She's since married a big strapping boy who lives in the middle of nowhere on the Ilevert branch of the Alabama River, and nobody's heard a word from her since.

If they ever put up a monument to Ruby Lee, it'll be a long list of names subscribed on the base. The thing is, Ruby could never get enough. Or maybe, the better way to say it is, Ruby could never give enough. She was the fact of summer, and nobody ever heard her say a cross word in her life. Such a monument should be a figure of Purity crowned with daisies, and holding a bunny-rabbit, if it would be true to Ruby, for with her one never once had that feeling of two in conspiracy in the act of love. Wickedness, even mischief, was an alien notion to her. Love was simply something that occurred when the sun went down.

That night in Philine's bed was the first time I ever slept with a girl of my own general social class. If one can imagine Ruby Lee educated and a little reserved, she'd be Philine, with the sole difference that Philine had a sense of complicity with the darkness, with the moon, with the season edging on a little each moment. Though my feeling for Ruby Lee was certainly what you'd call a *warm friendship,* my feeling for Philine was certainly what you'd call *first love.* Now, after my life has jigged its crazy way over a dozen different paths, I can still feel the sweetness of those embraces in all the fibers of my body, and nothing that has happened since can steal a whit of lustre from that night. And plenty has happened, as you'll see.

"Want a cig?" I asked Philine, at some hour of the morning.

[57]

"Unh-hunh," she asked drowsily, taking one. "Heaven knows, I never saw such moonlight."

"You must have the same thing on Lake Pontchartrain." I yawned.

"The same moon, but not *you*," she teased, tugging at my ear.

"Don't do that," I cautioned. I hate people messing about with my ears.

"Touchy," she said. I growled and bit her hand and she loved it. But after about a minute of that, she got up, and after another minute she sent me packing.

"No, no," she said, "it's almost morning. Go on to your room now."

So I did, after kissing her good morning in a most nocturnal fashion.

A few happy days flew by which followed the pattern of the first one; till Philine announced she was off to Romar on the Gulf of Mexico to laze in the sun and go crabbing in Pelican Lagoon or bathing in the surf. So off she went, with a little straw suitcase and a cartwheel hat. I carried her junk to the car for her.

"Now, listen, you behave and hurry home," I ordered.

"I'll come back soon," she answered lazily, puffing her cig, and staring me down. Her tone implied that she might or might not behave.

On the second night she was away I was about to lose my mind. I had eaten supper with Miss Fiffy but afterwards she closeted herself in her library cubicle and left me to my own devices; so after stretching out on my bed staring at the ceiling for a while, I came down and phoned Lola. Well, she wasn't busy but said come over in an hour, her hair would be dry (!) by then, and we'd go to the Saenger to see Joan Crawford. I had to tsk-tsk! her, she's so crazy, but I *was* glad to see her. For the first time I noticed how *much* lipstick she wore, and how much she laughed. Hello, Lola. Ha-ha-ha.

[58]

How're your folks? Ha-ha-ha. Too bad about Cousin Flo. Ha-ha-ha. Who gets her estate? Ha-ha-ha. Are you thirsty, what time is it, I like your red dress. Ha, ha, ha, ha, ha. She's what you call surenuff laughing girl. The thing is, it's all real, she really thinks everything is wonderful. Women have a way of setting each other off: it was because Philine is so quiet and smiles that indifferent smile that I first noticed Lola's laughing and turnabout, I never observed the manner of Philine's quietness until here I was with crazy Lola. Lola can't hide anything she thinks, it shows in her face. Philine hides everything.

Well, we went to see Joan Crawford (Lola is nutty over her) and this was one of her *sad* pictures (at the end she walks out into a blizzard in Canada to die) so Lola finished her handkerchief and started on mine. Just buckets. Afterwards she was all used up, starving to death, so we went and sat in the little back room at Constantine's to have a bite. It was deserted save for a group singing at a table in the corner. So Lola and I came as close to a quiet conversation as I guess we ever will.

"You know when I was little," she mused, biting a hangnail, "I read *Silver Screen* and *Photoplay* to shreds, and always planned to be a movie star. I studied expression, I studied toe dancing, and goodness knows I kept Kress in business buying Tangee lipstick to try on in my room. I went to every movie that came to both the Saenger and the Crown, sometimes the Empire. Except Westerns. I never could abide them.

"Then, later, when I went to California to visit my roommate from school—she's this precious girl, her father's in real estate like Daddy: Mary Nettles Rodney—*originally*, they're from Tennessee—well, when I went to Los Angeles and took a look for myself at that place, honey, I just want to tell you, I lost my ambition and my appetite all at once. I can't describe it. Couldn't *begin*. It's not hustlebustle like they must have in New York where they have rush hours: out there it's

[59]

traffic and racketing-around all night you try to sleep but you can't!"

"What you want it to be so quiet for?" I mumbled through a piece of rump-steak.

"*Everybody* owns a convertible or a station-wagon and they think nothing of driving *three hours* to go to a Coke party! Can you picture that? But the food! I thought that if I saw one more glup of whipped cream I'd toss my cookies, if you'll just excuse the expression. Whipped cream everywhere! I think they even rub it in their hair. I vowed if I survived to come home again I'd live on cornbread and turnip greens for a year. I never thought I'd lose sleep over turnip greens. Nossir. But I did! We won't even bring up the subject of oranges. Ugh!"

"My, sounds awful," said I politely.

"Oh, that's not all! Unh-*hunh!*" she chattered on, letting her steak get stone cold. "Well, see, I've never cared for stucco, never have—"

I mentally tuned her out for a minute, concentrating on what they were singing back in the corner. When I tuned Lola in again, she was still in California, then a minute later I heard her say, "But then we're all spoiled—that's what Mama says—says on the Gulf Coast we're all spoiled. Pretty places and pretty things."

"Fairly tol'rable food, too, when it's hot," I muttered, pointing at her steak, and she dove in.

That's life, I told myself. In seeking a little pleasant company I have flown myself right into the jaws of this talking-machine, Lola. Just then, out of a clear blue sky, she looked up, and spoke, over a forkful of tomato.

"Perrin'll be home soon."

"Ah?" I muttered, not giving a blue damn. Perrin is Son, and you can see why he'd be called Son, silly as that is, though I swear he's the Perrin type actually. Imagine, my own mother thinks it's a fine name! I've never been able to like him for an instant. First of all he's too pretty to be a boy.

I remember one summer, when we were little, we all

stayed the summer with Uncle Acis at Bayou Clair; we couldn't have been more than ten or eleven. On the first day we were there Uncle Acis took us in tow and walked over to Terriel—on that very day I decided Son was a perfect little snob. I have only to close my eyes to see him laughing and shaking his yellow ringlets and saying to me, "You don't know anything!" We had snapped at each other all day; coming back, Uncle Acis stopped and turned around and said, "One more word and I'll tie you-all tail against tail to a sweet-gum sapling, and you can woof at each other all night long." He would have, too.

Now Son was grown up and specialized in poetry-writing and swimming matches.

"For about two months or longer, I reckon," went on Lola, "I know he'll want to see you."

"I'd like to see him, too," I lied heartily, thinking Oh that snooty boy, like to see him, yeah, see him drowned in a privy.

"But you won't know him—he's changed much more than you. You probably don't remember him at all."

I considered this a moment, then Lola was left there eating as I flew off to Memoryland.

Son, as I remembered him, had unusually bright eyes. Even his mop of blond curls faded away when one was faced with those foxy clarities. Changeable of color, but unalteringly sharp and hellish in expression. In that summer at Uncle Acis' we might have become close friends in the way one can, in sharing one of the boundless summers of late childhood, develop that last possible moment of candor into a lifelong and comfortable relationship that is mute and changeless. The season itself had a climate of amity: when I ponder that summer, it seems that never before and certainly never since have such piled-up clouds existed, luminously white, blue-blurred on the edges with that dimension of heavenly distances that seems most to belong to music. Till the day I die, certain sounds of music heard over water will bring irrevocably to my mind the skies over Bayou Clair and those castellated clouds lumbering across them—I feel

[61]

again the heavy drowsiness of the air, the infinite afternoons, the green-almost-to-oppression greenness of the sweet gum, the bay, the burnished pine. That summer, so still, had the seeming length of all my life up to that point, and though I'm sure it must have poured down rain for half of it, my memory is all of the Southern sun literally exploding in the heavens, and of my sudden consciousness of being the creature inside my skin, which was well tanned and soft, and on which the shifting breezes fell with languor.

And Son, inside his skin, was just as out of reach as me. If I was the quiet boy, seeking the top of the oak tree, or rocking in the three-branched fork atop the tallest magnolia, Son was the little social gentleman and danced about the house, getting in Acis' way, and going through the bookshelves (Uncle Acis had hidden the too-lucidly illustrated Rabelais and Petronius) and expressing his almighty opinions on everything: he must have gotten pretty tired of Uncle Acis saying, "Boy, you will have fever of the mouth if you don't shut up. It's a wonder you can stop long enough to eat."

But Son had just discovered words I guess, not that anybody knew then he'd take to writing. On the other hand, I had discovered silence, or rather fallen into it. I dreamed crazy things in broad daylight, about long expeditions into Africa or Brazil, voyages around the world, things like that: I had a kind of mental continued story to which I added a chapter every day. I relied heavily on *National Geographic Magazine* (Acis' mother had taken a lifetime subscription; nobody ever told the magazine when she died) for my material, and my dreams were as marvelously colored as the picture therein, thoroughly in keeping with the brilliance of the landscape in which I rested.

The only times Son and I moved in the same orbit were when Uncle Acis took us out in the sailboat, then we fought as always. Lola was the baby and the tagger-along, no one ever noticed her especially save to pull sandspurs from her feet, or help her through barbed-wire fences. She must have been six-ish, I think. She had an old mongrel dog, woolly, small, that she adored, named Baby Ray. Once I did indeed throw Son into the Bay, just pushed him off the side of the sailboat, and Uncle Acis fished him in again and gave us what-for, said we'd have to take turns in the boat after that, because he was jolly well bedamned if he'd be responsible for the drowning of a pair of hellions. "Why do y'all get on each other's nerves so?" he'd ask all the time.

Yet there was a kind of invincible truce we arrived at on occasion when we were perfectly at peace, though never for a moment joined in any project. Son used to lay out miniature gardens with pebbles and soda water stoppers, buttons, beads, etc. Poor Lola was never permitted to join in, because Baby Ray always tore things up. The truth is, there were times when I'd have liked to work with Son on these lengthy projects but he was so bossy, and liked everything so exact, and I really couldn't think up paths and beds, rockeries and ponds like he could. So I'd swipe me a whole big box of matches from the pantry and tear out to a piece of beach beyond Flycatcher Creek. I'd stick those matches in the sand to make armies, whole battalions on march, finally I'd set them all on fire, and finish in a glorious burst.

So though we were known collectively as "the kids" we comprised three separate little worlds, which rarely impinged. Once we fought in earnest: over a little-old bird. Son was desperately afraid of bugs and birds. Snakes and alligators were nothing to him, I've seen him tease both. But a beetle crawling on his arm could send him hysterical, and as for a bird—! On the other hand, I'm a bird-fancier.

I put a sparrow in his room, and hid back of the linen press in the hall till he went in there, then held the door shut from outside. The bird didn't show itself for a minute, then I heard a fluttering, then a choking sound from Son—he ran to the door without saying anything, just breathing hard. I held fast, he gave up, and ran back from the door to the window. The poor bird was flying all over, crazy by then. I gave them a few minutes of each other then opened the door, and slid in. It was simple to open the screens, and

[63]

guide the sparrow out, but Son was wrapped tight as a mummy in his bedclothes, and I had to go over and shake him out. He was flushed, and his eyes were bright. When I saw him, I had that awful feeling of joke-gone-wrong. Incapable of speech for a moment, he finally blurted out, "You put that bird in here!" very bitterly.

"No, he just came in to see if you were as big a fraidy-cat as he'd heard," I replied, snippily. At that Son just got up and came over to me and dug his fingers into my neck, choking me and scratching me with his nails all at once. (I still have a little scar on each side; they're scarcely noticeable, especially in a collar.) We both overflowed with the accumulated rancor of the summer: over and over we rolled, locked tightly together, kicking, clawing, grunting.

Baby Ray found us first, and by her excited *ruff! ruff!* brought Lola, who yipped once and ran for Jenkins, the yard man; since both Uncle Acis and Modena the cook were away at the moment. That gentle brown old man, clucking regretfully, came in and lifted us apart as easy as separating seedlings. He shook us, not roughly, but admonishingly.

"Now y'all oughtn't to do that," he pleaded. "Plenty of time to fight when you is older and has things to fight over."

I sobbed a little, Son just glared, Lola cried, and Baby Ray took it all for a festival, and went about yapping joyfully.

"Go wash off your pore bloody neck, chile," Jenkins told me, then sharply to Son, "I reckon you oughta just file down them claws a little, Mr. Perrin."

He made us say we were sorry and shake hands. After that explosion I guess we might have put aside our differences, but that Uncle Acis was so furious with us he forbade us to speak to each other on pain of being shipped home instantly, and furthermore made one of us accompany him always.

So Son and I had a kind of solemn politeness enforced on us, we both enjoyed the high drama of it: sometimes I'd catch his face intently studying mine—two big eyes and a throw of yellow curls seen above the business of extracting a nugget of meat from a crab claw in the gumbo. I remember once he read my mind. I can't remember the text, only the occasion. He had smiled a very self-satisfied smile, amused not only at reading my mind, but at the knowledge that I respected the fact of his cleverness.

Having to follow Uncle Acis on alternate days is how I came to know my crazy uncle, that wondrous man, wholly angelic, wholly hothead. Following him is simpler sounding than the doing of it. I mean either in conversation—verbally he's a skylark—or in physical fact: he's a darter, a swooper, he'll start in one direction then go twenty others. If Uncle Acis said two o'clock, he meant either one or three. If he said front gate, likely as not you'd meet him at the back or halfway between. But I followed truly, and would have to hell and back.

Though the summer was marvelously eventful, I was happy at last to go upcountry, back home to the good red clay banks and rolling hills of Persepolis, to my own family. Since the moment Acis made us shake hands and say goodbye, since Son, stiff and gazing downward, mumbled "So long," then ran inside, I hadn't glimpsed his beautiful snotty visage. What would he be like, I wondered. But from deep inside surged up that old distrust, that instinct to hide the Silver Bells and Banana Caramels when he hove into sight.

"Honey, where have you gone?" asked Lola, lazily, breaking her roll.

"Oh, thinking," I replied.

"Rust your brain."

"Listen," I muttered. "You've been telling me all summer that Son is coming home. What's the truth, now tell me the truth, is he or is he not? What the hell is he doing all this time in New York?"

"Why he's just studying."

"Studying what, where?"

"Why honey, you'll have to ask Mama. She's the one corresponds with that boy. He don't study me, or Daddy, that's for sure. Doesn't know we exist. It's Mama gives him the extra money all the time: I just don't know what he does with it all, but it seems to me he goes through a lot."

"Is he still writing poetry and that kinda stuff?"

"Of course. Daddy and Mama don't know exactly what to make of it; he explained some to me, and I thought it was nice after I understood it. It's not like what we have in school, though. It's terribly modern. Some of those real serious magazines without pictures in them, just writing, have brought out lots of his things. I'll show you next time you're at the house. The last one he sent had an awful story about a man going in a bawdy-house in Morocco and a fight breaking out amongst the floozies: it was kind of sad, in a sloppy way, I guess Mama wouldn't have noticed it 'cept Perrin's poems followed right after this story, see, and it gave Mama a real turn, I guess. I told her she was old-fashioned."

"Is he gonna do that all his life, write poetry?"

"You ask *him*, 'cause he is coming on the L and N, and we can just go down to the station and see him come in, which will be late at night on the twenty-second, kiddo."

"Kiddo, yourself."

Lola regarded herself carefully in her vanity mirror. "Though I don't know if I can stand that old station, myself. I have spent exactly one half of my life waving things in and waving things out of that station. Someday I'm gonna disguise myself as a nun and rush up at the last minute and hop on that train and disappear in the direction of the nearest steamboat sailing for Switzerland."

I wondered for a minute if her geography was so hazy she really thought she'd sail right to Zurich or Lucerne on a dear little white steamer, like a toy. I guess she really thought so. I guess she thought she'd be met on a pier that looked just like the Alba Club by the King of Switzerland and old Heidi with her stinky goats, and a yodeling troupe, and I don't know what-all else.

When I took her up on her front porch, I was overcome with a dozen emotions at once, and when I told her goodnight I took the sweet fool in my arms and gave her a good hard kiss on the mouth. She drew back, startled.

"Now just how did you mean that?" she asked.

For answer I just smiled, then she slapped me. I still didn't move, it hadn't hurt me, but tears came into her eyes (*her eyes,* when it was me had been given the swat) and she touched my cheek gingerly, then kissed it lightly. "I'm sorry. I wasn't noticing what I did."

"Doesn't matter."

Then we heard Lola's mother scuffling around upstairs, and her voice floated down to us, her papery night-voice, neither whisper nor sigh.

"Is that y'all, Lola? Is that y'all?"

"Yes'm."

"Oh. All right. Turn out the porch light, hear?"

"Yes'm. I'm coming right up." Then to me: "You're impossible, just impossible. Thank you, I enjoyed my evening."

She looked searchingly into my eyes for an instant, before running inside and locking the door. I started strolling home, and saw that already a little nibble was gone from the moon. Philine, my darling, hurry home, I said to the night, and a boat on the River gave an answer: *Poop, poop, hooo-eeee!*

"Now, remember, your mother is a very nervous woman," Mr. Charlie told Lola. "Behave."

"That's something I always try to remember," said Lola. "But after all, Daddy, it's only Perrin coming on that L and N, it's not the President, or the Holy Ghost."

"But he's more important in this house than either of them, you oughta know that, baby," answered Mr. Charlie, puffing his cigar.

We three had been assembled on the front porch for thirty minutes, waiting for Cousin Annie to come down, so we could start to the station. Mr. Charlie was more talkative than usual, I guess he was pleased to see Son again, though he may have only caught a little of Cousin Annie's fever.

Feverish she was, too; the poor thing was beside herself. She'd rearranged the same couple of hairpins ten thousand times, checked the icebox to see that Son's cold supper hadn't walked off, lost her gloves, run upstairs and down, and all the time Lola and Mr. Charlie and I just bided our time on the porch.

"At this moment," drawled Mr. Charlie, "your mother is putting an envelope of money under Son's pillow: she thinks I don't know this; and she'd do it even if she knew she'd be horsewhipped five minutes after."

"I never noticed her skulking around *my* pillow," said Lola, bitterly.

"Now, baby! She knows you put the squeeze on me, just same as Son gives her a rough time at the old checkbook."

As I listened to them, I began to find it difficult to believe that Mr. Charlie, big, slow, high of color, thick of hair, could be father of Son. Lola, for all her foolishness, has something of her father about her eyes and her hair is akin to his lion mane. But Son is neither like him nor like Cousin Annie.

Cousin Annie is the nervous type for sure, you have the feeling she's jittered all her color away and has been left mousy. But you can see her bloodline in her proud bony nose, and if you catch her seated and start on family history, she'll work herself into a fine flush, and start twinkling. Just say *Vine and Olive Colony* or *Alba Tract,* that's enough, and that woman is gone. She's not prissy-proud, it's just that it's all so gone and so *romantical,* but can all be proved by papers. When Cousin Annie dies, it'll be in a seizure of enthusiasm over some map with squiggly writing.

Mr. Charlie, on the other hand, though "well-connected," has several good strains of bandit in his chart, maybe even Copeland gang. I heard him once say his family was all half-breed and only much later figured it that he meant half good family and half pure-dee wildness. Not that people pay much attention to that sort of thing any longer: it's the bank account that determines in this penny-pinch world, when all's said and done; though in a happier time they used to

[68]

have a saying in Mobile that went like this: "In Boston, they say who is his grandfather; in New York, they say is he rich; in Charleston, they say has he manners; but in Mobile they say can he drink?" Which reminds me of Grampa reading the *Genealogical Journal* and remarking that the *Mayflower* obviously had the same number of accommodations as the *Normandie.* Anyway, Mr. Charlie is difficult to know—smiles his drowsy smile for everybody, but just doesn't talk.

The L and N Station is the smelliest station in the world: by that I mean there is a greater variety of smells coming and going there than any place you might care to mention. It's only twenty paces from the Mobile River, and though they've changed it now, a year or so ago, at the time I speak of, it was an old one-story brick building, and a lot of sheds, and covered-over tracks. You can smell the heady saltiness of river water, sometimes fish, sometimes sewage, and quite often that old pee-and-orange-peel perfume that is common to all railroad stations. The choking smoke of the engines, the cooking smell from lower Government Street eateries, the onion-and-all-rooty-vegetables smell that holds forever on Commerce Street and Front Street, where the produce houses are, the really fine scent of coffee roasting—well, you can have your choice, according to the wind and the season.

Time we had collected Cousin Annie from where she'd flown off in every direction (she never did find her gloves) and gotten the car around to the river side of the station, and parked it, making our way over tracks, and dollies laden with luggage, piles of melting ice, toward the hallowed spot where Perrin would alight, it was nearly time for the train. There were all sorts of excited fools running around, waiting to welcome whoever; one group in mourning come to collect either the body or the relatives coming from afar, a lady with two noisy terriers, and the usual nonchalant railroad employees.

"Is it on time, Charlie?" worried Cousin Annie.

Mr. Charlie leisurely strolled to the blackboard, Lola hang-

[69]

ing on his arm. They studied the chalked figures then strolled leisurely back.

"Seems to be," he told her.

"Oh," said Cousin Annie, then turned to her daughter. "Now, Lola, don't you let me cry!" she blurted. "If you think I'm gonna begin, you do something to attract attention."

"Like jump in the River, maybe?" said Lola vaguely, peering down the tracks.

"Oh! If I thought you were giving me sarcasm, I'd slap you right here!"

"No, Mother: I was really just talking to hear myself talk. I didn't mean that."

"I hope not!"

"Besides, I think Etta Mae better do the tricks, 'cause I may break down myself," added Lola.

"Uh-oh!" exclaimed Mr. Charlie. "I better just split my handkerchief in threes right now."

"I ain't no weeper, thank heaven," insisted Etta Mae vehemently. "Misery never was my dish. Don't tear up no good linen for me, Mr. Charlie."

"Well, Son's been in New York City almost a year, Charlie, and I must say I'll be glad to see him home."

"We're all glad as we can be," said Mr. Charlie. "And he'll be glad to be back."

"It's been a long time since I've seen Perrin," I remarked, making conversation to Cousin Annie.

"Years and years!" she cried out, fixing me with a look that seemed to be pity for someone hadn't had the privilege of basking in the glow of her son. "Honey, you'll scarcely know him. You'll be a surprise to him, too, I daresay. Oh, it's too bad Acis couldn't be here tonight. But he wouldn't come to town even to see the statue of Admiral Semmes do a shimmy-dance; that's what he *says.*"

"What's the latest news on Uncle Acis?" I inquired. "Have y'all been down there lately?"

"I tell ya," Mr. Charlie intoned, "we hear all kinda tales

[70]

about Acis down there in those woods, but we've never gone down to check up."

"Now, *Charles!*" scolded Cousin Annie.

"This boy's not a child any more," said he.

"Well, *Lola,*" frowned Annie meaningfully, at which Lola addressed herself very seriously to Etta Mae.

"Etta Mae, hon, I hope you brought my bottle, and my cod-liver oil, also a change of didies, 'cause we're gonna have that Lola-is-still-a-baby routine again."

"Girl, you a mess!" hooted Etta Mae and we all chuckled; Cousin Annie even managed a little what-hath-God-wrought? smile.

"As if everybody in the whole wide weary world didn't know that Uncle Acis has taken up with some barefooted farm girl down there," added Lola.

Cousin Annie frowned preparatory to scolding Lola, but just then there came a sad drawn-out train whistle, sounding from far enough away to be in Chickasabogue Swamp still, but up and down the track all the little knots of people began to buzz. The way Cousin Annie was leaning over that track, bobbing her head and cooing, I thought she would run up the track, catch that train, and kiss its sooty face to thank it for bringing her boy home. She is a real fool when it comes to Perrin. Mr. Charlie must have had the same thought, for he put his arm around her to hold her to earth, and said, "It'll be a minute or so yet."

"I hate trains when you're not gonna get on them," sneered Lola.

"I know he'll really be hungry," remarked Etta Mae.

"I'm hungry myself," said Mr. Charlie.

"Me, too," I added, because I always am. I love to eat.

Then, before anybody could go up in a burst of feathers, or jump in the River, or die of nervous starvation, here it came: way up Front Street you could see it puffing unconcernedly along, already slowing down. In that moment when everybody craned their necks for a glimpse of the black engine, I had suddenly a flash of intuition, of brain storm, or

[71]

something, like the night of the storm, almost. I knew that the train was bearing down on my life in a certain way: I felt it. I knew that all my memories I had kept of that summer at Bayou Clair were doomed before I had sorted them out, or filed them—and saddest of all, before I had understood one thing of them. Now I can describe my feeling a little, but as that train puffed, hooted, and finally tinkled its mischievous bell, all I knew was that some profound unquiet had been dredged up from the rich muddy alluvium in the bottom of my soul.

But here was the train, and the porters were pulling luggage out. Our group was nervously looking in both directions. I watched them, since I didn't really know what Perrin looked like at this point. Dogs were barking.

"There he is, Miss Annie," said Etta Mae, pointing.

I looked, the others ran. Several young guys got off, and which might be Perrin? Cousin Annie could easily be an Olympic sprinter: by the time Lola and Mr. Charlie had reached Perrin, Cousin Annie had already embraced him hard enough to knock her hat off, and Etta Mae picked it up for her. All I could see as I followed them was a blond head in the middle of a knot of embraces and exclamations and suitcase-fumbling. I guess Perrin has had a line of people waiting to tote things for him all his life. There was some difficulty about his typewriter; he went back into the train for it. Cousin Annie was glowing, Lola was smiling and even old Charlie seemed animated; Etta Mae was civil.

Then he came out again, and Cousin Annie was saying, "Son, speak to your cousin!" Perrin turned to me: "Well!" he said, "it's been a long long time." When I took his hand, I felt I held the warm paw of the original Electric Monkey. I had the impression of a creature too apt, too clever, and too handsome to be any good at all in the workaday world. The blond ringlets were flattened out, the blue eyes now blue-gray, but the old shine was about him still, and my feeling still was *Hide the bon-bons, here he comes.*

"Hello, Perrin," I mumbled.

[72]

"We have a lot of catching-up to do, it's been ten years."

"I know."

"No, it's not too heavy," Lola was saying, struggling with the typewriter.

"No, give it to me," Mr. Charlie insisted, and took it away from her.

As we strolled toward the car, Perrin casually put his arm around my shoulders.

"Mother says you've come to work in Mobile."

"Yes, for a while anyway."

"I've come to work in Mobile, too," he murmured, smiling to himself. He intended a joke I didn't see.

"Where will you work?" I politely inquired.

"In people's hearts," he answered mockingly but grandly, "and on their sympathies. And in their checkbooks. I'm dying to go to Europe."

"Oh?" I smiled faintly.

"Who's going to Europe?" asked Perrin's mother.

"Why, Cousin here says he's hot to go to Europe," said Perrin with a straight face, patting my back. I frowned.

"He just came to Mobile," said Cousin Annie. "What is he, a gypsy?"

"I reckon, that's it, Cousin is a gypsy, and me—" He raised one eyebrow. "I am—"

"Come on, come on," drawled Mr. Charlie. "Y'all can chew the fat at home."

Back at the house, bottles were opened, lights lit, and the well-known fatted calf was trotted out and served up. Cousin Annie and Etta Mae had outdone themselves; we were partying in the kitchen till all hours. Studying Perrin, I began to see that look of somebody's lived in New York for a while, a kind of brightness that's part fatigue and part elation—it takes a Southerner a year to acquire this look in New York, but only a few weeks to lose it when he's home again. I don't mean to imply that Perrin had a case of wobble-eye like some people, but just that he seemed mighty flighty. He'd have had a hard time to be at ease, anyway, with Cousin Annie

[73]

waiting at his right hand to burn down the house if he said do it. All he'd have had to do would be say *Burn it down!* and she'd shout *Yes, sire!* and jump in the matchbox.

A few days later we had a holiday, and I slept late. When I came down at ten-ish Tony had the stable doors open out in the back yard, and was polishing Miss Fiffy's old ruin of a Hispano that sat up on blocks against a day of picnicking. Fern and Fiffy were making a mess and having themselves a time on the back porch. The sun was pouring in, and there they sat: Fern was shelling butterbeans; Miss Fiffy was reading aloud to her the comic strip of "Poor Effie" from dusty yellow *News-Items* she'd dragged from her storeroom.

"Then it shows Poor Effie going out in this rainstorm to take this warning letter to Mr. Furious, and she doesn't know she's being followed by this Arabian on horseback, as if anybody with two eyes wouldn't notice such a thing."

"Oo-ee," gurgled Fern, "I notice anything on four feet, or two either, trailing after me on a dark night."

"But this pore little fool doesn't. Neither does the dog notice. I don't know what good that dog is, save for her to talk to when there's no other characters about. Like here she says, 'Gosh, Nipper, I hope Mr. Furious is home. 'Cause Mrs. Lovely will be awful mad at me if I stay out any longer!' "

Fern dropped a handful of beans with a *plop!* into the collander. "What does that dog do?"

"He seems to turn his big perfectly expressionless eyes up to her as if to say, 'You talk too much.' She does, too, look how the words fill up all this space."

"That pore little girl never seemed the brightest thing on this earth to me," observed Fern. "But the pore child has had to wear that same dress with the collar for at least ten years. Must be made of real fine durable stuff, but God love her, I'da got sick of it long time ago. She only has that one dress: I reckon she must rinch it out overnight."

"No dog in Christendom is dumb as this Nipper," said

[74]

Fiffy disgustedly. "Once in a while he attacks the villain and keeps the dam from being blown up, but that doesn't save him from being the dullest animal ever."

"Did you know Mr. Kosta Reynolds' famous Baudauer?" I interrupted Fiffy to ask. She put down her paper and regarded me with a curious expression.

"Of course," she answered slowly, "that lovely beast. I knew him well. Very well indeed. He was the prince among dogs. But then dogs are only extensions of their masters' egos in certain cases. I'm not detracting from Baudauer one bit to say he owed his charm to Kosta. I swear to you he had some of Kosta's mannerisms."

I raised my eyebrows high as they would go at this, and she caught it, and laughed.

"Oh, that Kosta Reynolds!" said she, looking out into the yard. "He'll never get a medal for piety nor purity, but the saints I prefer are those that first were great sinners. A passive martyrdom is just not enough for me. Oh, yes, Kosta! His career has been somewhat blushful, but I forgive him everything for those paintings of Bayou la Batre and for the fact that he's a regular conversational *alpiniste*. He'll follow without blinking across the widest changes of subject. I'll overlook anything up to murder in people who know what I'm talking about, and will follow all the way." She continued to stare into the yard.

"I've 'bout finished the beans," interjected Fern. "But you've left me with one shoe on, and one off. *Is* Mr. Furious at home?" Then Fiffy scrambled around amidst the wreckage and found the rest.

"Yes, he opens the door and says, 'Why, Effie child, what are you doing out on a night like this? You and Nipper come in and dry yourselves by the fire.'"

"I don't guess he'll think to offer her a hot toddy," sighed Fern.

"No, he manages a cup of coffee for her, though." Fiffy put the yellowed paper down again. "Baudauer used to drink tea, you know. Kosta had a special large cup for him, and

[75]

Baudauer would always be furious if he didn't have his part of the party."

"Excuse me . . ." I interrupted again. "But I wonder if you've heard when Philine is coming back?" An urgency seeped into my question in spite of me, the two women looked at me, exchanged glances.

"Matter of fact, I did," announced Fiffy. "In this morning's mail. Next Sunday. She's gone on to stay with friends at Camp Catiebelle for a couple days. She sent you her greetings. The card's in there by the telephone."

As though hearing its name spoken, the telephone gave a loud ring just then. I ran to answer; it was Perrin calling me, saying to save Saturday night for us to get together, so I said all right, I would, and that was that. After I hung up, I stood there thinking how I'd never get accustomed to Perrin being real, after him being a childhood memory for so long. Fiffy's voice came from the porch, still reading "Poor Effie."

"All this time he's reading the letter and the Arabian is staring in the window bold as you please."

"Is he on his horse," asked Fern, "or has he just climbed up somehow?"

"I can't tell, Fern, I think he's hanging on to the vines. Anyway none of them see him."

"Fine watchdog that Nipper is!"

I stood in the hall, gazing absently into the engraving of the Palace of Chambord which hung there. My mind was full of Philine, my mind was full of Perrin, two poles. When I wandered back out to them, they were saying something about Brother John. I hadn't given a thought to that old hellion for days. There was too much else on my mind.

Saturday night after supper we sat in Fiffy's big double-parlor where the lamps and unnumbered bunches of flowers gave an air of party. She was sitting there cutting the pages of some new French biography that had come in that day's mail, from New York. She had brought a knife from the supper table, and was making a series of *zzzzips*, stopping

[76]

occasionally to read a paragraph, then hurry impatiently to finish cutting. I was puffing smoke lazily up toward the gold-and-white ceiling. We were quiet 'cause we had talked ourselves out at supper, and had to regather our strength. Perrin was due to call for me, and all I could think was: what did we really have to talk about together?

Then we heard the doorbell, and shortly after, Fern ushered in the golden boy of the Moreland household, he was all dolled up, his eyes bright. He stood there grinning at us like a real Cheshire Cat, confident of his own radiation and expecting us to fall down and cry out praises, I guess. He strolled over and took Miss Fiffy's hand with a flourish and kissed it with a smack, which pleased and alarmed her.

"Have to watch out for this one!" She laughed.

"He musta learned some pretty fancy manners in New York," I said.

"No," said Perrin. "My mama taught me to kiss charming ladies' hands, when I was three."

"Praise to the face is open disgrace. Sit down," said Fiff.

"I've known Miss Fifield much longer than *you*," he said. "We're old old friends."

"That may be so," tittered Fiffy before I could reply, "but this young man and I are more than friends—" she indicated me with a wave of the hand—"we're *compatriots,* and we both live in the rocky province of Stubbornia. Charm cannot melt us."

"They lotta places not shown on maps," I observed, thinking of Zuolagaland and Lola's Switzerland, as well as this rocky province.

"But charm's still the best passport," insisted Perrin, as though he had invented charm single-handed. He was almost dancing, he was so conceited.

"Oh, sit down and behave," I shouted impatiently. "You're so charming you make my teeth hurt!"

"Tum-te-*tum,* just move that pile of books," said Fiffy, smoothing down her wild locks. Charm might not melt that lady, but it could certainly make her feathers ruffle up de-

[77]

lightedly. She picked up her bell and gave a loud *plonkle-plonkle,* and Fern brought the coffee tray after a second.

"Two, thanks." Perrin took his cup, then she handed mine over, and poured her own.

"I have it on excellent authority," stated Fiffy, "that you've published some fine poetry. Is this true?"

"Well, I have published a few things," he answered. "And I've written a *Masque of Death.*"

"Oh? Hmmm. I see. Death muted or Death flamboyant?"

"Flamboyant. I'm not a Southerner for nothing."

"You must tell me who the new poets are," she said.

"Richard Wilbur, first of all! I'll lend you his things."

"I want you to lend me Perrin Moreland. Don't you have copies I might see?"

"Yes, I'll bring them over."

By then I'd finished counting the scrolls around the mirror top, and was starting on the plaster acanthus leaves from which depend the chandeliers. Then Perrin, with his usual trick of reading minds, turned and cast his impudent eyes at me.

"I guess," he remarked, "that we're boring my cousin here to death. He reads nothing but law and hot-cha stories. He certainly doesn't read poetry."

"Oh, he doesn't have to—*yet,*" chimed Miss Fiffy. " 'Cause he lives it, he does indeed." I saw by her eyes that if it ever came to a choosing of sides, she'd be with *me,* against Perrin, for all of his charm and glib conversation. I smiled at her.

"Nobody ever died of boredom," she said. "Of course some people are too tender, and some too mischievous, to live in this world: they either die young, or turn fuddy-duddy. Some, like Kosta Reynolds, choose the clown's immunity. But nobody ever ever died of boredom."

"Hear, hear!" I shouted, and Miss Fiffy, thus encouraged, cascaded on for a full twenty minutes, mentioning Greenwood LaFleur, a purple suit worn by Henry James, went to look up something Jefferson said, went on talking, brooked no comment from Perrin, finally came around to literary

[78]

matters again. Shortly thereafter we excused ourselves, Perrin being in a kind of pet.

"Now don't forget," Fiffy told him as she walked us to the door, "to bring me the poems, and the new man Wilbur."

We walked in silence a moment. I could see Perrin had to be shaken out of his mood, so I began making clever conversation.

"Tell me," said I, "how did you happen to get into this poetry racket?"

"You impossible boy!" he cried, "it's not a racket! . . . oh, but it is in a sense of being undercover. Poetry *is* undercover."

"Is it?" I asked, not sure whether to laugh or cry.

"Yes, it's dealing with the truth about truths."

"You manage to wade," I told him grimly, "in water that's over my head."

"Hell's bells, Cousin, you're a poet, too; you're making little ole metaphors dime-a-dozen. I do believe you're smarter than you look."

"And you're very pretty, too," snorted I sarcastically, at which he took my arm lightly, and leaned toward me laughingly.

"Come, come, come, come, come! Let's begin again. We mustn't be snippy with each other. I want to get to know you, I don't want to play mutual insults. You're my unknown cousin: my parents say you're uncommunicative; my sister says you're cute. Me, I haven't located you yet."

"All right," I agreed. "We'll have a truce. But it's you that will cause the first ruckus."

"No, no, I'll keep the peace, 'cause you set me off to such advantage. I'm sure you have more brains than me, but I'm perfectly certain I have all the imagination. Then you have that marvelous black hair: sometimes it's very trying for me to be blond."

"Ever think of India ink?" I asked.

[79]

"Don't joke about brunets wanting to be blond and vice versa: it's the history of the world."

I could see this was leading nowhere but to gloom again, so I threw down my cigarette and jumped up and down on it, then ran a few yards, jumping up to touch tree branches overhead.

"Where we headin'?" I demanded.

"I thought I'd better take you on a tour of the more interesting bars and dives."

"Suits me," I said, kicking an imaginary ball.

Here's Cockatrice!

THE BLUEBIRD ALL NIGHT LUNCH ROOM is down on St. Julian Street, just off lower Conti. After all the brokerage offices, the small job printers, the garages, the umbrella-repair shops and such-like in that dilapidated but busy part of town have closed up shop and gone home, the Bluebird is the only brightly lit place between lower Government Street and lower Dauphin. The streets are dark in the waterfront section, the old buildings gloomy and beetle-browed—that gloom of empty upper stories, wharf rats, the eternal waterfront sensation of departures amidst hustlebustle, and returns to things familiar for one moment strangely seen. Down by the wharves, there are coffee-joints and beer-joints full of noise, pouring yellow light into the street, but around St. Julian Street the Bluebird rules supreme.

It's a former maritime supply store, a big room with a pressed-tin ceiling in diamond-shaped designs and with fleurs-de-lis in the corners. The only thing blue about the Bluebird is this ceiling, which is painted a kind of puky blue; varnished with a fine layer of time's grime. The walls are ornamented with mirrors, over which rosettes and streamers of crepe paper sport in attitudes of wild abandon. There are several calendars, a blackboard with the Business Men's Lunch for that day chalked on it—for instance: *Virginia ham, F. Fries, t. greens, salad boll on side.* Naturally, the eternal soft-drink signs. There's a busted-down piano there, and a guy who plays pretty well until he gets likkered up and passes out, then anybody can play. This certainly keeps the program various: sometimes you get some sad guy off a foreign ship (ships from all over put into Mobile) who'll play those sad slow things that have everybody in the joint drowning in their beer glasses, all down-eyed and shuffly-foot.

As luck would have it, on this particular night, when Perrin and I came sauntering in, after quick glimpses of half a dozen other places, the pianist was still sober and going fine. He finished "Big Leg Mama" with a crashing chord (one out of three notes is hopelessly and irrevocably out of tune) and started tiddlyfingering a muted version of "Wanta Get Something Straight Between Us," causing a couple of chubby whores sitting near him to sing a few lines. The place was crowded (Saturday night!) but we caught a booth just as some folks were leaving, and ordered beers.

"I'll ask you to 'scuse me," said Perrin, rubbernecking, "while I just case this joint. *Beaucoup de monde* here tonight. This is my second home, you know: I love it. Now there's something special!"

I turned to see; it was a Spanish-ish or Italian-ish sailor in a black sweater, his head crowned with a whorl of black ringlets, one gold earring shining insolently. Between his black clothes and his black hair, his face was almost hectically bright, being suntanned, and his total apparition *foreign*. He was casing the joint, too.

"Everybody's here tonight!" crowed Perrin, banging his fists lightly and quickly on the table top. "Look, there's the Tiger Woman."

It was a tall girl, with slanty eyes, much too heavily made up—she didn't need it, she was good-looking—with the most impressive mound of whirls, swirls and sausage-curls atop her head that ever you saw. It added a foot to her seven. She was dressed all in white with a red belt and in that elaborated coiffure she had pinned a miniscule red celluloid airplane. She was followed by a dumpy woman of fifty-ish in a flowered dress and a Bradley sweater, and a mean-looking man with a handpainted necktie. Their booth was obviously reserved for them, for the old eunuch who wiped tables gave them a big gummy grin which the tall girl ignored completely, establishing herself on one side of the booth, sitting perfectly straight, her companions opposite. She was so tall she towered up out of that booth like a lone sunflower in a daisy patch.

"You see, isn't it operatic?" exclaimed Perrin, pink with pleasure.

"Hmmm," I replied. Sitting opposite Perrin, I began to study him. No doubt about it: he was more than handsome, he was beautiful. It's the quicksilver face of the Electric Monkey I'm talking about. His eyes were blue, not the candid clarity I remembered from childhood, but darker and changeable, shadowed by his lids and briary blond eyebrows, narrow but adamant. His complexion was high and light. It's the face of one who can carouse and drink for ten nights running and never show even a smoky smudge under the eye. Me, if I don't get eight hours, I look like Death's little brother Joe. But this Perrin, he had a shining tireless face that never gave anything away. The kind of face that makes certain fat old men mad just to see it pass, makes other men thoughtful, the kind of face that makes young girls and old ladies stare; and makes young married women whisper together. I asked myself what lay behind it.

"Perrin," I began.

"What?" he said absently, still casting his eyes around the noisy place. But I didn't know how to phrase my question, and finally he turned to me. "What? What, what, what? What are you saying?"

"Oh, I was just about to say it surprises me, your coming to this place. I remember you as such a little gentleman when we were kids."

"You," he nodded, "I remember as glum, and as my persistent tormentor."

But he couldn't make me mad. We drank silently for a bit.

"This *is* wonderful, isn't it? There's nothing in New York to compare. Never having been there, naturally you wouldn't know."

"I'm popping a gut to go to New York," I said, then glanced around. I was wondering what Perrin would say to

[85]

those roadhouses in central Alabama, places out in the middle of nowhere where you *really* see things to make your eyes bug out—places where those motorcycle clubs congregate, swaggering around in their reflector belts. Fights are customary, and love-making almost public. A Saturday night of the full moon is something to see, whereas this place was just a waterfront joint going full blast, that's all.

"Yeah, it's nice," I said to please Perrin.

"Tell me the truth," he coaxed, suddenly looking sharply at me. "Are you and my sister lovers?"

I blushed at his suddenness and for certain dreams I guess. "*No,*" I protested firmly. He gazed at me a second.

"Well," he laughed, "for your sake I'm glad. 'Cause I was going to say that if you *were* you must not be a satisfactory lover, 'cause Lola is right now as peevish as ever I've seen her."

I suppose only our lifelong acquaintance made it easy for him to say something like that, but hell, he'd say anything that popped into his head. Because then he said: "Who *do* you sleep with?"

But I never answered, for our second round of beers came. Not that I'm a damn bit shy, but it was the feeling of Perrin coming with a greedy smile after the chocolate drops: I wanted to hide everything from him, even the tinfoil from the long-gone candies. He was busy watching the crowd again. Some college boys had come in, trying to look old and bold.

"Wouldn't you like to start a good fight?" asked Perrin.

"Not specially," I said. "You got wild ideas, boy."

"It's little you know," he replied, with a tantivy air.

We drank more beers, then still more, lapsing into a comfortable silence. The Bluebird was becoming noisier and noisier and conversation difficult. Something made me look up from where I'd stared into my glass, and I realized instantly that a duel of eyes was going on in the café. Perrin was one point; the sailor with the earring and the Tiger Woman were the other two points. The sailor was standing alongside the piano flashing his pearlies at the world, but leveling his gaze first at Perrin, then at that sloe-eyed girl. Perrin would look at the sailor, then would turn and give a funny little almost-smile at the girl. They're all crazy, I thought, and took a long draught of beer. I lit a cigarette and puffed a cloud of smoke up toward the ceiling. When I considered Perrin again, he was still tangling eyes with those other two, his counterparts, coldly meddlesome yet aloof as he. Watching them, I almost expected the three of them to rise and make an airy round and circle over the mob like dragonflies over a green summer pond. They were that bewitched and eye-involved.

"What the hell is going on?" I inquired.

"You're too young to play," he said mysteriously. "I am creating chagrin. Chagrin . . . and desire."

"You're screwy," I told him. "Crazy as a cootie-bug." I also cursed him with an elaborate oath, very pleasant to say, very expressive.

"Envy, Cousin, and extreme immaturity. Your nasty mouth should be washed out with yellow soap."

"If my mouth was full of yellow soap," I railed back, "I'd blow out big old bubbles and it wouldn't take Madam Kay to see the future plain in all of them."

"The future in a soapbubble?"

"Yeah, about your appendicitis."

"Beg pardon?"

"That you'll have from swallowing the teeth you'll swallow when I hit you as hard as I'll hit you someday, just on general principles."

"Touchy, touchy!" He laughed, and proffered a cigarette. I knew suddenly that sooner or later he'd feel my fist in his face. But Kosta Reynolds entered the café at that moment, going back to the Tiger Woman. He saw us, and after greeting the tall girl and her friends he bore down on us, grinning and rolling his naughty old eyes.

"Dear loves! What are you doing in this dive?"

"What are *you* doing?" bantered Perrin, coquettishly.

[87]

"Ah!" He grinned. "The business of the night. Looking for models."

"Then you're not satisfied with me," moaned Perrin.

"My dear Perrin, you're my favorite model, but you're not quite anonymous. This is the place to pick up windbirds."

"Windbirds?" I whispered to myself, and shrugged.

"Kosta, we're dying to meet your extraordinary friend there," cried Perrin. Well, we're dying now, thought I, when it hasn't been ten minutes since we were making chagrin.

"Hey, Ione!" Kosta cried; with a kind of marvelous dazed-giraffe start, she turned and came over to us.

"Ione, I want you to meet some friends of mine." Kosta was showing her off as a kind of prize package. She looked at us with unbelievable amber eyes—enormous, luminous, edged with a curled fringe of perfectly spaced (real) lashes. On top, those formidable clusters of blond hair tightly curled.

"Hey, how you?" Ione said seriously in the voice of a five-year-old girl. She scrutinized Perrin, then smiled at me, a perfectly natural smile, charming and childlike, showing big healthy white teeth, and exorcising forever, by one note of that childish treble, all associations save green groves and cotton fields. Hardly able to contain our wonder, we murmured polite greetings.

"Ione has been sitting for me," said Kosta proudly.

"Mr. Kosta"—Ione smiled—"is painting of my portrait. Several."

"Are you a Mobilian?" Perrin asked Ione.

"Beg pahdon?" She glared at Perrin.

"Where's your home?"

"I uz born at Three Mile," she said. "Know where that is?"

"Of course."

"Lotta folks don't," she said, gazing about the room, then added through half-closed lids, "That's just their hard luck."

Spellbound, we sat silent for a long instant, then Perrin

[88]

hurriedly asked Kosta, "Have you finished Baudauer's monument?"

"Not yet," said he, his smile melting.

"Mr. Kosta is all broke up over his poodly dog," drawled Ione explanatorily, and sadly, gazing down at the tiny Kosta from her great height. Her face showed she regarded him as too cute to be true. "Come have a drink." Then to us: "Baudauer was *some* dawg."

"Baudauer was an angel," sympathized Perrin.

"No," said Kosta wistfully. "Not an angel, but the most perfect of poodles on this earth. He understood three languages perfectly from birth, and detested hypocrites."

Ione's expression in hearing this was worthy of a whole series of paintings cataloguing the nuances of Confusion and Doubt. But she said to us, "Pleased to have met y'all," and led Kosta away, after giving Perrin a hard look.

"From what hollow tree did *she* spring? It's a perfect example of appearance versus reality—the soul of Sunbonnet Sue in the body of the Queen of the Night."

"I like her voice," I said.

"It's a shock to hear her speak, after having seen her from a distance so long. Just think, if the world had arranged itself only a small bit differently she might be our Aunt Ione."

"What!"

"I mean if . . . life were different . . ."

"Well, it's not."

"Anyway, Uncle Acis knows the lady well."

"That don't make her our aunt." I grinned.

His reply was lost to me, for the high tide of commotion and noise in the Bluebird had now been reached. After, it would ebb till closing, for the customers would get drunker, or calmer, or leave in pairs, or pass out, or be put out, or be transported to a glassy-eyed state where the eyes see inwardly. Of music there was a surfeit: two idiots playing a duet at that beat-up piano, while in a booth a sad thin-faced boy, accompanying himself on a guitar, sang a hair-raising

[89]

ballad with the refrain of "But it never lost its elasticitee" to his companions, all unsmiling youths deep in their fifth or sixth round of drinks. I smiled sleepily. The last I recall, as I lapsed into a beery Saturday night trance, was the old waiter picking up pieces of a broken bottle, making *tsk-tsk* sounds.

"You can shore tell a night of the full moon!" he complained. " 'Cause everything obstreperous with two feet and the price of a beer drags itself to the Bluebird."

Rainy rainy rainy Sunday. Down it fell. When I woke, my teeth were all wearing little cashmere sweaters, and I felt generally stupid. I cautiously rolled over to face the window, watching the gray drops droning down tirelessly. The trunks of the magnolia and the oaks were stained black with wet, and the wisteria vine bedraggled. In all my body there was a kind of luxurious ease, and the warm bed was sweet to lie in —I stretched and turned one way and another, running my tongue over my teeth. My clothes, I saw, were all over the joint.

As I climbed up into the world again, I asked myself how I had gotten here. I remembered the glitter and racket of the Bluebird swirling before my eyes and then at some point everything merged. Oh yes, Perrin carrying-on his strange three-point flirtation with Tiger Woman and the foreign sailor . . . and the distinct smell, beery stale, of the table top . . . my head had surely laid there. After . . . Perrin's face framed in a dark square . . . the taxi window. He had sent me home and stayed behind at the café. A twitter of resentment shot through me: was he then not human, incapable of intoxication, remote and untouchable forever? For what pleasure had he stayed behind?

Down it fell. The fall is hinted and winter will come. How quickly the time has flown since my arrival in Mobile. I thought, I must write my folks today. Everybody has good intentions when they wake on Sunday morning after a wild

Saturday night. But rainy Sunday goes quickly for all its flatness: the letters never get written.

At home, in Persepolis, they'd soon be dillydallying over breakfast with second and third cups of coffee, and the Sunday paper. Still it rained. I glanced at the clock: 8:47. I had waked as though it were a weekday. I'm the only person I know who is awake at this moment I told myself, save Fern downstairs. Lola is curled up like a little cat, her hair wilder than wild, Fiffy not stirring, Cousin Annie and Mr. Charlie dead to the world (I bet Cousin Annie snores), Etta Mae out cold. Oh, Uncle Acis! He's the original early riser. Acis used to be always up busybodying with Old Sol himself, mucking about his garden, messing about with his boats, sometimes fishing, sometimes pulling the sun up out the bright waters of Bayou Clair by reading to it from his old books that he lugs down to the pier. Thinking of Acis, I vowed I'd write him a note too; maybe even pay him a visit: I didn't write him then, but much later, as you'll see, I did pay him a visit.

Thinking of Bayou Clair, long-gone and sunny forever (perhaps my true Zuolagaland), I went back to sleep, with the rain rub-a-dubbing on the leaves. I dreamed, though dream is too foursquare a name to give to the pictures melting one into another that flashed through my mind. Perrin and I were children again, Lola too, in a place that was maybe the Bluebird, maybe the side porch at Bayou Clair. There were people there, in the dream, from Tutwiler High in Persepolis, that I haven't even *thought* about since we graduated. The Tiger Woman was sitting in the booth with us, only she wasn't the Tiger Woman any more but Ruby Lee Jimson laughing and cutting up. It was all crazy, and there was something wry that wouldn't announce itself.

". . . going to sleep forever?" Ruby Lee was saying mockingly, leaning across the table, and I woke with a bang. There was Philine, bright and sassy as new paint, sitting on the foot of my bed. The rain had dwindled to a drizzle. It must have been eleven o'clock.

[91]

"Baby!" I groaned, rubbing my eyes.

"I'm back," she said, coming to me, and tousling my hair. I pulled her to me, and nuzzled my nose against her warm neck.

"You smell bad," she said, with a grimace. "Beer and cigarettes." But she made no effort to escape.

"I'm still asleep," I grumbled, stretching and groaning.

"You must have tossed a fine one last night," she said.

"Did you have a nice time?" I managed to grunt as I turned completely around, straightening out my kinks.

"Oh, sure," she replied lightly, then: "You should see yourself sleeping. You look like somebody else."

"I always sleep incognito."

She brought me some coffee, and while I struggled to consciousness, she demanded to know where I'd been the night before. I told her a little of where we'd been. She had to know all about Perrin.

"Sounds like you don't like him."

"Baby," I said, "if only you knew. He's all right for other people, I suppose, but we've always gotten on each other's nerves."

"This I must see. I must really see what gets on your nerves." All this time Philine was driving me slowly crazy by touching my arm, my hand, leaning close enough for me to get the benefit of her perfume. I put down my cup with a small crash, and reached out to take her in my arms.

"Now, now," she laughed. "No Saturday night business on Sunday morning."

And though my instincts were swarming, hers had been more perceptive, for there came a knock at the door, Philine jumped off my bed, I shouted, "Come in!" and Fiffy came billowing in, like something traveling on a high wind. Her hair was like a hurricane, for all the dozen combs like a flotilla of storm-threatened fishing boats.

"Good morning," she sang out. "Are y'all having a morning party in here?"

"Near 'bout," answered Philine.

"John had a terrible night," said the old lady. "I'm afraid the time is coming and I dread it."

"Ah, too bad. Poor old thing," sympathized Philine.

"Yes," I added, as though I'd been personally acquainted with his symptoms for years.

"I suppose it'll be all for the best, like the stupid saying goes. I'll be as bereft as poor Kosta Reynolds, who'll die yet over Baudauer. I shall have to wear black (relieved with a few touches, never fear, of white) and receive condolences. If I were Perrin Moreland, I wouldn't write a *Masque of Death*, but a sort of *Etiquette of Grief,* in which I'd disclaim all the old forms, and invent new ones. I'd rather have all my teeth pulled out, one by one, in the fiery office of a demon dentist in hell for eternity, than receive condolences. I love being loved, hated or envied—but being pitied, or worse, being sympathized *with*, makes me break out in spots, like hives. When my papa died, that delightful bad-tempered man—and he died quietly and knowingly after a three days' sickness—all Mobile and Sophia counties, half of Baldwin, with a few driblets of Marengo County as well, descended on me and set up such a riptide of sympathy I very near drowned. Worse, I started to believe for a minute that Papa was a saint, which he wasn't. But they all came, the sisters and the cousins and the uncles and the aunts, you know, and moaned and groaned and gnashed their teeth (those that had 'em): rehearsing all their private griefs for me. I wasn't fooled—they were sad for all the mean things they'd done in their lives, not for Papa's death. The worse were the silent *understanding* ones who'd press my hand, look into my eyes a little damply, and utter some shattering cliché. I do wish I'd written down their words: I could have taken up burnt leather work, and immortalized all those gems of sympathy on pillow tops, worked in a genteel script across the sky in a view of Mobile Bay."

"Hoo-hoo!" I cried, impressed.

"In two days I was ready to either enter a nunnery, or close

[93]

all the shutters of this house and become grief's recluse. Then I had two signs from heaven that all was well: one was that I found Papa's pornographic library where he hid it (there's a part of the masculine nature I'll never understand) and the other was that I received a box of sugared ginger from a lovely friend. Between the two things I was saved: those awful satyrs and fauns seemed to say of Papa 'Not an angel, and not yet to be,' while Miss D'Été's ginger said sharply, 'Be gingery, be caustic, breathe fire in grief's face.' So there you are: that's how it was. But in the case of Brother John, how's it going to be?"

"I hope," I said quickly, "that you kept your papa's books."

"Oh yes, never fear, I just locked them back up again, and keep the key handy."

"I'm very fond of fauns," said Philine. "I don't know, however, 'bout those satyrs."

"Hmmm," said Fiffy. I never heard her utter expression more succinct. I suppose we might have had a morning party well into afternoon, except just then Fern appeared.

"Miss Fiffy, Son and Lolo are downstairs asking after you."

"Well, do! Say I'm coming down tereckly."

"Yes'm."

"You come on, too, Philine, and let this night-owl get dressed. And you, night-owl, come on down, too, you hear?"

"Sure thing," I answered, wide awake and in good spirits. Philine was home, and Fiffy running in high form. Let it rain. Let it pour.

"Who are they?" demanded Philine.

"My cousins, Perrin and Laura Moreland."

"Come on, Philine," urged Fiffy. "He writes poetry, and she likes Switzerland: you can talk to them both."

"Oh, this is the cousin," mused Philine.

While they were getting themselves out the room, the sound of the piano came up to us, I don't know who was playing, but that crazy Lola was singing in a lusty little-fool voice:

[94]

*"Down
       fell
              the pony in a fit!
   Guess
           we'll have to all walk home!"*

All alone in my room, I began to laugh to myself, and suddenly realized I had contracted Mobile madness, and—thank you very much!—was mighty proud and happy to have it.

I'm in a dream, I told myself, none of this is real at all, and I stared hard at my clothes as I dressed, hoping to convince myself of reality. Hey, boy, I told my puffy morning face in the mirror, either the trolls or monkeys have bewitched you, you better try to get conscious. But I stayed in the dream, content.

I put down my hairbrush, straightened my tie, and went out into the hall to go downstairs. But in glancing across the stairwell, I saw up in the front hall, the door of Miss Fiffy's room was standing open. At that, I stopped dead still, my heart pounding. I stared: I could see her cluttered dressing-table with the oval mirror over it, which stood between the front windows. The shutters were closed, but slits of rainy light came in. The curtains were silk, patched, cracked, sleazing, but still bright. Stiff, they fell from gilt cornices like waterfalls in an amateur canvas. Pictures, chairs, work-baskets, writing-kits; naturally, bunches of flowers. The other side of the room was invisible to me, save for a stack of books reflected in the aqueous oval and somewhere there presumably lurked the mysterious and insular Brother John.

I'm not really a snooper, or even particularly a pryer, but I knew I had to enter that room, and withdrew my foot from the first step where I'd placed it. I stood clutching the banister, ashamed of my curiosity, but popping to settle the question of John. What could I say to him? Oh, I hoped to peek in that door without being seen in the half-light. Or, if seen, I could certainly always just say, "Excuse me," and withdraw. Or so I hoped, at any rate.

Still I waited. Downstairs they were chattering: I could make out the words of Lola and Fiffy, but Perrin and Philine were too soft-spoken to carry well. Fiffy was speaking.

" . . . truth? What *is* truth, after all, but a hag living alone in a haunted house? She doesn't have many suitors nowadays, but the ones she has are . . ." Well, I thought, that takes care of truth. Then in a flash I was consumed with jealousy. Perrin and Philine, and they were downstairs together, and Perrin's the oldest bon-bon thief in the world! Yet I had to see John. Well, now or never, I told myself, swallowing hard.

I tiptoed quickly down the hall toward the front of the house. The floor, accustomed to Fiffy's aerial tread, betrayed me: *creak, creak,* it said, and I stopped dead still. From the room came a thin querulous old voice. I didn't quite catch what it said, but it was a question. *Yes?* or *What?* At that, I jumped, but I had to go on in then, I'd been heard skulking in the hall like a shy burglar. I stepped inside Fiffy's door decisively. An enormous and fanciful bed dominated the disarray of furniture and objects. Piled on tables either side, and in enormous hummocks on the floor, were books, old and new, magazines, papers: a complete library. At first I thought I was losing my mind, for there was no one there. I pressed my hand to my forehead and gaped in disbelief.

Then I saw him, a huge old yellow cat that must have been a thousand years old. Fat as a pillow, he rested in a plumped-up nest of pillows, taking his imperial ease in a gilded rattan basket at the foot of the bed. He was certainly half-blind, and more than half-dead, I'm certain, but I have to hand it to him: he was one hundred per cent sure of himself. Giving me this twin-moon stare, he seemed to say, "What the hell, young man, are you doing here? If you wanta see *me*, you better just write for an appointment."

What he actually said was "Rrrrrrrreow," and that in a very mean tone of voice. I went quickly out and downstairs.

When I reached bottom (that was a long trip down the stairs, for my mind had tumbled over so many precipices, and

[96]

flown back up to so many peaks, that by time I reached downstairs hall I couldn't remember beginning my descent: all this commotion was going on over John, it goes without saying, since now my whole conception of the household was altered, and the image of Fiffy bulwarked or bedeviled by a kind of midnight-conversation companion—long since fixed in a human frame of reference—now had to quickly give over for another of Fiffy as the protectress of the beasts, which conjured the statue of Diana with her hound that rain and time were wearing away in the gardens of Dexter Plantation near Gadsden) they were, naturally, still making birdy-birdy in the parlor.

It had become a double conversation, I grasped—Perrin and Philine on New Orleans compared to New York; Fiffy and Lola on cooking. When I sidled in, still mentally gasping at the sudden reduction of Brother John, the aristocratic idiot child, to this hunk of dingy yellow fur in a basket, I must have shown confusion in my face, because they all stopped and eyed me.

"What is it?" asked Miss Fiffy. "Are you unsteady? Regard Mr. Moreland here: he's fresh as can be." She turned and explained to Philine. "These two were out till all hours, carousing."

I looked at Perrin: he broke off looking at Philine and turned to me. "Good morning," he said. He was fresh as always and damnably full of smiles, but I saw his eyes were a little bloodshot and it pleased me to think he was, perhaps, after all only mortal flesh.

"You never really told me about your cousin," reproached Philine.

"Well," said Lola snippy as you please, before I could answer, "we try not to mention our black sheep." It was plain she was annoyed at someone in the room.

"Pardon *me*, Lady Audley," I said kissing her hand in mock of Perrin's airs and graces. She didn't take it that way though; she giggled delightedly and made me sit by her.

"Lovely boy," she cooed. "Where *have* you been lately?

I haven't seen you in so long. We used to have such times together." Was it Joan Crawford? I don't know, but it wasn't Lola. Then I caught on: Lola was playing this scene for Philine's benefit. Lola had cut her hair very short, in cute curls, and was wearing her jet eardrops. She couldn't have been cuter, and she knew it; and she couldn't have been flipper, because of knowing.

Philine was studying this fireball with a fishy eye, obviously an instant dislike had exploded between them with the natural ease of the thunderclap. Perhaps Perrin had abetted it, who knows? He was dividing his attention between radiating charm toward Philine, and studying my reactions. I wouldn't look at them, but stayed by Lola.

"Perrin and I find we have several friends in common," Philine told me.

"Ah?" I answered. It's one of those statements that have no possible answer, though when people say things like that I always have a great temptation to smile and say, "Isn't that disgusting!" or "Oh, I'm *so* sorry!" But I never do.

"Mama sent you a message," Lola told me. "Says she hopes you remember to write your family and also please to remember a cash offer she made you for some secret information." This eluded me for an instant till I remembered the recipe that Cousin Annie was so hot for.

"Okay," I murmured.

"And Etta Mae says some of your shirts are still there from the last wash 'fore you left."

"I'll come by fetch them."

"Please do, 'cause . . . well, I have something to show you. . . ."

"Okay."

I had to regard Philine and Perrin: those two were clicking like fury. They were chattering about books and painters and such. Fiffy had withdrawn from the conversation, and Lola had launched on a description of a murder mystery she'd read, so as to prove to all present that she, too, cracked a book now and again. Every word was *clever,* 'cause Lola

[98]

always has a word of the week and you might as well stand back, boys, and let her kick it to death.

"What I couldn't get is why she wanted to kill the old man. I knew from page one she was the one did it, I certainly thought it was *clever* the *way* she did it, I mean I'll never be comfortable around flypaper again as long as I live, but I can't figure what she *gained* by killing him, the pore old soul. If she'd 'a' had a long talk with him about page fifty, the book could have gone on to be about something else. I reckon it was more *clever* to kill him and keep you guessing, otherwise they couldn't have used the detective, after all he's the main character in these books, nobody cares who's killed if the detective is *clever* and knows a lot of English Literature quotations by heart, and all about poison and psychiatry and *clever* things like that and is good-looking."

"Lola doesn't understand the point of detective fiction, she has too kind a heart. She's not real interested in puzzles and has much too kind a heart." Perrin smiled, turning his face toward his sister.

"What is the name of this epic?" inquired Philine regally, deprived of Perrin's gaze.

"It's called *I, Said the Fly* and I *do* understand it."

"I, said the Sparrow, with my bow and arrow," mumbled Fiffy.

"I'm reading *archy and mehitabel* now," said Lola. "My roommate in school—she's this precious girl named Mary Nettles Rodney, well she knows it by heart, the whole book. She learned it driving from St. Louis to Los Angeles, said it drove her pore daddy crazy. You oughta hear her recite it."

"I'd love to," said Philine, with scarcely a trace of enthusiasm, her tone not being lost on Perrin, for he turned back to her and put on his charm full-blast, enough to give that girl a suntan. God, his conceit! Fiffy, sensing undercurrents, looked off into space and said, "It must be lovely in New Zealand today." I didn't listen to anybody for a minute, till suddenly I heard "Does it interest you?" spoken to me.

"Pardon?"

"Perrin suggests we might make a night of it next Saturday, and see the famous Bluebird and such."

"Wonderful!" cried Lola, with real joy. Then a kind of terrible momentary silence fell, in which it was plain to everybody save Lola, that Lola wasn't invited. But I certainly wanted her along, if Philine was going to go culture-club with Perrin. That moment of silence was my downfall: I darted a glance at Philine, who returned it, Perrin intercepted it and smiled. Well, thief, I thought, now you know who I sleep with. He did, too.

"You'll love it," I told Lola almost ferociously, and had the pleasure of seeing her brown eyes light up with that ecstasy of pleasure anticipated.

"Damn tootin' I will," she chuckled, in a wicked tone, already casting herself in a new role, ready to sing a waterfront blues. Philine resigned herself to Lola, even defrosted a little. I think Philine *could* have liked Lola but it seemed that Lola's simple-minded fox terrier enthusiasm for almost anything made Philine feel oh so old and oh so worldly and thereby oh so remote. But Philine obviously didn't like other women. She liked undisputed reign and no doubt. She conceded Lola's presence as a kind of mascot.

The next week flew like nothing at all, time moving like dandelion fluff. Even the office seemed vaguely pleasant to me, not that Hastings Martin wasn't always nice and interesting, but even the others I detested so didn't seem so bad. The nice weather, I guess. The fellows and the two typists and Mrs. Moddy, the receptionist, had a certain set of running office jokes, with a certain set of running laughs that killed me dead, froze me in my tracks. The worst was Elise, who was "cheerful" in the mornings. But like it says in the poem, "Hell's dull school is an office clerk on an office stool." You can see that by contrast with Miss Fiffy, Philine, Lola and Company, anything would seem commonplace, but by the same contrast the already-commonplace became suffocating. During that sunny lull of a week, though, they were bearable, and Elise twice forgot to sing out, "Good morning, *everybody!*" upon entering.

I won't pretend that Philine's return didn't have something to do with it. I need a certain amount of love-making. We took up where we had left off but with a difference. Something had altered imperceptibly. Difficult to explain. I don't mean we took each other for granted, but we lost a need to be better or showier than ourselves. We lost that wish to explain ourselves to each other. Thereby, a fine sense of conspiracy vanished which might have betrayed us to the household. Fern and Tony certainly knew I was not always in my own room, but Miss Fiffy with her old-fashioned delicacy about closed doors and her addiction to the midnight symphony on her bedside-table radio seemed completely unaware. So Philine and I spent some lovely nights together, never the magical occurrence of the first, but fine, fine.

"I can't decide what to do with myself," she said one night, as we lay in semi-darkness. "Daddy wants me to come home to New Orleans for a while. Says I oughta work in the place for a while: he'd like to see me paint some pretty views of the Vieux Carré, which I am constitutionally unable to do. I spose I oughta try to please him. After all, it was his well-rubbed greenbacks put me through school and sent me off to Paris, he deserves a little return. Mama is the real problem, though. No matter what I paint she's surprised, and says, 'but, baby, why do you paint things like that?' She's the reason I haven't worked harder at it. When an oil of mine —of old tumble-down house near Lake Borgne—won a prize, she said, 'It's wonderful you can paint like that, but I don't see why you'd want to paint anything so tacky.' Mama is a case: for her the subject matter of pictures is exclusively a matter of flowers, maybe a few portraits. Once in New York I took her to see the things from Vienna, and she'd look at those big Rubens nudes and sigh, 'Meat market, meat market,' over and over. But she loved all the Dutch landscapes, and had a fit over a little-bitta thing of two monkeys sitting in an arch eating nuts."

[101]

"I like monkeys," I ventured.

"Anyway," Philine went on, "I guess I should decide something."

"Decide to stay right here."

"Nope, have to be on the move."

"You," I stated, fondling her arm, "are a complex little number."

"And so are you," she said seriously enough. "At first glance I thought you were just a nice physical backwoods type—you know, a sweet naïve stallion, but now I'm seeing more."

"Thanks," I said doubtfully, then snickered. "My story is this: all I know is that I want to be myself, but I haven't decided which self to be."

"Oh, the modern world!"

"I mean, I could be pure-dee Sophia County, or pure-dee Mobile."

"A dear two-headed boy."

"Kiss me twice, then," I insisted.

One afternoon after work I went to the Morelands to pick up my shirts, and pass the time of day with Cousin Annie and Lola. I pressed the bell-buzzer and it *zzzzzzed*, and I very distinctly heard Cousin Annie on the side porch say, "Go see who't is, Son," and heard Perrin sass back, "No." Then after a long time, Cousin Annie came and very delicately twitched the curtain at the sidelight to see who it was, then opened up.

"Why, hello!" she said very pleasantly, bobbing her head. "Come on in, we're sitting out on the side."

"I'm not going to stay long," I told her, as I followed through the darkened living-room and dining-room to the side porch. In the center of the grass rug was Perrin, in blue jeans, barefoot, with the tails of his shirt tied together to make a bare midriff. He had two chair cushions under his head, and was holding a book in the air over him. Next his head was a Coke bottle, with a straw bent just at the right angle so he could turn his face a little and have his lips meet the straw without having to turn his eyes from the book.

"H'lo," he said, without change of eyes or position.

"Hello," I said non-committally, studying him.

"He's been frozen like that since lunch," said Cousin Annie. "He'll take supper intravenously no doubt."

"It's such a good book."

I craned my neck to read the title: *The House in Paris.*

Cousin Annie was sewing something ruffly, either curtains or clothes for Lola, I dunno. I suppose Perrin had reached the point where he could close his ears.

"Had a letter from your mother," announced Cousin Annie. "Says that you might as well be in darkest Africa for any news she's had of your doings. You're all alike, you villains: Son thinks he's virtue personified if he manages one letter to me in a year."

"What about those postcards?" Perrin said faintly, not quitting his book.

"Postcards!" she sniffed, and put down her sewing. "Look at him! Why mothers get gray."

"I do owe the folks a letter . . ." I began, but Cousin Annie had an audience for her plaints, and interrupted me. She liked talking about Perrin.

"You know what he did? The other day I was trying to find out how he occupies himself in New York—"

"Giving me the third degree is what she means."

"—and I said, 'Come, now, spit in Mama's hand!' meaning of course 'fess up' or 'Come clean' and you know what he did? Well, if he didn't just lean his head over and spit—*really spit* —right in my hand! Did you ever hear of anything so nasty?" Oh, but she was proud of him—virtue or fault, if Son did it, it was already special.

"He's terrible," I agreed mildly, not giving a damn.

"Who was it?" came Lola's voice from upstairs.

"Your cousin."

Then Lola gave me a turn. "Oh, squeegicums," she gurgled from on high. *"Comme juh swee hooroose!* Send him up! *Qu'il mount!"*

I made a face of doubt and surprise, with my tongue stuck out, and Cousin Annie said in a hushed voice, "Don't discourage us. We told her she couldn't even consider going to school abroad unless she learned French, which is what she fondly imagined she was speaking just now. Not that you could prove it by me."

"Lola is speaking a foreign language all right," said Perrin. "Only it just turns out to be it's not French—it's Lola-ese."

"Leave your sister alone, Perrin, if you want to stay on good terms with me," his mother said.

"Well are you coming up?" hollered Lola.

"Scuse me," I murmured. "I'll go see what she's up to."

There she was (she had washed her hair and rolled it in a towel) with a book in her hand: it turned out to be an 1880 French phrase book that she'd turned up—it had things like *Shall we stroll into the conservatory for a lemon ice?* and *Do you think they will play the polka-schottische this evening?* with snappy answers like *Thank you very much, I should find an ice most refreshing* and *I certainly hope they will favor us,* in English on one page, and in French on the other.

"Miss Fifield is going to coach me some in French," she explained happily, tossing the book, and sitting cross-legged on a couch in the hall.

"Then all this foolishness about Switzerland is true," I marveled.

"Have your laugh." She shrugged. "Wait till you see me smiling off the cover of *Vogue,* dripping diamonds and glamor."

"You're dripping now." I smiled, teasing the damp curls at the nape of her neck.

"Stop it!" she yelled ferociously, then said softly, "I want to show you something I made."

"Okay."

She darted away to retrieve a manila folder, clacking back with eyes shining.

"I wonder what you'll say." She smiled shyly.

Then she drew out a large sheet of white drawing paper on which was a smudgy gray image I recognized as *supposed* to be my face, copied who-knows-how from a family photograph that circulated at Christmastime. She had copied it in typewriter characters, making a picture entirely of *M*'s, *X*'s and *O*'s. It must have taken infinite pains. I didn't know what to say.

"Oooo" is all I managed at first. Then collecting myself, I said, "Baby, how you must have worked!"

"Three days, that's all," she said offhandedly, proud as a peacock. But the question most full of wonder: why had she chosen my face for this scrupulous honor?

"It's the first of a series—" she tossed her head "—I'll do all my friends and make an album of them."

"That's very original," I observed.

"I may not be able to paint, like *some people,* but I have my own ways of making pictures. I embroider too, sometimes."

God bless us one and all, I thought, now comes it out—it's a counter-attack against the wiles of Philine. I could have put my face in my hands and laughed and cried at the same moment. How could anybody explain to Lola how adorable she was for being so silly, or how touching for being so adorable, and how silly for being so able to touch without knowing it. Perrin, in company, might have an unbreakable charm, but Lola had something better for my money. Her charm came all unexpectedly, like a sunbeam entering a tinsel factory, the result was dazzlement everywhere. I think I might be said to have come of age at that moment since for the first time in my life I recognized the quality of *being in process of being young.* But I only said: "I'm very flattered. This deserves something in return."

"I suppose you're too involved with that Philine to think of taking me out ever."

"She doesn't run my life."

"She'd like to. She's after Perrin, too. I suppose you know they spent the morning at Kosta Reynolds'." I didn't, but I wouldn't admit it.

"Oh, yes," I said airily.

"She is just about the most stuck-up person I've ever met." Then I was given free of charge Miss Lola's impression of Miss Philine, and it was really something. Drooped lips, hunched shoulders, dangling cigarette, and a low drawl dying away with what Lola was pleased to think was the rumbling echo of boredom and world-weariness.

"Listen, Joan Crawford, you dry your old messy wet mop. I'm going down to see Etta Mae."

"Go on," she snapped. "Who's keeping you?" Then she disappeared.

So I went back downstairs to search out Etta Mae, and we greeted each other effusively.

"Did you see Priss-Ikey in there?" she inquired confidentially.

"Yeah." I grinned.

"Ain't he the one? Ever since lunch he's been laid out on the floor like sumpin that fell out a tree. I begin to ask myself if my cookin's got so heavyhanded folks can just leave the table and no more. You better hurry get that pea-cake respie we worryin' over." She relished a peal of laughter and I joined in. "His maw," she went on, whispering, "has ben holding the watch over him the whole time, just settin' there snortin' and pawin' the ground. But she can't budge *him*. She's ben talking three hours solid; she only stopped to come out here get the Cokes, then she took up again where she left off. She keeps askin' him when he's gonna marry and settle down. She dint ask me. If she hadda, I coulda told her. When pigs fly, that's when. Yessir, when pigs fly!"

"No doubt about it, that boy is no-count."

"And just tell me what's he sposed to represent in that do? Some kinda cowboy?"

"No," I replied very nastily, "plainer than that—he's sposed to represent Perrin Moreland showing off his belly-button, and hoping all the world's gonna pass by and throw new dimes in it, to see such a pretty sight." That pleased Etta Mae mightily, she gave a great whoop, I thought she'd pop a gusset, I caught the fever and joined in. How we both haw-hawed (better than tonic) till Cousin Annie came back to see what the ruckus might be. We both sobered up then and made our adieux; I went back to the front of the house again.

"*Juh voudray unn dimmy-killo duh pomes!*" shouted Lola exuberantly.

"Awright, awright, awright," I yelled. She giggled, invisible in the upstairs hall. Rave on, hellion, I thought.

"Can't you stay and have supper with us?" asked Cousin Annie, after a harried glance upward, her big eyes shining on either side of her big nose.

"No'm, I'd like to, but I'm expected."

"Oh. Well. Well, come soon, you hear?"

"Yes'm, thank you, I will."

Perrin came to life suddenly, and closed his book, though remaining recumbent.

"See you Saturday night." He smiled.

"Don't forget my recipe," crooned Cousin Annie.

"No'm, I won't. 'Bye."

After I had gone out the door, I could hear her pick up her lament against Perrin. ". . . why don't you get up from there . . ." I heard her say.

Philine, no doubt of it, had taken a fancy to Perrin. They spent every afternoon at Kosta Reynolds' studio. It was Philine herself who told me, though Lola had mentioned it. But Philine regarded it as something amusing, and since she volunteered the information, I couldn't really say anything. I was jealous, though, as all get-out, and determined to flirt outrageously with Lola right under Philine's nose Saturday night, which was destined from the start to be fraught with drama.

Lola and Perrin arrived in their papa's car, already amidst

a bitter quarrel. Perrin, that afternoon, had seen the Iberville Antique Shop burn right down to the ground, and hadn't called Lola to come see it. She was beside herself with fury, and refused to sit in front with Perrin. Perrin, therefore, was magnifying the glories of the fire. Crystal chandeliers, he said, had exploded with a jangling like of crazy bells, and thrown gleaming pendants as far as one block away. Bronze figurines, he claimed, had melted and run in rivers of gold, hissing as they poured into the sewers. He kept this up till I almost felt I should be angry myself for his not having invited me to see it. Philine was amused, and wasted no time establishing herself in front with Perrin. I sat in back with Miss Mad, who was acting out a tremendous anger.

Philine, on the other hand, was being terribly Philine that evening, all poise, and regal. They just made each other (as before) twice more their selves. I made a mental note not to ever have to cope with them at the same time again, and funny thing is, that's last time, that Saturday night, that the four of us have been together.

We decided to drive out to a honky-tonk beyond Spring Hill, it was so early. The night was faintly cool. Perrin clicked on the radio and found some four-piece combo playing real Dixieland, and some sweet and lowdown blues. When we'd gone past the Loop, and were all out Old Government Philine and Perrin began a conversation, with "Gotta Get Going Blues" for background.

"I've really got New York on the brain this night," said Perrin.

"This is the nicest time of the year there," mused Philine.

"Mobile's not bad," muttered Lola.

"It's the music," dreamed Perrin. "In New York, I always play my Dixieland records when I get homesick for Mobile; now it's working contrariwise."

"Ninth Street at seven o'clock on a summer evening: cocktails, and music from an open window across the way. That's my favorite view of New York," Philine stated.

[108]

"No," disagreed Perrin. "For me it's a rainy Sunday afternoon, real drowsy weather, coffee and music at four o'clock."

"I'll take vanilla," whispered Lola to me, then, "Gimme a ciggy-butt." So we lit up in the back seat, and watched the shaggy darknesses of Wragg Swamp roll by, flat marshy stretches alternating with shadowy woods. I sighed.

"Why don't we just head this car for New York right now," suggested Perrin.

"I'm game," Philine said, then smiled back at me. "What about it?"

"No," said Lola firmly, "it won't do. I have to have about a week to get excited beforehand."

"Wouldn't you be excited, if we just took off now?" Philine demanded of her.

"It's not the same," insisted Lola. "I like to go to bed knowing that in a week such-and-such a thing is going to happen, and wake up knowing it's one night less till then."

"You got Miss Anticipation back there," observed Perrin. We all chuckled, including Lola.

I started thinking about New York myself. I'd always thought vaguely I'd go there sometime. I tried to imagine Perrin in New York but somehow couldn't. Nor Philine. But Lola I could picture in her white shoes and big hat, peeping up at something big: a statue or a building, but not at all dwarfed by it—it would have an air of peering back. No doubt about it, we were all thinking of New York that night. Foolish, too, for Mobile was at its loveliest. Long after sunset the sky still held an apple-green glow tenaciously, giving up only for that luminous and velvety blue that colors the very air, and makes windows and street lights seem more yellow than usual. The trees on Spring Hill were all slumbering darkly, save for an impromptu breeze now and again that seemed to turn round several times in a single treetop like a restless bird settling itself to roost. I studied Lola's face, close to the window on her side. In that pale oval, her eyes were fixed, her thoughts distant; seeing her so was seeing another person really, her repose was so unwonted.

"Perrin," she said, with a rising note.

"Hmmm?"

"What's French for *early* and *unhappy?* And for *earrings?*"

By the time he told her, and spelt it all out, we'd reached our beer-joint, and parked the car. Inside, the others chattered as usual, but I meditated in my turn.

Lola said to me, "You're communing with the other world again. Who do you know there?"

I laughed and held up my glass of beer, looking at her through that amber sphere of cold sparkle. "Nobody," I answered.

"Are you moody or something?"

"No, not at all," I insisted.

"I just wondered," she said.

"How's your French coming along?"

"Fine. Miss Fifield is just wonderful. If I had had teachers in school like her, I'd be a real quiz-kid today."

"Don't scare me," I beseeched.

"She makes it so simple. She says I'll be speaking in no time."

"All I know is a little Latin and a little Dog-Latin," I said. "You won't be able to speak to me."

"You aren't difficult to talk to, like some people I could name. At least you show it when you're listening, or show it when you're not. Perrin is a real pill when it comes to that: He'll smile and nod and say, 'Hmm' and 'Oh?' then afterwards you discover he hasn't paid attention to a word."

"That's where you're wrong; I listen to every word you let fall from your ruby lips, dear sister." Perrin barely turned from his chatter with Philine to answer.

"They're not ruby, for your information," tartly replied that child. "They're Dark Chrysanthemum, and I inaugurated the color tonight."

"Either way, when they part, I bend my ear, I do, I do."

"The hell you say." Lola shrugged, rummaging for a cigarette; "Gimme a ciggy-butt," she said imperiously, this time in an approximation of Philine's manner, so I did. Lola was

[110]

studying Philine all this while, spoiling for a fight with somebody, but strictly on her own terms.

Later, after an hour or so in the establishment Philine said, "I'll be ready for some air soon, won't y'all?"

"Oh, no, not yet, the night is young!" said Lola, who could be dying of suffocation but would still contradict Philine. Lola had already yawned several times.

"It's bad for the complexion," said Philine, tossing her black hair back, "all this smoke."

But we decided to have a couple of more beers, and drank them quietly, listening to the college boys and their dates laughing and carrying on. Even without conversation Philine and Perrin were somehow joined: one would say they had reached an understanding, that each had one ragged half of a treasure map, and only together could they find the cache. Yet Philine wooed me with her eyes, throwing me conciliatory glances, while Perrin gloated over his triumph in charming Philine.

"Know what I'd like to do?" exclaimed Lola, her eyes shining.

"I can't imagine," responded Philine, not cattily but meaning that really she couldn't. Neither could I.

"Well, it's fun; it does something for you. My roommate at school, Mary Nettles Rodney, and a bunch of us used to take a car and pile in it, and go way out in the country and speed on the highway, and yell out all the dirty words we knew."

"Oh?" Philine wasn't sure whether to fall out in a dead faint or not.

"Real loud!" burst out Lola enthusiastically at the same time.

Philine broke down and laughed, this annoyed Lola. She shut up right away. But the party, finally, after these hours, had shaken itself down into a unity. We were, at last, double-dates on Saturday night. I suppose with enough beer, or else enough quibbling, any group grinds its own rough edges off

[111]

and in the wee small hours, just automatically coheres. We did.

Much later, after the Rose Room and the Bluebird, we strolled about downtown. Bienville Square, when we reached it, was full of darkness, shadowy against the façades of shops and hotels around it. The unsleeping fountain dripped lazily all by itself, the pool mysteriously black and gleaming.

"The goldfish are sleeping." Lola yawned, leaning over the barrier, and staring into the pool. I leaned over and stared, too. There were Lola and I staring back, faintly grayish in the black water.

"They have better sense than us." I yawned back. "What time is it?"

"One must always live as though tomorrow morning might—eh?" Perrin said, cocking his head at Philine.

"Sometimes, Perrin, you make me mad," she told him to my great delight.

"Stay up all night," sassed Lola. "Sip a pint of champagne with a fresh peach in it, and you won't have to sleep at all."

"She's thinking of Ingrid Bergman in *Saratoga Trunk*," said Perrin. "Only that's just half of it, kid; you have to have Gary Cooper to rub your feet at the same time, don't you?"

"Hell, no!" roared Lola, suddenly skipping around the fountain. "I don't want anybody to rub my feet except me. I'm ticklish. But—" by now she'd circled back, and stopped breathless, looking at us. "—I know who I'd have if somebody *was* going to rub them, and it wouldn't be Gary Cooper. Anyway, all I need is that champagne with the peach in it."

"But that's all any of us in this world need, hon," said Philine.

"I need sleep." I yawned.

Back in the car, and this time Lola was with Perrin in front, Philine leaned her black head on my shoulder, and put her hand inside my coat, holding my waist. Lola had started cussing Perrin out in a low tone, and the rest of us

[112]

were silent. Just when Philine and I had both sighed and locked ourselves in a long kiss, ole Perrin had to start talking to us.

"Philine, I'll bring that . . . book . . . tomorrow . . . you'll be up?"

She hastily pulled her mouth from mine to say, "Never you mind, I'll be very much up." Perrin laughed and said, "Okay."

"Not me," snapped Lola. "Catch me stunting my growth by lack of sleep."

We pulled up in front of the dark house, a faint gleam from the hall light being the only sign of life. Perrin, full of flourishes, got out to open the door for us, and say goodnight. Seemed curious; later I understood. Anyway, he took my hand and clasped it, smiling his insinuating smile, kissed Philine's hand, and got back in the car. Philine made some silly remark, while Lola, taking this all in, threw herself down on the car seat and wouldn't answer anybody.

Upstairs, Philine took my hand and led me into her room. She threw down her purse and jacket, closed the shutters against the gathering light, and turned to me.

"Well?" she said. I went to her and took her in my arms. She threw her arms around my neck, and pressed her whole body fiercely against me. The girl had turned tigress. I was amused at her, and thought it was part play acting, and pretended to roughhouse with her. Then I saw her face, which was the naked face of desire, her dark eyes shining. Our love-making was of the wildest. It would be difficult to say whether it was love or a duel. Some challenge was involved, and certainly some curious anonymity.

Afterwards we lay quietly for a long moment, then rose at the same instant. While I was gathering my clothes and preparing to flee down the hall, I heard the milkman rattling in the street. Philine came suddenly from her bathroom, wrapped in her white housecoat. She stared at me unsmiling, then dragged over to me, studying my face intently.

[113]

"Goodnight," she whispered.

"Goodnight, Philine," I replied. Still she wouldn't have me go, but drew me back. I pulled away.

"Do you know what time it is? Do you want them to find me strolling out your room like this?"

"At this moment," she said, "I don't give a damn. I might later, but not now." Then she smiled her most radiant smile, which illuminated her whole face, and chased away her expression of fatigue. She pushed her tangled locks back, and stepped over and kissed me lightly on the cheek. It was pretty chaste after what had gone before.

"Goodnight, goodnight. You have so much to learn—but I'll teach you."

"So? So what?" I inquired sarcastically, not finding the path that led up to this observation. I was still annoyed at that prissy-proper kiss of dismissal.

"We'll talk about it some other time; it's not important. Only don't go away mad."

"Hell, who's mad?" I asked her. "But I'm beat-up; we both are and it's not surprising." I grinned meaningfully toward the rumpled bed.

She still stood there as I softly closed the door. I stole to my room; shortly after fell into bed, immediately into a deep dreamless sleep.

I think it must have been around twelve noon that I was awakened by a gentle persistent hand on my shoulder. It seemed I'd been in bed ten minutes, I'd slept so soundly; in that strange foreshortening of time I woke thinking Philine was tapping me, but I saw the delicate brown hand of Fern, recognizing her gold wedding ring. She carried a little tray with orange juice and coffee. I sat up, dazed.

"Hmmm? What is it, Fern?"

"I'm sorry to disturb your rest," she said gently and rather mysteriously, "but I need your help."

I gazed at her in disbelief. The tragedy factory which is part of every imagination began to heave and puff furiously in mine. Fiffy—? Philine—? Tony—? Maybe Brother John, the Yellow Ragbag?

"Don't be scarified like that. I'd tell you right away, wouldn't I, without stopping to tote up orange juice and coffee, if it was a death in the house. I'll tell you what it is. Maybe you'll understand it, but I won't ever. I'm gonna tell you sitting down." She pulled a chair from my writing-table over to the bed, and arranged herself in it. She had, I saw, a harassed air, and kept folding and unfolding her hands in her lap.

"Well, something's done happened that is going to upset Miss Fiffy something terrible. I amt told her yet, no sir, and don't hope to. 'Cause that I left to Tow, since he knows more about it. He is in with her now, bringing her up to date to this minute."

"How do I come into it?" I asked, by now thoroughly confused.

"Well, Miss Fiffy thinks the wide world of you, as I hope you do know. Of the folks left in this house today it's you can take the sting outen it."

"What about Philine?" I demanded, with a sinking heart.

"Well, it's Philine has gone and done this thing I'm talking about."

"In sweet Jesus' name, Fern, tell me just what it is you *are* talking about."

"Miss Philine. She's done gone to New York."

"Gone?" My voice broke in a high squeak of disbelief.

"Her and Son. They done took off, them two. Spread their nasty wings and *flew*, without a 'Merry Christmas' or 'Go to hell' from either one of them. Just plain took off. Miss Fiffy is going to be sick over it, just sick. For several reasons. Besides, you know how that lady is—she gets upset by people being rude: she says she understand perfectly well when people rob banks or shoot somebody they mad at, but she can't cope with it when people are mean. She'd rather have somebody steal the silverware than do her an impoliteness."

With folded hands, and a great sadness in her brown eyes,

Fern continued her lament. But I heeded her not. I was unable to comprehend what she'd said, and thought to run to Philine's door, fling it open, and wake her from a sound sleep. I sat speechless.

". . . that she left for you," I heard Fern say. She had produced a note from her apron. I recognized Philine's neat hand. It was a little square envelope.

"That's more than she left for anybody else. Maybe it'll explain something."

I tore it open: *Dear Naïve Stallion,* it began before my unbelieving eyes. *Perrin and I are gallivanting off to New York—exhausted, excited, but refreshed by a sense of scandal. Don't try too hard to understand. Or, if you like, come on to New York and I'll explain this and other things to you. Tell Aunt Netta not to worry and I'll send her a long letter soon. Ah, sir, 'tis a wicked world! Hastily, P.* There at the bottom of the page was the print of her lipsticked mouth, insolently red on the white paper.

I read it several times in a trance. Perrin. *Perrin!* Perrin and Philine gone off to immeasurable distances in the unknown North. New York . . .

"Did you see them, did Perrin come here?" I breathlessly questioned.

"I was sitting in the kitchen with the *Register,*" began Fern, "and Tow was out in back. I heard somebody whistle in the front, whistled a tune two times over, then I heard Miss Philine whistle back, and I peeked through the latticework on the back porch, and saw Son by the driveway, all dressed, with a raincoat on his arm. Then Tow heard them, and came tippytoeing around and went right up to Son.

"I didn't know what was going on, naturally I thought Son had come to fetch you swimming or some such, and I thought he was pretty fresh waking Miss Philine so early.

"Afterwards Tow came back and told me: Son had come in a Yellow Cab, and Miss Philine brought out her baggage and they piled themselves in it, and headed for the L and N. *New York bound!* is what they yelled to Tow. First thing

[116]

I did was run to her room to see what I could see. They was this note for you, and a terrible mess, lots of her things strewn about, and that's all. So I waited a while and talked to Tow, he said wake you up." She heaved a sigh. "He said let you talk to Miss Fiffy."

Who, I wondered, would talk to me. If I'd access to those two just then I would have crowned them. I was furiously jealous, mad at being left out, and under all sad—sad to the profound depths of my heart with a terrible foliated sadness. I reddened to think that all the time we'd spent together those two had known they'd be long-gone today. Gone goslings! And last night in Philine's room—her duplicity was surely unequaled. When had they decided? And why, for what possible reason? How had I failed them, and how had they failed me?

"What she say in her note?" asked Fern.

"Just that she's leaving."

"Don't you tell Miss Fiffy you has a note and she don't have one! Let's us just forget this note, you hear?"

Fern was in the hallway, hovering there like a timid phantom, when I tottered out my room, still reeling with the news. Happily for me, I had been recruited to temper the gale said to be blowing in Miss Fiffy's room: but was it? It seemed mighty peaceful to me as I went toward the door of her room. When I knocked, I heard Fiff stir slightly in her great bed, then a wispy voice trailed through the door: "Ye-es?" and I said who 'twas and sailed in, upon her invitation.

She was propped up in a kind of nest of pillows, bolsters, books and flowers in her huge bed. A lamp with the shade pulled awry was on one side of her, and a tray with coffee things on the other. The Sunday *Register* was everywhere. She discards the business and farm sections right away, begins by reading the "Betty Bienville" social notes. A chiffon handkerchief was tied around her head, over it cascaded her extravagant *chevelure*. Brother John was in his gilded basket on a tabouret near her. When I came in, he attempted that tigerish flicking of the tail's end that cats love to do when

[117]

they're impatient, interested or annoyed, or just feeling hellish; but all he managed was a kind of sad palsied little twitch. Then he trained his milky old eyes on me, and uttered a plaintive "Rrrrreow." I suppose he was putting to me the eternal feline question of *So hot, my little sir?* but it only managed to be an echo of the infantile *Ma-ma!*

"Now you shut up," she said to him affectionately.

He turned very slowly and looked at her, the poor mothy old beast; it was so jerky a movement that for a moment I wondered if maybe he wasn't mechanical after all, and if maybe every morning Fiffy didn't have to take a key from a ribbon round her neck and wind a spring in the small of his back. But then he stretched out with a very small sigh.

"Brother John is very sensitive to storms, climatic or climactic," said Fiffy, leaning sadly in her cushions, and looking at him. She turned again to me, but he opened his eyes, hearing his name, then wheezed once and closed them.

"What," asked Miss Fiffy almost shyly, "do you make of all this?" Fern had followed me into the room, still hovering about distractedly. Fiffy pointed to the coffee pot.

"I'm sure we could have a little more coffee, please Fern."

Fiffy listened to her descending footsteps then sat up straight.

"Fern is more upset about this than me, outwardly that is. Ever since Fern's son Ben went to live in N'Orleans, she's had nobody to worry about, and I've had to double-duty as a problem child." She chuckled and rearranged her cushions. "Come sit here—" indicating a hassock by the bed, "—so I won't have to shout. Now, tell me, what do you know of this?"

"Nothing, Miss Fiffy, nothing at all."

"They didn't even hint it to you?"

"No, ma'am . . . or if they did I didn't catch on."

"Then you are, too, so to speak—bereft?"

"I reckon."

"There's lots to consider. Philine's folks will be furious with her and with me. Naturally I'll bear the brunt. What

[118]

the wretched girl does is her affair, but why involve me. I love her, of course, but I have always found her trying to my patience, and positively corroding to my good nature."

"Don't know what possessed them. Cousin Annie is not going to be specially pleased either, I can predict."

"You," she said, fingering the counterpane. "You."

"Ma'am?"

"I'm so happy you're not part of this escapade. Don't misunderstand, I did lots more fanciful things in my time than this running off to New York. But this trick lacks a sense of style. There's a way to do everything."

"Fern seemed to think you were knocked for a loop by the news."

"Hardly. I've always sided with whoever kicks over the traces, or kicks up his heels. If anything I'm annoyed, most *modestly* annoyed, but annoyed—a delicate and flower-like chagrin. Listen, look out that window!" I ran to do her bidding. "Do you see Carrie Danville on her front gallery?" I nodded, 'cause I saw her plainly sweeping leaves off it. "I know her for a mean silly gossiper, and she knows me for a dreaming old hag. Yet we long to comfort one another. Only catastrophe, alas, can make us one. But have I called her over this morning? *No, no, no!* So you see, Philine's elopement is not as if we'd had a death in the house, or as if the pipes had frozen and burst."

"Elopement," I gasped, bug-eyed, suddenly filled with new ideas.

"Elopement," she restated flatly.

"You don't think—?"

"Oh, I see what you're thinking. Well . . . flight, then, not elopement. Whatever it is, it's a case of the beautiful and baleful, it smacks of *art nouveau*. I don't know how sad you are for either of them; please don't tell me! But 'tween you and me and the gatepost, I'm not too desperate over it. I'm saving my energy for facing Philine's folks, and for talking to Annie Moreland on the telephone: that oughta burn the wires for an hour or two. Wait till Elissa Moylan gets hold

[119]

of the story: it'll end up a legend of rape. Perrin may end up *having* to marry Philine. Let this story get three or four steps away from Elissa's inventive mind and they'll have me running a real *bordelle* here, with Witches' Sabbaths by appointment. Not that I mind contributing my bit toward myth, you understand, but I have always hated being ghost-written."

I was laughing, when we heard Fern coming back.

"Ssssh!" shushed Fiffy. "We must be serious."

Fern came in with coffee, and put it down on the table, peered inquisitively into our faces, then left the room. Fiffy poured the coffee—black, strong, bracing.

"Ah," she said. "The elixir of life. They won't have coffee like this on the train. You couldn't get me onto anything moving in the early morning without some of this brew. When did they decide to go?"

"I dunno," I replied. "Oh, Miss Fiffy, I don't understand anything about either of them, or when or how they took it into their stupid heads to run off. They were talking about New York last night, but . . . who would stop them if they announced they were going? Slipping off like this makes it seem like more than it is: I'm convinced they did it just to be show-offs, and I've a mind to go after them, just to give them a turn." It came as a surprise to hear my own voice saying this, but I realized that I'd made up my mind when I read Philine's note, to traipse right on to New York myself.

"Ah?" said that lady, doubtfully. "That might be very good for you. Sad for me. I'd have to ask either Kosta or Fresh-Air Charlie over to pay me court. But you're ripe for New York, I think."

"Why don't you come along?"

"Ah, no. New York? Never again. I'm fine, Mobile is fine, everything is just fine. But you'll never see how fine Mobile is, or Persepolis either, unless you go away to Pavement Land for a while."

I began to answer, but she went on.

"If I thought—" she added, staring out the window "—that life wasn't *excellent,* I'd slash at my wrists with a dull paper knife and shout 'Murder!' in a lusty voice. *Think* who'd come running: psychiatrists, psychologists and basket-weaving instructors! I'd hold a kind of dark court." She sipped her coffee and giggled. "Don't think plenty haven't done just that, who really only needed to fall in love with somebody or something, or just take a good strong purgative."

At that I really had to break out in a loud haw-haw. That silliest of creatures!

"It's true, it's true," I cried, wiping my eyes. "St. Valentine or calomel."

So we drank coffee and laughed together.

"I wonder what they'll do for money?" I thought aloud.

"Oh, rumbun, what they don't have they'll get. Spoiled, both of them."

Slowly I realized that Miss Fifield was playing for me, too, on a different level than for Fern, but deceiving with great gentleness. She was upset deeply by the flight of the two idiots; though I shared her pretense of flat sadness to feed Fern's solicitude, her real mood, hidden deep, was shared by none: I sensed it and tried to name it. Yes, Philine and Perrin had wounded that old lady in some subtle acute way: something to do with a sense of time, of flippant alteration in the comfortable flow of events from day to day.

We went down for late dinner in midafternoon, eating, silent and picky, on the back porch. The house was full of ponderous Sunday quiet. We both expected the telephone to explode in the hall, and produce Cousin Annie amidst lightning flashes, but it didn't. After dinner, which was magnificent since Fern believes in feeding misfortune and had made potent cajoleries, Miss Fiffy went up to nap and write letters; I sat in the double-parlor, reading "Betty Bienville" and the sporting news.

The front doorbell after a time gave the faintest nervous

[121]

titter, and I opened up for Lola, rather pale, with her jet earrings.

"Hey."

"Come on in, baby," I said.

"It's much quieter here than at home," she said.

"Ah?"

"Yeah, Mama just found the note Perrin left this morning; she thought he must have gone swimming; she started worrying when he didn't turn up for dinner."

"We've already had our to-do—we knew about it early this morning. Come on in, and sit down."

"Okay, thanks. I suppose everybody with two eyes and two ears has known about it for a week: Etta Mae says he was very particular about having his shirts and drawers for yesterday. He packed yesterday afternoon, I reckon."

"Is Cousin Annie . . . very . . . uh . . . ?"

"Hooo-eeee! Don't visit us for a week. Home presents a dreary picture and then some."

"All I know—" I nodded my head—"they must be pretty beat-up by now, up all night then hopping an early train."

"They planned it pretty well. I took myself over to Kosta's just now, and brought it all up casually, but I needn't have: it was no secret to him. They'd talked it all over, and asked him to take care of certain things for them. Kosta didn't even know they hadn't told anybody."

"Why, those nips," I muttered bitterly, and she replied with a dazzling oath.

"If you want *my* opinion," Lola said after a bit, "that precious Philine is nothing but an old-fashioned slut, and my brother is nothing but an old-fashioned bonehead." I didn't answer that.

"Don't you think so?" she insisted.

"Oh, they're crazy."

"Well, I'm glad they're gone. I'm probably the only one, but I'm glad."

"Why, baby?"

She rubbed her hand up and down the arm of the sofa

[122]

where she sat. "Because . . . well, because . . . the only time I have what might be called a private life is when they're neither one here."

"You're a mess, Lolabelle," I teased her, "and before you go on maligning people who go to New York, I better tell you I'm going, too."

"Going to New York?" she quavered. She had stopped dead still and regarded me long and carefully, like a child who understands the tone but not the sense of some adult expression.

"Yes."

"What for?" Her eyes were bottomless.

"Cat's fur," I rejoined solemnly, "to make kitten britches. I thought I'd go up and chaperone those two."

Her frown made one fierce line of her eyebrows; in her eyes a whole series of ideas chased one another. She stood up, and walked around the sofa, then turned to me.

"Leaving *me* to sit here in Mobile, and put flowers before *all* y'all's pictures, I guess? Not on your tintype! No, *sir!* You won't see *me* again, not for a good long time. I will be long-gone myself next time you come sniffing round this part of the world."

She was laughing flightily; soon those big round tears came plopping out her eyes. She stumbled toward the hall, rummaging in her pocketbook, bawling the while, found an old lipsticky Kleenex, blew her nose, then ran to the front door. She fumbled furiously with the latch, finally got it open, then she turned to me standing there just inside the parlor door, and shouted, her face a sight to behold:

"You blessed Epaminondas, you! Just be careful how you put your feet in those goddam old New York pies!" and she slammed that front door after her just about as hard, I'll wager, as any front door in the state of Alabama has ever been slammed. Alabama comes from an Indian word meaning *Here we rest.*

I stood there, shattered, until utter soft silence had enclosed me again. Outside the street was quiet, inside the

[123]

house seemed muffled in a heavy noiselessness; Fiffy was asleep, Fern and Tony away, and I had a galling sadness, a feeling of being all alone in the great empty house.

I don't know what I expected to prove by running off to New York, but run I did. Just like I don't really know to this day what Perrin and Philine hoped to prove. Anyway, I went to the First National and drew out my savings that I'd transferred to Mobile, listened patiently to Cousin Annie laying down the law over the phone, as if I were responsible for Perrin's behavior, then took a laplunch Fern prepared, pecked Fiff on the cheek and set out one afternoon for New York City in the far North.

Miss Fiffy had given me a brown-paper parcel to return to Perrin—his manuscripts and a book called *Ceremony* by Richard Wilbur, poems: I read them all while piney woods and a thousand upcountry towns flew past. Perrin's poems were mostly to or about his Yankee friends it seemed—all poems about "Night" and "dark," full of strange words, and impossible to follow. The poems in the book were varied, more interesting. I laid them all aside finally, and already at Washington, before the grim mudflats and gray skies of New Jersey presented themselves, I knew my journey was a fool's errand. Yet I moodily found a kind of cheerful inevitability in my following Philine and Perrin—it was as if they each had a rein, as if they both pulled me straight to the old house on Ninth Street where Perrin kept a disorderly top-floor apartment looking into the tops of ailanthus trees.

They weren't particularly surprised to see me. Or rather they were surprised enough, but they were too taken up with life in New York to worry with me much. Philine was trying to get a job in a swank Fifth Avenue shop; Perrin was on the telephone night and day. Sure enough his mama's child. But he was manipulating a hundred and one strands of gossip and backbite like a regular little master spy returned from exile.

After one evening with them, I saw several things in a

flash: that they were no more interested in each other than two stones, that all was forever over between Philine and me, and that Perrin's New York self was a kind of sad monster who delighted in creating confusions. It gave me plenty to think about, as I gradually discovered New York City, amidst growing realization of the inanity and folly of my being there.

"Now tell me what it is that's eating you?" insisted Philine one afternoon.

"Nothing's eating me," I answered.

"Ah, ah, ah!"

"It wouldn't do any good to tell you," I said at last, " 'cause it wouldn't change anything if I did."

"You're peeved—" she smiled—"because Perrin and I ran off together."

"Why *did* you?"

"Perrin's idea. Drama. I didn't need much persuading."

"Well, I . . . I swear I . . ."

"Look," she said, "Perrin is my honey-boy same as you but in another department. I like you in the bedroom, and Perrin in the parlor."

"Well, my God!"

"Would you want roast beef for every meal? I doubt it."

"When we first met," I obstinately told her, "I thought we clicked. You can't deny, Philine, that the first time we were together was something pretty special. But you just fizzled out on me. Instead of growing closer, we kept growing apart."

"I'm not sure what you think you can expect from me, you know."

"I'm not sure myself. . . ."

"Any fool should have known," snapped Philine, "that my invitation was purely rhetorical."

"Well, baby, let's don't fuss," I said mutedly. "Might as well be nice to each other."

"I'm sure I don't know why," she sighed.

[125]

"That's a bitchy thing to say."

"Sorry, I feel very bitchy right now. I don't know how to explain to you. Don't you see, I like being around Perrin, knowing he's always up to something. Making things happen, creating little emotional storms."

"Just 'cause *I* don't send up storm warnings every hour doesn't mean my weather bureau is deserted."

"But I *like* storm-warnings, in fact I like storm-warnings far better than storms. That's why I like Perrin. I like being amused, in fact I *have* to be amused. Otherwise I might just fall asleep and stay that way. You must try to understand that Perrin and I are very complicated people with very complicated needs in this world. Now you, you're complex, but you're not complicated."

I made a very rude noise. "You and Perrin both need a swift kick where it'd do you the most good. You both so busy roughriding over the whole world you don't know where you been or where you going."

"I reckon," mused Philine, "that my name and Perrin's will be linked together till the last trump of doom just because we happened to take the same train to New York."

"Kid," I snarled, "y'all have *always* been on the same train —it's the Mean People's Dreary Limited, y'all are in the selfish car."

"Well, here *he* comes," said Philine, as Perrin appeared in the door.

"Secrets?" asked Perrin, studying our faces.

Stubborn me, I decided to stay in New York. Since I'd dragged myself up there, I felt I *had* to stay a while. After some empty weeks of sight-seeing, with Philine and me running around together very civil and comradely, seeing very little of Perrin, I started job-hunting, and one fine day found myself filling out forms and filing them, in a loan bureau on Twenty-third Street. Some weeks later I moved into a dreary little hotel not far from the office, though every night or so I trotted faithfully down to Perrin's neighborhood.

My dear, began Fiffy's spluttery-looking letter of several pages. *My house, always haunted, has two new ghosts— yours, which your return will exorcise; and Brother John's, which will remain. My beloved animal died during the night Tuesday, in his sleep. When I woke I knew he was gone—I sensed it, and couldn't bring myself to speak to him. When Fern brought my coffee, she took one look and she knew, too. I had an old doll trunk which served for his coffin and he was buried in the side yard. I know I shall be considered an utter fool, but by association, by magic, by time, by a dozen workings, he had become more, much more, than a cat, a plain dumb beast. Much more, much much more. I am bereft of you, my conversational companion, and Brother John, my attendant in contemplation, my familiar. But enough of sad news. What of you? Write me all, immediately. Lola comes to me four times a week for French, and it has been great pleasure for me to teach her. She's quick as a wink, and a marvelously impudent creature to have about the house. We went together to Kosta's studio last week to see the finished statue of Pan he's been making. There was a mob there, and Lola was the flirt of the day. We wished for you, and Kosta and others (Ada Mary Stewart, Eddie Backenburger, etc.) all enquired of you. They've cut down the big oak at the corner of St. Francis and Perichole. Do you need anything? Fern and Tony send best regards, and I say "Here's my hand, with my heart in it—" and when are you returning? and why don't you write me?*

Dear fool! I smiled to myself. So her old yellow ragbag is dead! I dragged out paper immediately to write, and found myself full of sympathy and the wish to cheer, even though the death of that pore cat was nothing to me.

I had realized immediately upon arriving in New York that emotions change when their décors change and that some sentiments, like wines, change in voyaging, some indeed, like rare vintages, not surviving travel. Another realization came much more slowly: that Fiffy was a sorceress, exercising a magic that touched all surrounding her; that Philine seen in Fiffy's light was not the Philine wise-cracking with Perrin in New York. And Perrin, no longer laved in his family's adoration, was seen as a rather wry, disconsolate, disagreeable young man. I puzzled over these things as the cold and dark time came, and as December brought the first flurries of snow. I spent Christmas in solitary state, by choice. Not being sad, or homesick, or anything, but just being alone for the first and probably the last Christmas of my life.

Christmas Eve had brought a greeting that gave me pause —from Miss Lola. Another of her typewriter masterpieces— this one was a reindeer with bells on his antlers, shown dancing, all done in X's with the red ribbon on the machine. Folded inside was a scrawled note from the silly child.

"Going to Switzerland! it began. *Going to be there to start Spring Term. Have a black coat that is chicer than chic! Hate you for not writing! Mary Nettles Rodney is coming for a visit before I go!* Then it rambled on, dwindling away to *Merry Merry* and *Happy Happy* and all written in alternate red and green letters. It made me sit and stare at the brick wall outside my window. But there were cards from Persepolis and a letter from Miss Fiffy, so I kept reading.

On Christmas Day I opened my packages from Alabama, then wandered through the snowy streets an hour or so before eating my Christmas dinner in an expensive French restaurant. I ended up in the highest and brightest of moods. I am my grampa's child, and solitude and privacy have a magnificence to be sought. That Christmas alone in New York had a clear frosty happiness that I'll never find again. May never need or want again.

I went to a New Year's Eve party at Perrin's, full of artists and theatre people—wild, loud, and wonderful. Philine had gone to Connecticut with her new beau, a guy from NBC, and I sat alone in a corner with my drink and watched Perrin turning charm off and on like a faucet as people came in. I kept feeling there was unfinished business with **Perrin**: something that needed to be said, even shouted.

"Did you hear, *but did you hear!* that ironic fatalism in the bass?" Perrin was saying in a conversation about music.

"If you divide a human being at the navel, with the heart for treble, then hell, the bass is always ironic," I said to myself, thinking I'd like to be in bed with Philine at that moment. Even though we were scarcely speaking by then.

"I think Cousin is homesick," Perrin said to me in passing.

"Drop dead twice," I told him sweetly.

Toward the end of March it was trying to be spring and I had a letter from my mother that bowled me over. My Uncle Acis, she informed me, the inveterate bachelor and swamp-dweller, had married fat weepy Ada Mary Stewart. They'd run down to Pascagoula and gotten hitched it seemed, then took their time about telling anybody. This had me shaking my head in wonder. I'd have said *Uncle Acis*, if demanded the name of the first Bachelor of the World.

But Ada Mary! She's about a year younger than me; Acis is twice her age and maybe then some. Some weeks later than this letter I received the wedding announcement from Acis, and there scrawled in pencil at the bottom it said "Come see us." I smiled at this, it was so typical: I mean all that elegant engraved italic, then the penciled scribble. The years since I'd been to Bayou Clair fell away, and I could see the tanned face of Uncle Acis, hear his irresistible guffaw ringing out over the bright water.

One night shortly after, I happened to be in the subway and a soldier sitting opposite asked me if the train went to Times Square. I assured him it did, without knowing what I said, for I had heard his voice, slow and endearing: he was speaking pure cotton country.

"What part the South you from?" I grinned at him.

He blinked a little. He was a big boy with big feet encased in heavy clod-hoppers. His face was weathered with

[129]

a lifetime of working in the fields; it seemed fiercely bright in the dinginess of the subway. He heard the South in my mouth, and very very slowly he smiled: he was sure enough what you call a stretch-mouth rascal, for that smile took up all his face, reducing his eyes to sketchy lines skirted by networks of sun-grin wrinkles.

"Oh," he drawled, "I'm from nowhere at all in Sophia County, Alabama." I near split a kidney to hear that sacred name.

"I'm from Persepolis," I said.

"Ho, now," he said, eyes widening. "We a long way from whar we belong, huh?"

"Whereabouts in Sophia County?" I questioned.

"Like I tol' ya—nowheres. We have us a place on the Ilevert branch 'bout twenny miles from Bessie Town."

"D'chu-ever know an old girl named Ruby Lee Jimson?"

"Jimson's *my* name," said the soldier reflectively. "Yeah, that's my name. But I never heard tell no Ruby Lee."

"She's from up there."

"Ruby Lee Jimson?" drawled he. "Naw, that name don't chase out no gophers fer me."

"Well, Jimson's an old Alabama name, I reckon there's more than one." At that, the soldier laughed low in his throat.

"More'n one? You oughta see my maw just sweeping Jimsons off our front porch. We got plenty of Jimsons. I got five brothers, they all married."

But our conversation ended there, for the Times Square stop appeared outside the grimy windows, and the soldier pulled his big body up and clomped out.

"So long," he said, from the door.

"So long," I replied, with a gesture. "Good luck."

"Yeah," said he, then disappeared.

I had that drawl ringing in my ears. Sweet music. It wrenched me out of my trance after a cold crosspatch season in New York. I looked about me: the dim lighting, the littered newspapers, the sleeping drunk. Fool, I told myself, why are you chained here. Go home, dumbbell; think what it is in Mobile now, in green Persepolis. With mounting excitement I mentally composed a letter—to Uncle Acis! For the idea had come from nowhere and possessed me to go to Bayou Clair and visit Uncle Acis and his butterball crybaby of a wife.

I couldn't sleep for excitement, so did indeed write to Uncle Acis, to Fiffy, my folks, and a letter of resignation to the head of my office, with my week's notice. To hell with the heavenly twins, I told myself—cold-hot Perrin and hot-cold Philine. I didn't even tell them I was leaving. Just left New York one day, as bemused and up in the air as the day I arrived, but happy that my strange vacation had ended, beside myself at going home.

From Venice was that afternoon

IMPATIENT TO REACH Bayou Clair, I checked my luggage save for one satchel, and caught a kind of chug-chug bus that goes down the highway, then turns toward Bayou Clair, leaving one with only a couple of blocks to walk. All the way down, I was hot and cold by turns, saying inside myself *Hurry, hurry, hurry* to the bus driver, who doubtless was unacquainted with the word.

The sun was ferocious, an angry yellow patriarch, the pine needles shone brilliantly, air ponderously heavy with musk of pine, and spiciness of willow oak. Bayou Clair had become in my mind the brightest of citadels, the most delicious of pleasure-gardens seceded from the world, and scarce obtainable. When the rattletrap coughed to a stop and let me out, chugging away afterwards toward Terriel, I stopped dead still to collect myself; all impatience vanished, the peace of midsummer drowsiness drowning my unrest.

Summer in the deep South is not only a season, a climate, it's a dimension. Floating in it, one must be either proud or submerged. Sleeping in it, one must be either mute or inspired. Fighting it, one is always left either frazzled or dead, perhaps made mad. Loving it as I do, one has the pleasure of seeing time stand still, of knowing sound and scent resume their old importances.

The pebbly, needle-strewn road winding from the Terriel road down to the white gate set in thickets of camphor trees and Cherokee roses had shrunk considerably and seemed not one third the length of my childhood memory of it. The bridge over Flycatcher Creek was new, and I missed one of the two old cypresses that had guarded it. The topless sweet

[135]

gums and magnolias were seen now as measurable, the wreathy boskets of chinquapin and holly now seen to only half-conceal the gleaming waters of Bayou Clair lying beyond. The hot brightness of all this greenery, the hum and murmur of leaves, insects and birds, the bagpipe snore of—near bee, or far motorboat? both are summer's thoroughbass—these things were more vivid than memory provided. I marveled, poking along the curving road, at the lavishness of this little green world.

Impulsively, I threw down my satchel, and pulled off my shoes without bothering to untie the laces, by dint of a hard jerk or so. Socks I ripped off in a wink, and stood there, foolishly wiggling my feet in the cool powdery dust in the shade of a blackberry thicket. New York seemed no more real than a tale read in a book; all the history of the "charming" Perrin and the "fascinating" Philine took swiftly its proper dimension: a scene in a frieze, meant to be noticed, but after all rather flat. All had been preparatory and youthful, now something new was beginning. I felt a fine weightlessness; I was basking in the most complete aura of *let-loose* one may ever attain, complete because I was conscious of being so.

I turned the curve in the road, and saw the gate, needing paint, at a small distance from me. A few heaped-up cloud towers were trundling across the heavens, engrailed with tinctures of blue distance. A mild breeze frisking in the camphor leaves brought to me the sound of a dog barking and a creaking of oar-locks somewhere on the Bayou. My heart made flip-flops: I was perfectly happy, in the South again, back in the green and crazy land where I do indeed belong.

But I couldn't lift my feet. I stood rooted in the dusty road, the monkeyshines of light and shadow moving over my body, dappling me, as though happy ghosts stippled me with ghosts of spangles to suit me for a midsummer Mardi Gras. I studied the persimmon tree I had climbed as a child; the pale green globes were hanging now amongst the leaves.

[136]

Along the ditch I saw the widow's-tears, their ink-blue buds closed tightly; the bees were grumbling in the sweet pepper, and against the dazzling green the flowers of the rhexia were as illogically bright as candy or the rosiest nail polish.

After thus holding time dead still, and for a long moment refusing the world its right to turn, I walked on. I lifted the latch of the gate, and shivered slightly as a double consciousness raged through me. I saw coming toward me, hidden under her sunhat, much altered but instantly recognizable by her plump outline and her manner, Ada Mary Stewart, switching along in a white dress, my contemporary but my uncle's wife; across the lawn, in a grove of mimosas, I saw at the same instant a terra-cotta statue which I knew instantly was "Pan Grieving" set to mark the grave of the celebrated Baudauer. I dismissed the statue from mind, and regarded Ada Mary.

Ada Mary belonged to no category whatsoever—never did, and wouldn't want to—but must be described as beautiful in a different kind of way. When I knew her years ago she was dumpy fat, neckless, and always in tears. Now she was no longer dumpy, she was simply a round young woman, round face, ripe round breasts, impressive hips, but everything tapering off toward delicate ankles and wrists, fingers whittled off to tiny little tips; she seemed made to float in air, high up over the highest tufts of green, guided by a silken string. Her forehead was domed high, and set off her fine brows and great gray eyes which in certain lights could be blue. She smiled a peerless smile, and showed me the complete Ada Mary Stewart Dimple Collection at one fell swoop.

"Well!" she said softly, giving me her hand.

"Well," I echoed. We looked each other up and down, a little embarrassed, but pleased to see each other.

"I was just thinking you'd be along soon," she said. "Here, let me help you." She immediately took refuge in busyness, snatching my satchel away from me. "Come on in, Acis will be back directly. We're very glad for your visit. Acis

[137]

was very pleased to hear from you, thought you'd forgotten him."

"Who'd forget Uncle Acis?" I smiled, putting down my shoes and socks on the porch.

"Do you want to wash first, or will you have a drink?"

"A drink, if you're having one too."

"I've had tumblers frosting all day."

"How's Modena?"

"Couldn't be better, she's at Terriel today. What have you been doing in New York?"

"Oh, I'll tell you later. Not now, please. I just want to hear 'bout y'all."

"Acis and me being married is still the big topic. Lot of people can't understand."

"Lots of fools in the world. How long have you known Uncle Acis? Did you ever come to Bayou Clair when Perrin and Lola and I used to be here for summer? I can't remember."

"No. First time I met Acis I didn't even know he was kin to y'all. No, Daddy had business with Acis; after Daddy died I came down here to straighten out some things, and well, that was it."

We reached the porch, Ada Mary pulled off her rough sunhat. Her brown hair was pulled back tight to a great bun at the nape, and this severe coiffure made her seem more matronly than her eyes and dimples would concede. I fell into a rocker, sighed, and stretched out my legs. She carried my satchel into the house, remarking, "Now just relax, I'll get the drinks." I listened to the sounds of summer in process till she came back.

"Try this one time," came her soft voice, as she handed me the tumbler, and I did; it was exquisite.

"Mighty fine," I said. "Mighty fine."

"How you've grown up," she said, eying me shrewdly.

"Time catches up, you've grown up too."

"I don't mean getting full growth," Ada cried out, but in a softer voice she added, "I mean shedding a couple of skins,

[138]

and acquiring an eye that looks with a look. You understand?"

"You mean finishing with being a child."

"No, no." She smiled. "I mean not stopping being a child,
but taking on adulthood as a part-time job."

"How well," asked I, "do you know Miss Ninetta Fifield?
Did you study with her?"

"No, I began with Miss Garnett."

"I don't mean piano lessons," I exclaimed. "I mean saying things calculated to make people jump. Adulthood as a
part-time job!"

"Hoo-ee!" giggled Ada Mary. "Go way!" she added to a
yellowfly.

"Are you still a weeper?" I asked teasingly. "I remember
you were always bawling when you were little, you always
were."

"You always needed your face slapped, and I might oblige
right now." But she was showing her dimples. We both
laughed.

"Well, I'm mighty glad Uncle Acis chose you for his wife,"
I said seriously, realizing I had to acknowledge the match in
some manner.

"We chose each other," she said quickly, then— "I better
warn you now. I better just warn you against calling me
Aunt Ada Mary, or anything like that. Or Aunt. It's true
I'm married to your Uncle Acis, but I'm not anybody's
Aunt Ada, thanks just the same."

"All right," I said.

"I depend on you to stick by me," she said.

"Sure thing," I answered, wondering if she was warning
me, enlisting me, or about to give a confidence. She went on.

"It's not easy being married to somebody who is not only
somewhat older than you, but a famous character besides.
There's lots of people think of me not as Acis' wife, but as
his latest invention. But I'm not. I'm Ada and I'm his wife.
The minute Acis and I set eyes on each other we knew what
we wanted. Now we have it: we're married, and we're

happy in spite of fools and know-it-alls. But I'm not any-body's Aunt Ada, you'll have to understand that. I'm Ada, like always, to you. You'll never be other than you, either, as far as I'm concerned. You're sure the hell not my nephew, and—" she waggled her finger at me "—if I ever catch a nephewish look in your eye or a nephewish tone in your voice, you can start ducking your head, 'cause the nearest brick has already started toward you."

"You trying to scare me or something?" I asked her. I was tickled at old Weary Weeper turning out to be Miss Boss Lady, but I was damned if I'd give her an inch. But her look made it all right, I reckon. She wasn't really being biggety. I'm perfectly willing for ladies to have opinions, because if there's anything more richly interesting than the opinions of ladies, I don't know what it might be. I mean when they have arrived at them by themselves. But ladies that are big-gety—that's another thing, I can't stand ladies that are big-gety, and there are plenty nowadays, don't kid yourself.

"I know better'n to try scare you or any of your clan. I ought to by now, after all I'm married into it. No, I just spoke my mind. Don't look like that! We've been friends since childhood, no reason to be anything but frank."

"Sorry," I mumbled. "I forget sometimes and show my Sophia County scowl."

"Lemme show you your room," she said, getting up, and I followed her into the house.

The inside of the house was considerably altered, what with the living-room enlarged and elegantly paneled, the whole wall of the old pantry become cupboards, and every-thing more citified and comfortable than when I was there as a child. Originally a summer house, it had slowly taken shape as an all-the-year house, had a silly add-a-part look that I liked: for example, one hall in the middle of the house that went from dining-room to kitchen had windows giving into a back bedroom. This window wall was clapboarded just as though outside, for they'd simply built on that hall and what was beyond it. There were coathooks in this hall made of cypress roots, which sprouted from the wall like the antlers of some beast that never existed save maybe at Bayou Clair.

All the furniture was different—fine old walnut and rose-wood pieces from Acis' mother's home up in Carroll County, Mississippi; at least three splendid mirrors, one framed in plain wood, the others gilt with doodads—then scattered through with the more solid stuff were old wicker things discarded years before from the now non-existent town house. It was carefree and lackadaisical, being open to the Bayou on one side, and the green world on all others, but it had its own elegance and an elegance of surprise as well, like a lady in a Paris frock chewing bubble gum. Above all, one look and you knew it was the stronghold of such a one as Uncle Acis, for even if you never heard of him, you wouldn't have to be the brightest thing on this earth to figure out who lived here and what he was like. No, you wouldn't have to be Sherlock Holmes, nor his little brother either.

Uncle Acis operates on the same wave length, I think, as old Miss Lulie Stewart of Belle Fontaine who is now older than God, but who can smell somebody nailing a sign to a tree as far away as a mile. Miss Lulie will traipse out and just plain smell the wind. She can't *see*, that's certain, and everybody knows she's half-deaf though she pretends she hears *everything*—in fact she's so busy hearing everything that you get the feeling sometime that she hears Voices. But she just *knows* when somebody is up to what they shouldn't be in her opinion, and draws her old mouth down to a pretty scary line and gets her hatchet and is gone. That's Uncle Acis, too, same way.

Even if she lives to be three hundred and can only sit around and give orders, she will always have my Uncle Acis for her deputy. He's just as fanatical: he'll just set out some-times, in fine weather, to see what's happening along the road. The real sport is finding somebody putting up signs: some busy mousy little man in a double-breasted suit, with a

[141]

mouthful of tacks and a magnetic hammer, out cluttering up tree trunks.

"Ho-ho!" Uncle Acis will roar out. "So it's you that's punctuating creation with this crap?"

Every time he'll swear he owns the property, and that the man better move on. He's had at least one fine row when he accosted the owner of an acreage out putting up signs on his own property and gave *him* a rough time. But he tears them all down, that's where the kindling comes from. Every time, he'll come back twinkling with enthusiasm for what he's accomplished, just like Miss Lulie. If you want to see something heartwarming you want to see Miss Lulie sashaying back with this real pleased look, puffing for dear life, more dead than alive, but triumphing by simple unquenchable ire over time itself.

Then there's Uncle Acis' desk. He bought it real cheap from the Marine Junk Company. They got it from the Southern Hotel when it closed. A family of four could easily live in it. Rolltop, naturally, and rolls with a sound puts me in mind of the Offstage Battle Noises they had for Senior Class production of *Journey's End*. I mean rich, impressive, unexplainable, but definitely *wood*. In this desk one finds the index to Uncle Acis' interests. Besides the world's greatest concentration of pointless pencils and unanswered letters, there are little caches of seed corn, a few shells and pebbles, a drawerful of snapshot negatives that can't be identified, a genealogy of the Foxe and Wingate families, a few old screws and bits of ormolu from who-knows-what, several dried-up bottles of ink remover, a *Souvenir of the St. Louis Exposition* knife with fourteen blades (of which one is an earspoon) and years and years of Henry A. Dreer seed catalogues from Philadelphia.

This object is smack in a corner of the living-room, and Uncle Acis has it arranged so he can move his chair a little and see out across the Bayou. Acis' mother had hated this desk, and would sometimes sit across the room from it, looking pained, after years of trying to persuade Uncle Acis to throw it away or at least move it out the living-room. She even suggested he might build a little detached room around it, with shelved walls. But Uncle Acis had been adamant and the desk had remained.

"I think that's the biggest desk in the world," Ada Mary said, eying it. I could sense that she had her own feelings about it. It's funny how ladies take instinctive dislikes to certain *things,* and how without visibly communicating with each other, they'll all have the identical reaction. "But Acis made me promise never to touch it. Nothing could prevent me, though, from giving him a pencil sharpener for Christmas."

We wandered out onto the other porch, which faced the water. The salt wind, fresh and bracing, blew in my face. Ada Mary stood there looking out across the shimmering blue and green.

"Bayou Clair's nice, isn't it?" murmured she, dreamily.

"Certainly is."

"I hope," she went on softly, "you'll stay a long time. Acis would like it and so would I. We're having some friends down for a couple of weeks, I think you know them all; after that it'll be just us. You must pass a real old-fashioned visit."

"Thanks, Ada Mary, I hope I can."

"Oh, I'm just Ada now," she remarked. "No more Mary, just Ada alone.

"Where is that boy?" she added, shading her eyes to look across the Bayou as she stepped down to the yard. I followed. "Come on see our pretty garden."

"Tell me," cried I, remembering suddenly, "the famous Baudauer is buried here, isn't he?"

"Yes," she turned to me saying, "come see—the statue is nice."

On the land side of the building were shrubberies and garden beds new since my time, and over amongst the mimosa trees, a good stone's throw from the house, was the grave of Kosta's beloved pet. There was a brick pedestal

[143]

four feet high, and on it, just smaller than life-size, was Kosta's terra-cotta figure of "Pan Grieving."

"My incorrigible Acis refers to this as our *terror-Kosta*," said Ada. "But that's 'cause he preferred always coons for pets, and has never been real excited over cats and dogs."

It was a fine statue. Pan, standing dejectedly, had his hands up hiding his face, but not touching it. By craning you could see his sly face drawn with grief, his eyes closed. His syrinx and his wreath were at his feet. The goat half was modeled in almost poodlish curls, and in the human half all the curves of the muscles were full of that arrogant sensuousness that seemed to occupy old Kosta. There was a flippant goat-tail whisk on the backside of the figure.

I couldn't help feeling the sadness of old Kosta somehow, for all the bright sun, and the sprightly garden-party air of this spot with the pink puffs of mimosa smelling warm and confectionate, the heedless green all around. I think the statue spoke true, and put forward a more solemn grief than one would think, to see crazy Kosta tossing his crest of white hair, or to see the drawings and paintings of the poodle. It was not, this statue, simply a pretty ornament for the corner of a garden; it was a real goatling god, sexy and curious, albeit in repose. To see this Pan was to meet Kosta straight on for the first time.

I reached up to pat the impudent tail.

"Everybody does that!" Ada giggled. "I waited to see if you would. That pore little tail's gonna be worn away before this pedestal loses its new look." She rubbed her hand on the rough bricks. "We hope for moss," she said almost under her breath, leaning down to pull a knot of wishing grass. Then she offered me one end of a stem, after pulling off the bloom. "Make a wish!" She pinched her end of the stem, I pinched mine, then we pulled very carefully, our heads almost touching. It made the square, easily and perfectly, all sides of equal thickness: we'd have our wish.

"Ah!" we both sighed at the same moment, delighted, then dropped the stem and laughed. I realized I hadn't made a wish! Or at least not consciously. But somewhere in the dark pantries of the heart, you know I believe I *did* make a wish: the grass said it would come true. On we strolled.

The sound of a boat bumping the pier and the clatter of oars thrown ashore made us rush to the water. As we reached the pier there was Acis just stepping onto the landing platform from his rowboat. He was engaged in unloading his supplies from Gaspard's Landing, and didn't see us till our footsteps reverberated on the sun-silvered wood of the pier. He turned, shaded his eyes, and broke into a great grin.

Uncle Acis is muscular, compact, and springy. He bounds up from chairs; is never uneasy on a shaky ladder or a thin limb. He's a jack-in-the-box, he likes to climb things, and jump over things. He belongs to that race that watches the earthbound over its shoulder as it skips on ahead, eager to be first at the picnic ground.

"My God!" is all he'd say, giving me a rough bear-hug. "My God!" He was glad to see me, but after a minute was embarrassed at Ada being there, for Ada and I were so close to the same age, and that's a great rapport in the world. He gave her a basket of okra he'd brought from Gaspard's, then we all began to talk at once.

Uncle Acis was brown, that old expression "brown as a berry" would have new meaning for you if you'd seen him, though in all my life I've never figured what berries are supposed to be so brown. But brown he was, and the hair on his arms was bright gold. On top his hair was sunburnt to cornsilk color, the sides and under layers being the same brown as his skin. His face had filled out since I'd seen him, and he had developed a filigree of squinch-lines from being out so often on the Bayou in bright sun. He wore faded seersuckers, hanging from his watch pocket was the little gold lizard that had served him as fob all his life. Most of all, he was reassuringly himself.

"And Perrin?" he asked, in a tone speaking volumes. "You two still at each other's throats?"

[145]

"Yes!" I laughed.

"Well, hell, that's no surprise. What of Lola? Have news of her?"

"Just that she was hot to get to this school in Switzerland."

"Too bad we couldn't have a grand reunion here. Though on second thought it'd probably be too much to bear. But we'll drink on your being here, won't we, Ada?"

"Yep."

"Soon some people you know will be coming down—we're having a kind of sloppy house-party for a few weeks."

"Who, Uncle Acis?"

"Why your erstwhile landlady Queen Ninetta Nut-etta, and Kosta Reynolds (he's in mourning) and Miss Fiffy's Fern, and Miss Fiffy's Tony, and Miss Fiffy's old Hispano with the yellow wheels, but *not* Brother John: he's dead and buried happily elsewhere, in Miss Fiffy's front yard I think (that's cheerful) and for that I thank heaven—'cause I could see Bayou Clair becoming the South's most famous pet cemetery. I told Miss Fiffy to throw that mangy corpse on her compost heap, there's nothing better than a little animal fat. Reincarnation in the form of flowers, I told her, but she wouldn't listen. Between Miss Fiffy and Kosta it'll be gay here this season, yes it'll be gay! Though Kosta's the worst and he's had over a year to get shet of this Baudauer obsession."

"Don't forget Aunt Lulie!" chimed Ada.

"I'm coming to that: in addition, we have lured Miss Lulie Stewart here for dinner; you'll see for yourself."

"She does it with her little hatchet," put in Ada vaguely. "I'll go ahead and fill the glasses, y'all come on, hear?"

I helped Acis put the oars and fishing things away, then we started toward the house.

"Well," he said casting a shrewd glance my way, "last time you were here you were a little bitta boy, now you're a man. Makes me feel pretty ancient. Do you have a girl?"

"No, unless you count Fiffy."

[146]

"Haw, that sweet bat. Every man and boy worth two cents has her for his girl some time. She's wit's whetstone. No, I mean a *girl* friend."

"No, I'm a free spirit right now."

"Well, that's hopeful." Acis grinned. "Your father was looking pale and preoccupied at seventeen already. Angie Olivet, that moron; never mention her name near your mama. But not me. Horses at twelve, then boats at fifteen, then I took up reading. Are you set for law?"

"No, I'm not set for anything."

"Never mind, you've got one hundred good years to decide."

"No, Uncle Acis, the thing is, I've caught up with myself all of a sudden; and I've realized that everything I learned in school and everything people have told me, is all crap, and I've got to start over from the beginning."

"Why, there's my heart! Bayou Clair is the climate for you, you just stay here. Maybe we could persuade your folks down for a visit. It's been donkey's years since I've seen them."

"I haven't seen them myself for over a year, spite of 'em being so close."

"And you've been helling around in the Nawth, huh? I'll just have to hear about that. Come on, let's go in."

I waited patiently to see some sign of affection, or passion, or even conjugality between Acis and Ada, some look between them that was a "married" look. But never saw it. My jovial uncle was much the same as I remembered him, Ada was very much like a guest in the house, though a familiar one. They'd seemingly not lost their separateness. They set each other off. But Acis no longer hopped up from table twenty times during the meal, as formerly; and Ada, passing the gravy boat, or murmuring to Modena, had achieved a grandness unexpected in one who'd been Weary Weeper, and shy, and nervous and unpredictable. Why, old Ada passed the gravy boat like the goddess of gravy herself:

a simple magnificence. I marveled, as we dined by candle-light, at the shine on her hair, the freshness of her plump face. Had Acis conjured this glow, I asked myself.

Acis, still a talker, and certainly unchanged in profusion and fieriness of his opinions, had a new shine too, difficult to name. Anyway, they were illustrations to an argument for marriage.

After supper, while we were sipping coffee and smoking on the front gallery, Ada excused herself and went inside. Minute later, surprisingly there came a ripple of frolicsome music through the open windows.

"You have a piano!"

"Sure, Ada's. I want her to always keep up her music."

Remembering the soupy-sad pieces I'd always heard her play, I was real pleased to hear all this gaiety. It was the sort of thing Miss Fiffy played, up and down and all over the place. It sounded fine, with the background of crickets, katy-dids, treefrogs, bullfrogs, and the distant drone of a motor-boat out on the Bayou some place. It made perfect the night, which exhaled the scent of willow oak very strongly, as well as a heavy sweetness of some night-blooming shrub.

"We have a concert most every night." Acis smiled. "Some-times people out in their boats row up to our pier to hear Ada play."

"What's she playing?" I asked, charmed by the crazy chasing of the tune.

"Scarlatti." He puffed a lazy swirl of smoke as the house, the dark trees, the starry night itself were all pervaded by Ada's music, an airy complex melody—full of sudden shifts—that seemed trying to budge all solid things and make them dance. Finishing one piece, she took up the next, as rapid and as mischievous.

"Music is excellent for the digestion," observed Acis.

On she played, while Acis and I brought each other up to date. Naturally I told him nothing explicit of Perrin, or of Philine, but I think he sensed I was holding something back. He told of improvements to the estate, of the acreage planted

[148]

in tung trees, satsumas, of his plan to dam a branch of Stella Creek to make a swimming place. We talked a deal of Sophia County and of my folks, while music still poured from the windows, then, abruptly, ceased with an upward swoop, and the soft clatter of the night rushed into its wash of silence. The katydids and frogs were especially loud. Ada rejoined us and we listened to the insects till we all began to yawn and went in.

Every day began with a swim before breakfast, then after breakfast came the projects of the day: picking blackberries, caulking an old rowboat, helping Acis paste entries in his Camellia Culture scrapbook, then midmorning Cokes, then a swim before lunch, lunch, a nap, Cokes, then a turn about the garden (this including weeding, spraying, picking) a trip up the road, or across the Bayou to Gaspard's Landing, then watering and weeding, then a cocktail, then supper, coffee, music, then bed again—all of this accompanied by a riptide of talk from Acis and Ada and even me, and the oft-repeated observation, "Well, we're not getting much done today," but this was a kind of customary refrain. Ada practised her music, I laid a few bricks: beginning of a path leading to the statue; some mornings we crabbed or fished off the pier for that night's supper. Acis, all the time he wasn't busy with the Cottens, who lived and worked on the place, spent tending his camellia cuttings: he'd been bitten by the camellia bug for sure, and was fussing over a group of Charlotte's Reds from Spring Hill. In a sense it was childhood recaptured, pristine and unexpected, without search. I lost the date, all sense of time, bathed in a sunny suspension, though I anticipated our visitors.

One morning, finishing breakfast, I had just put my napkin in the napkin ring when I was startled at the sound of a husky Klaxon booping, and a chuckling kind of motor turning in at our gate. I rushed to the side porch: it was the dilapidated Hispano, grandly upright, fixtures gleaming, with dusty yellow wire wheels. Driven by Tony, it contained a be-scarfed Miss Fiffy, a sunhatted Fern, and a great number of baskets and cardboard boxes, including a wicker animal cage, from which peered a whiskered visage. It was nothing less than a sight.

It shuddered to a stop, and all the doors seemed to fly open before I could get down the steps. Ada and Modena and Acis had come by then, and everybody talked at once. Fern, lifting Elissa in her basket out the car, greeted me first. Tony and I shook hands, and I took the animal, then Miss Fiffy got out.

"Oh!" she cried to me. "Oh, oh!"

"How's my girl?" I asked and gave her a light kiss. She held my free hand between both of hers.

"I really thought you were lost to us, how happy I am to see you!"

"No, not lost!"

She pulled me aside, turning her back on the others. Acis had gone straight into the motor with Tony, who was proudly showing it off; while Ada and Fern were bucket brigading the baskets to the porch.

"I'm glad you saw fit to come home; I'm *glad.* Let those two naughties stay in New York." Then she fixed me with a quizzical look and said, as she took off her scarfs: "I never said, did I, that Philine was an angel flown from heaven's coop and moulting now on this earth."

"No, you never said *that.*"

"Well. But we'll talk later. Where's Lizzie?"

"Right here. That's not Elissa, is it?"

"The same. She's gotten right pretty, we call her Lizzie now."

Then hearing her name, the animal wailed from her basket. "Lemme out!" is what she said.

"Proper compost," Acis yelled, a muffled voice from inside the hood, where he bent into the motor.

"Fiend," laughed Fiffy. "Come, Lizzie!" And Lizzie stepped warily out.

"My, how good the car looks," I said.

"We haven't had it off blocks since Mardi Gras. I like the parades best from a closed car. Yes, we polished it up to come here. We created a sensation at Government Street loop when we stopped for gas."

"Don't doubt it," I said admiringly.

"I hope you note we have new cushions, too. But I felt that this house-party was *tellement speciale;* I had almost a sense of embarkation for Cythera."

"Nope," roared Acis, "it's Smuggler's Island. Nothing but outlaws here."

"You," Fiffy questioned, "are you a smuggler, or a smug-glee?"

"I'm a smugglaree," I countered. " 'Cause I smuggled myself down here."

"Well, I think you're the quietest roaring-boy of all, but still a roaring-boy, that's what I think," said she.

So it went, better than a comedy, and much more confused, all chattered at once, vying for attention, full of news.

Lunch was giddy, and a gabfest for sure; afterwards Fiffy was the star performer for afternoon. She had brought with her from town an old red-and-gold book from her childhood days, full of tricks, stunts for parties, directions for objects to be made of paper, and instructions for shadow plays, all that sort of thing. In a chapter on "Garden Fun" there was a fantastical passage which stated in matter-of-fact prose that lilies could be made to waltz. It seemed that a music-box sounding beside the *Lilium regum* would cause noticeable movements by that flower. Fiffy, in great glee, had brought book and music-box to try this experiment in Acis' garden, where the Regals were in full summer bloom. Acis, full of party spirit, had fetched his own music-box into the garden, and they had lugged out stools and all, Ada and I standing by, amused, while Fern and Modena watched suspiciously from the corner of the house.

[151]

"Why don't you bring your piano out, Ada?" I inquired. "I'm sure that's lots better than an ole music-box."

"Shut up," she said, then to the others, "If y'all intend to make these lilies dance, you better get going, 'cause it's surely fixing to rain."

"You remember *Little Ida's Flowers,*" commented Fiffy to nobody.

"Whatchall gonna do?" asked Modena, frowning.

"Why, Modena, we're gonna have these lilies here dancing a waltz."

Modena laughed uproariously at this. Going to the corner of the house she said to Fern, "They plan to make them lily-buds cut a trick! I do wants to see it!"

"—tell me!" replied Fern dubiously. "It's the boobyhatch, come Monday."

"How long does it take," asked Acis, "before they dance?"

"Well, I guess they have to get accustomed to the rhythm," answered Fiffy thoughtfully.

"Creepy," muttered Fern.

Then Acis and Fiffy each clicked on his box, and amidst our watchful silence and the sound of a new-sprung breeze in the treetops, the interwoven spiny music plunked away: a double waltz, the tunes hopelessly tangled. The sky was clouding over, the air had already cooled; there was certainly a squall headed up the Bayou from the Bay. Lizzie ambled around the corner of the house.

"*She* may dance sooner than these proud vegetable creatures," said Fiffy.

"It's gonna pour down cats and dogs," admonished Ada, squinting at the sky, while the music played on.

"It's gonna pour down," echoed Fern from the corner of the house.

"Damn!" exclaimed Acis, for his box had run down. He pulled the key from his pocket and hastily rewound. "Damn!" he cried again, for he'd dropped his key in a clump of plants. Ada helped him search for it.

"I believe that one is moving," observed Fiffy, but resignedly, for she saw it was the wind. A few big drops fell, stirring her to action. She snatched up her music-box and ran inside. Ada took the second box, I took a stool, but adamant pigheaded Uncle Acis was still thrashing about in the leaves —I had to laugh seeing him bent double in the flower bed.

"It'll rust if it stays here," he said.

So we hurried in as the rain, cold and torrential, crashed in the lush summer foliage, thundering on the roof. Ada, once inside, took an umbrella and ran to the window to toss it out to Acis, but the latch of the screen was stuck and she couldn't open it; Acis was already soaked anyway; his clothes hung on him, and his hair was plastered in silly bangs on his forehead. A sudden gust shattered the poppies, a flash of color. Still Acis searched.

"Now you come in," insisted Fiffy at the window. She had that eternal feminine need to bring the world in out of the weather. But Acis might as well have been carved in agate for all he heard.

"Go ahead," taunted Ada, "catch ground-itch."

"You girls might as well shut up," he replied calmly. "I don't study putting foot one in the house till I find my little old key. I've had that music-box and that key too since I was no age at all."

But then Fern came out with a raincoat over her head and found the key. She reached her slender brown hand under the leaves and fished it right out triumphantly. Fern can always find things. "I know how people throw things down," she says.

"I guess," Fiffy grieved to Ada, "we'll never know the truth about lilies."

"Come on dry off, Acis," cried Ada, "and we'll have coffee."

The next day was cloudy and damp, but the rain had stopped for the moment. Inside the house, all was tempestuous preparation for the dinner party, Ada's first as mistress of the house, and she intended to impress. At daybreak,

Tony rattled off to town to pick up Kosta, peppermints from George's Candy Shop, and such. I carried garbage to the compost heap and the pit, enjoying the spectacle in the kitchen.

We drank Cokes midmorning; Modena, Fern and I sat down on the back porch to drink them and have a cigarette. But Ada, barefoot, in blue cotton, her hair in a knot that was coming undone, was going like a dynamo and nothing could stop her. Her round face was flushed and her cheeks blooming. Watching her mashing avocados for the sherbet that would climax the feast I fell suddenly, unexpectedly, foolishly and thoroughly in love with her. She had the tip of her pink tongue stuck out the corner of her mouth, and my sole desire was to gather her soft roundness in my arms and bring my mouth down over hers, to catch that pink tip in my teeth, and tease it.

Ada, spoon poised, looked up and looked into my eyes. I think she read every single thing there. For then she looked down, then looked sideways at me, humming to herself.

"Well, we're all working like Trojans today," she said, then she wiped her hands and said, "Gimme a drag."

I handed her my cigarette, and she took it carefully and took a long puff, a smile lurking in her dark eyes. At that moment, happily—a silence had fallen, and there was a roaring in my ears: possibly I was flushed—there came a call from Acis in the dining-room, to help him put the extra leaves in the table.

"I don't much care if it does rain," he confided. "I like parties on rainy nights."

"Me, too," I agreed.

Hearing a motorboat on the Bayou, we pulled back the curtains and peered out to see the Reverend Macklin, who lives near Revenue Point, and preaches at Gaspard's Landing. He was Uncle Acis' pet hate. He was puttering along, cautiously close to shore, his daily custom. Acis stopped dead still, like a bird dog pointing.

"*Oh!*" breathed my uncle with voluptuous disdain, run-

[154]

ning to hold up the curtain at the next window. "Medi-
ocrity's angel, there he goes. Going out to corrupt the
innocents and file the great sinners down to pocket-size.
Make 'em all fit the mold!" He passed, mumbling, to the
next window. Reverend Macklin was hidden for a moment
by the pine on the lawn, and Uncle Acis ran into the hall to
peer from the front door sidelights.

"Go on, hurry up, the devil's after you with his long-
handled spoon!" roared Acis. Then holding to the doorknob,
he kicked up his heels, a kind of shuffle dance in place, partly
morning-of-the-party gaiety, and partly disdain for the
preacher man. When he skipped merrily back to the dining-
table to resume his labors, I saw that his eyes were shining
with real pleasure, for all the world the expression of a fox
terrier that's given chase to a flivver.

"What in the name of heaven," came Ada's soft voice from
the door, "is going on in here?" I turned, all jellified, at her
voice. "Are y'all having a morning party?" she asked.

"Uncle Acis was just cussing out the Reverend Macklin,"
I explained. "He just passed in his put-put, going to corrupt
the innocents, Uncle Acis says."

"You're terrible," Ada chastised him, lifting the curtain
herself for a glimpse of the preacher, but he was out of sight.
"The pore ole bastid's disappeared." Then she went to Acis
and brushed a feathery kiss across his cheek that I felt on my
cheek too, by proxy, by proximity. I daresay I felt it more
than Acis—a fiery imprint, infecting my veins with the sweetest and wildest desire. She smiled as she went back to the
kitchen.

Kosta Reynolds, tanned, silver-maned, impudent-eyed as
ever, burst in with luggage and painting equipment just in
time for lunch, saying, "I live for parties. I date my life according to the most successful of them," and hugging everybody impartially. Also pats and pinches. Fiff, engaged in
manufacturing elaborate place-cards, was holed-up in her

[155]

room till Kosta zoomed in, then she descended with her flower cut-outs and bold Spencerian inscriptions.

At four in the afternoon, we heard a car rattle into the gate, and everybody stopped to listen.

"Ah, that would be the archdruidess," observed Fiffy.

Which is who it was: Miss Lulie Stewart, chauffeured by Allan Stewart, her great-nephew, a big boy of nineteen with a crew cut and thick eyebrows who is a lunatic for old automobiles. But Lulie—! Greeting her was exactly like going to the Egyptian part of the Museum and saying *hello, there* to an authentic mummy, receiving in reply a possum handshake. She wore a silk turban that was terribly zoot and was probably Ada's choice rather than her own. Otherwise she was all shawls, scarfs and silk kerchiefs, nothing corporeal, and mere slits in parchment to serve as eyes, lips that were never still. She made little comments to herself, and to this day I suppose nobody has figured how much she intended people to hear and how much she thought she was saying to herself.

"It's a pretty day, it's surely a pretty day," she babbled (at that moment the sky was black as ink—there's *her* humor), looking a little shaken after her ride.

"Oh, Aunt Lulie's just like a little kid," explained Allan as we chatted on the porch. "She'd rather speed on the highway than eat. She's mad if I don't take her for a spin every evening."

"She's never scared?" I knew he was a hot-rod kid, with a hopped-up motor, who raced on the highway.

"Aunt Lulie dud'n know the word. Besides, she can't see well enough to read the speedometer, even if she knew what it was, or to see if things are rushing past at ten miles an hour or ninety. She knows she's moving by the wind busting past her ears and she likes that."

At last, after day-long endeavors and anticipations, we sat to table, lit by candles, and transformed by the brightness and formality into creatures more handsome and more witty

than ourselves. Ada in a new blue dress, with white ole-
anders stuck in her chignon, seemed a veritable animation
of Good Cheer. She lacked only a golden cornucopia. Uncle
Acis was bright, though with a watery eye—he'd caught a
summer cold—while Miss Lulie, by her matter-of-fact peev-
ishness, set off the airy spirits of the rest.

"What's *that?*" asked Miss Lulie, pulling a finicky face at
the watercress.

"It's watercress, Aunt Lulie," said Ada patiently and
grimly. "You don't have to eat it."

"Grass," intoned that old lady, very much as Lady Mac-
beth might say *blood,* so Ada quietly removed it from her
plate. Miss Lulie has been known to spin a lamb chop across
the room if it didn't please her. Over at Stewarts' they'll be
happy to show you the grease spot on the dining-room wallpaper.

"Quickest path to an early grave," mumbled Miss Lulie,
"is through the salad bowl. *Weeds* . . . and *raw.*"

"All right, all right," cautioned Allan, "if you can't behave
I'll take you right home."

"Miss Lulie Stewart shouldn't oughta worry 'bout no early
grave," said Modena very softly, as she went into the pantry.
Her remark was lost to all, for the pretty tinkle of glassware
and silverware was the music that prevailed: everybody was
hungry and the dishes superb.

"Baudauer would never even smell carrots," observed
Kosta, during the main course, as he refused the vegetable.
Acis gave him a look.

"Kosta, we all love you—" he began.

"We all loved Baudauer," said Fiffy. "But we think—"

"I know, I know!" answered Kosta, shaking his white
cockatoo crest.

"If I hear the name of that sweet goddam lamented poodle
just one more time," snarled Acis, "I may flip a ruby."

"We love you," put in Fiffy gently, "but think you should
let poor Baudauer's memory rest in peace."

"Mr. Kosta oughta eat his carrots," Fern added. "They have iron."

"Oh, well," sighed Kosta. "But you know I *did* love that creature very much."

"Stop it," said Acis, "we may all burst into tears. Why don't you entertain us instead? Here you are, with an international reputation for pure deviltry, and you're still moping over that nice but dead poodle."

Kosta smiled sheepishly. "Lulie and I are going to do the Castle Walk for you after dinner, eh, toots?"

Lulie was so busy she didn't hear, so Kosta gained her attention by stealing a pickled peach from her plate. She slapped the back of his hand with her butter knife and smeared butter there, very delightedly.

"You pesky humbug!" She tittered, thoroughly amused and pleased with Kosta. Everybody laughed.

"Well, see, I *have* entertained you," said Kosta as he licked his hand.

"You're redeemed," Fiffy admitted, "but Lulie won the points."

"I'll just have my peach," said Miss Lulie, and grabbed it back, licking her fingers after.

"She gets sloppier every day," Allan declared, embarrassed.

"Oh, listen!" shushed Miss Fiffy, her eyes shining. It was the sound of rain in the black night outside. It had begun quite suddenly and with it came faint rumblings of thunder far away. We heard Tony running up the back stairs to close the windows. In the dining-room, suffused with light and wine, the sense of fête was even stronger—the circle of light in the center of the storm.

"Blessed rain," crooned Ada, with a turn of the head. "It means we'll have some late green beans, after all."

"I'm thinking of the camellias. They needed this," said Acis.

Miss Lulie had her head lifted, sniffing the freshness of the rain, but the sherbet of avocados came now and Acis opened the champagne which was its accompaniment. When

[158]

the first cork popped, she sat up straight and shouted, "Mardi
Gras!"

"Let's drink to the happiness of the house," said Kosta.

"No," exclaimed Fiffy, "the happiness of everybody under
this roof tonight. For ever and ever."

"Now, absent friends," proposed Ada for the second toast.
With mingled regret and anger I thought of Perrin and
Philine. . . .

"You're so quiet, more so than usual," Uncle Acis, quite
rosy, shouted at me. "Are you in love?"

"Yes," I said simply and truthfully. Ada lifted her eyes
with hardly perceptible movement, looking at me with spoon
poised.

"Who, pray?" she dared ask.

"Well, everybody here . . ." I began evasively and truthfully. Then I saw the look on poor Allan's face: hopeless
confusion. "I mean . . . the party . . . and . . . all . . ." I finished lamely.

"To parties," said Acis gaily.

But Miss Fiffy, perhaps the wisest of all, turning her clever
eyes from one to another, made another toast, quite lightly
said, "To love!" and Kosta leered and said, "Aaaah!" then
we drank. But I'm sure they were thinking of different
matters.

No one showed an inclination to leave the dinner table,
though coffee elsewhere was the custom of the house, so Fern
brought the huge pot of black brew into the dining-room.
Fiffy and Allan and I had lit our cigarettes. Miss Lulie, like
a tired old monkey, was dozing bolt upright in her chair;
Allan had gone to fetch from the front hall her extra wrap,
a purple afghan to put over the knees. The candles had
burnt halfway down, and Ada was peeling the solidified drip-
pings off the candlesticks, very abstracted. Her face, close
to the flames, was almost orientally expressionless and moony,
save for her bottomless eyes. Acis had lit a cigar and was
puffing away, watching her. Outside the rain beat down, full
timpani.

[159]

Miss Fiffy said very confidentially to me, after a gesture in the direction of the absent Allan, "Don't you think Southern men are at their best before twenty—" nodding sagely "—before they're corrupted by the world," she nodded then ever so slightly at the sleeping Lulie: "Southern women at seventy —*afterwards?*" She was about to continue her thought when Allan came galumphing back, all eyebrows and legs, to protect the sleeping monkey from chill. But Miss Lulie woke up, and petulantly refused to have her afghan, set her mouth and fought her grandnephew.

"I just can't do a thing with her," apologized Allan. "She's *bad.*"

"Where's my coffee?" piped that little old terror.

"Sometimes, Aunt Lulie, you just try my patience," sighed Ada, pouring her a cup.

"Thank you, Ada," replied the incorrigible creature, "and sometime you must just try mine." Then she splashed a spoonful of sugar into her cup from a high altitude.

"Have a cig?" asked Kosta, fliply proffering the pack to Lulie.

"It's your kind sets fire to the piney woods, with your nasty cigarettes," she snapped.

"I believe sometimes Lulie thinks she *is* Mother Nature," chuckled Acis in a low voice.

"Aunt Nature, it's a big difference," said Ada, regarding the antics of Miss Lulie rather coolly, as Kosta lit up and blew a puff of smoke across the table.

"Meddler, meddler!" she cried at him.

"An evening with Miss Lulie is an evening of good old-fashioned bear-baiting," observed Acis to me. At this Allan unexpectedly laughed, a great big guffaw that shook the windowpanes. He coughed and turned red, and there came an echo of laughter from the kitchen: another party there. Acis sneezed.

"Where's the brandy?" asked Ada, and as Acis poured it, she turned to me. "Has Lola traveled any in France yet?"

"She's there now," put in Miss Fiffy. "Likes it better than

Switzerland even, though anyone could have told her that. She should be in Paris just about now."

"Why don't you tell us a story?" Acis prodded me. "You've been too quiet. Now you must amuse us."

"I envy Lola her chance to travel there," sighed Ada.

"Very well," I said. "Have y'all heard about old man John Lussac, and what happened to him?"

"You'll go there yourself, someday, you and Acis."

"I pray."

"Why he's the old man at Sweeteye was killed in cold blood in his own house. His house was haunted."

"John Lussac? He's *dead*," said Miss Lulie adamantly, as though that told all of *his* story.

"Well there's lot to it, y'all sit still now, and I'll tell you how it was," I began. So they all turned to me, and I started my tale, against the steady roar of the rain, while Ada replenished cups.

"Well . . . see . . . when old man John Lussac was young, he went to school at Harvard, I don't know what he studied, it didn't matter, 'cause he certainly didn't plan to work, his family owning all that corner of Mobile County as well as acreage in Sophia County and Baldwin County as well. I think he dillied around in New York for a while, then dallied in London, then after a while, when his papa was so sick, he came home to Sweeteye to stay for a while, and the thing is, he never left again. He had assembled a mighty nice library for himself, and he settled down to read it. He could read Greek and Latin like you read the morning *Register*, just matter-of-fact like, with his coffee. He was real struck with Greek history, and people would come sometimes on Sunday afternoon pretending to want to settle questions of Greek history and literature, but really just wanting to take afternoon coffee in his old house—it'uz the only real showplace within spitting distance of Sweeteye. They had real fine French furniture that had mother-of-pearl set in it, real fancy, you know, and crystal chandeliers. But even people that didn't know beans from boathooks would get carried away when he started reading in Greek to them: he had a good floating style of reading, and a good voice—it was all impressive.

"My grampa knew him slightly, we went once on a Saturday in November and had a good visit with him. Very handsome old man, you know, his eyebrows had stayed black when his hair turned white, and he was tall and slender. There was nothing in this world for him but Greek wars—just get him started. Though later he got interested in magic, too. Anyway he lived at home, till first his papa died, then his mama, and his brother moved to Demopolis—the brother was married, had a family—so finally he was left alone. He didn't work, as I told you, so gave up keeping the gardens, then closed off some of the upstairs rooms, then finally just had this one couple to take care of the house, it was the daughter of his old nurse, and her husband. The money was draining away, and he lost some investments in the Depression, and finally sold most of his land, and just when he was beginning to wonder if he might not have to either go to work, or sell the house, he was saved by fire from heaven, I mean to tell you he was photographed miraculously by a flash of lightning."

I had all their eyes, Allan was a sight to see, and Lulie slept again, while outside the rain was being buffeted about by a breeze that had sprung up.

"Well, see, there was this fine thunderstorm one summer afternoon, you know a real crasher like we do have, and Mr. John Lussac was roaming around in the double parlor of his old drafty house, when there came this blinding flash of lightning (some people passing in an old Chevvy later said they saw a big ball of fire roll along the rooftree of his house) and afterwards a *tremendous* crash of thunder—not just one big crash—but several horrible crashes amidst a steady bombard—oh, I forgot to say that he didn't have the blinds drawn, he's the type likes a thunderstorm—"

"Hmm, not me!" exclaimed Ada, nibbling peppermints.

"—and anyway, the thing is, that he was dazed for a min-

[162]

ute, for the bolt had struck the pecan tree right alongside the house (it's a miracle he wasn't killed *then*) and burned right along one side of it into the ground, and he rushed out to see if his two servants were all right, they were but were pretty scared, so it wasn't for an hour or so that he discovered what had happened.

"Well, at the exact moment the lightning flashed, he'd been standing in the center of his double-parlor, and it had huge mirrors at each end that reflect each other, and the lightning acting on the mercury backings of those old mirrors (they don't make 'em now like they used to) had photographed him on both of them, two perfectly recognizable profiles on the mirror surfaces."

"For do!" Fiffy was charmed.

"I did hear talk of this," added Acis.

"Well, don't you see, this saved Mr. John's life. It didn't take longer than twenty-four hours for all Sophia and Mobile counties to know about it; Baldwin, too. I have to tell you the best of all now: one of those mirrors was badly flawed, and so one of the images had perfect horns, though if anybody with two eyes would stand still and look at it, they'd see it was a watery stain in the glass, nothing more. But people see what they like to see and overlook everything they *should* see, so it became the Good Image and the Evil Image of Mr. John, without he could do a thing about it. They said the lightning split him in two for one second in eternity, and the mirrors had reflected his two natures and caught them. So it wasn't but ten days later the first excursion bus was put on, that led right to the porch of Lussac Hall. They cleared away a part of the old vegetable garden for a parking lot, and Mr. John set up a kind of refreshment pavilion on the side porch, and he got the Dixie Rose Ice Cream concession, and had Cokes and Nehis, and lemonade that he made right there, sandwiches, too.

"At first, you know, he was mightily amused by this Good and Bad theory, but they say that after a year or ten months of people staring at him as he showed them through the house, that he began to go in that parlor on Saturdays, when the house was closed to the public, and stand there looking at those smoky wraiths of himself stained on the glass. But, anyway, in a year, he salted away a nice little bank account, I can tell you, and published a little pamphlet he wrote in a rolling straight-a-way style, called 'A Burst of Light, or Between Two Reflections.'

"Then, after about a year and a couple of months, he noticed those lightning photos were fading, and he was mightily depressed, thinking his source of revenue would be lost if they went. He experimented (out in the stable) with painting on glass, but couldn't get the right effect. One day when Stebby Martin came back from Mobile (that was Mr. John's best friend; he told my grampa this story, and that's how I got it) and Mr. John said, when he met him on the front porch, 'Well, I'm ruined, 'cause I'm annealed; my two natures are reconciled. I mean, those goddam mirrors have played out at last.' He didn't know what to do. He told Stebby seriously that he wished he could cook up some ghostly bloodstains on the floor of one of those closed-off rooms upstairs ('cause the house had already come to have the reputation of haunted, and people now said—people who knew perfectly well it was Greek—that he talked in an unearthly language to ghosts and zombies; and his poor cook, a good woman and an artist in the kitchen, came to be thought a conjure woman) since he couldn't replace the images faded from the glass. Stebby said why not retouch the mirrors, but of course Mr. John showed him how that couldn't be done. But Stebby did promise to find some dragon's blood pigment at a pharmacy on Davis Avenue in Mobile, to try bloodstains, and that's when this terrible thing happened that cinched the history of Lussac Hall. Some poor ole loony escaped from the County Farm and killed Mr. John with a hatchet, and made a pretty mess of bloodstains about the upstairs hall, I can tell you. I didn't see it, thank you, but Stebby did, and he told my grampa he never hoped to see the like in his lifetime. Anyway poor ole Mr. John Lussac got his wish. An-

[164]

other thing, the mirror in the front, that had had the Good Image, was broken the same day; they claim it shattered by itself at the moment he died, but I say bull to that—somebody just took a brickbat and let fly. But the other mirror, that's the best and most unbelievable part of the story. See, Mr. John left the money to his brother and family, and the house he left to the County. He always thought they'd want to have it a museum. But the County didn't entertain any such notion: they emptied out the house right smack out, and sold the property to a real estate investment company in Virginia, and that big ole mirror, too big for anybody's house nowadays, and too ill-famed for anybody to pay cash for it, went to the dining-room at the County Farm—so the glass of Evil Image went to where Mr. John's murderer had come from, and that pore loony, well he died in the jail, before they'd even charged him with the crime!"

"Gosh," drawled Allan, his jaw sagging for an instant.

"Was he dressed or undressed when he was photographed?" inquired Kosta.

"Dressed, it was daytime."

"That don't prove a thing."

The candles were pretty far down by now, so Ada fetched fresh ones, began to whittle the ends. Allan, the rosy and abashed, looked sheepishly about.

"I know a story. . . ." He grinned. "I don't know what you'd think of, I kinda like it . . ."

"Go ahead, everybody has a turn," boomed Acis. So Allan, husky with shyness, turning his glass round and round, told his story.

"Well, there was this sailor . . ."

"Aaaah?" said Kosta.

". . . that was on leave . . . and he went to a lawn party and met this swell girl, you know . . . Pensacola, I guess, some place like that . . ."

I looked at gentle Ada, wondering what tale she could tell, she'd probably play a *scherzo* and let that serve. I stared at her until she lifted both her eyelids ponderously and looked straight back. We both felt Acis' gaze at the same moment, and without turning her head, she shifted her eyes to Acis and smiled very slowly, like a flower opening in a fast-motion film, never ceasing her scrupulous peeling of wax driblets. Miss Lulie, not understanding one word of it, was following with her eyes Allan's elephantine leisure of narration.

". . . they found that they liked the same books, and movies, and this girl said, 'Well, what a coincidence, I can see I have good taste in movies and reading matter,' and when this sailor offered a cigarette, she said, 'Well, it's the same like I smoke; I guess I have good taste in cigarettes.' So the way it was they went on talking and found they both liked *Dardanella* and Tschaikovsky, and she said, 'What a coincidence, 'cause I do too: I can see I have good taste in music.' Just about everything you can think of they talked about, they found they liked the same, and that girl would say that identical remark about a coincidence, and how she reckoned she had good taste in this or that or th'other. . . .

"So she invited him to come for Sunday dinner next day, and he did, and he admired the house and all from the outside, but then he was real surprised when she opened the door 'cause there in the center of the living-room rug was the engine of a 1927 Bugatti racing car; it's the type 44, you know, with the cambered front wheels. . . ."

This last he said very earnestly to Miss Fiffy, who obviously had not the remotest idea what such a vehicle might be. But she was game. "Oh, of course." She nodded politely.

"When he looked through the open door of the bedroom . . . he saw the body of the car on her bed . . . the front fenders were in the bathtub. The sparkplugs were everywhere underfoot, and the battery was sitting with the biscuit dough on the kitchen table . . . anyway, this girl noticed the sailor staring blankly at all this, and she said, 'What's the matter with you?' and he answered, 'Please just tell me what is all this?' and that girl snorted and replied, 'Hell's bells, I never said I was *neat*, did I?' "

Well, Acis and Kosta and I roared, Allan smiling from ear to ear at his success, but it was one of those jokes that are simply not amusing to females, so Ada and Fiffy ha-haed politely and let it go at that. But old Miss Lulie, seeing Acis and her favorite, Kosta, knocking themselves out, joined in with her strident giggle.

"Hee, hee, hee," she pealed, looking at Kosta for encouragement.

"Speaking of mirrors," murmured Miss Fiffy, sending a long trail of smoke into the air, "invariably brings to mind Biddie Sayres, who might be said to have lived *in* mirrors, practically."

"She's Mrs. Something Inge now, isn't she?"

"No," Ada explained. "She's Mrs. Bailly Creston, she's Tinker's mother."

"Well, anyway, she'll never be anybody but Biddie Sayres to me, and I'm fixing to tell you why."

"I think I know this story." Acis grinned.

"No, you're thinking of what Biddie Sayres said to the traffic-cop who thought she was drunk that time; everybody knows that story. This is different—this is one hundred years before that."

"Tell us," I encouraged.

"Well the demented girl had been to England for a long visit. The family had cousins there, in Worcestershire, who were as delighted and amazed at her beauty and ignorance as she at their worldly-wiseness and sheer Englishness. It was a real English county family, at that time rather wealthy I believe, and much given to riding and hunting, and that sort of thing. Well, Biddie was too stupid to be afraid, and certainly a healthy specimen of Southern womanhood, with rosy cheeks and cornsilk curls that hung to her fanny when she took her hair down, so she proved a marvelous horsewoman, and pleased her English cousins mightifully. They were certainly loath to let her go. But Biddie had to come back to Demopolis, and delight and amaze her family and friends with a *kind* of English accent appliquéd over her pure upcountry Alabama one, to say nothing at all of her nip-ups on horseback.

"Well, after her papa died, and Biddie got the upper hand in the house (Mrs. Sayres was a real mouse) she thought she'd inaugurate a hunt, yessirree bobtail! a real English hunt, right in Alabama. *Tally-ho*, as they say; and as *I* say, *Tilly-loo!* 'cause the only, the *only* kind of hunting I could ever see—I mean I don't give a sneeze in a cyclone for your hunting: I'll cook and eat all the wild turkey in Christendom you can catch, and I'm partial unto madness to quail when it's stuffed with little sausages and rests in a contemplative pose on a dear little *chaise-longue* of grits—" with what delicious pantomime she sketched this image! "—but the only hunting I have done, or ever will do, is to go out frisking through the woods for the first violet in March. No, I take that back! Three kinds of hunting for me: the first blue violet, the first white (they're sweetest), and the first dogtooth —they're the yellows with the jaggy leaf. But all this riding to hounds I give to you freely—you are *welcome* to it! Miss Fifield's compliments, and go fall in a bog. Let alone quicksand!

"Anyway, Miss Biddie was going to hunt to the hounds, and the Devil in a tailcoat couldn't have changed her mind. That girl had a real battering-ram whim, as all know who ever opposed her. So the first thing was to go to her dressmaker and have some pretty fancy habits made, naturally. Hats with ostrich tips, habits with demi-trains; you know, all that. Though how she got this conception of a hunting costume, I'll never know, after the chic plainness of the English get-ups. Me, if I chose to ride, I'd go as Mazeppa.

"They brought the hounds for this affair from North Georgia where they was a county hunt established at that time—brought all those sad-eyed animals and their master and trainers and what-all down to Demopolis in wagons: you can imagine, this was fifty years ago. Biddie had the horses, of course, and they dug up this man with a hunting horn who could almost play it. It promised to be a real exciting hunt 'cause old man Donald John Ashwander had his boys and his servants mounted in chinaberry trees along his property, with their rifles stuck out through the leaves—he'd let it be known what could be expected when horse number one set its hoof in *his* fields. Let alone humans and dogs! (He was planted then in cotton and watermelons, as I remember.)

"Naturally Biddie would make it baroque, ah yes. They were going to start with a hunt breakfast of dazzling proportions, I asked Biddie at the time (naturally I went for the affair when she asked me—I was going to wave them off when they left and wave them back when they returned: two trips onto the upstairs gallery just outside my bedroom: they could exert *themselves* as they pleased) I asked Biddie, I said do you hate horses? I said the breakfast was obviously designed to break the horses' pore backs, but my pleasantry was two or three miles in the air over her pretty head.

"Well, see, they had taken the piano out of the double-parlor, (which had mirrors either end, like Lussac Hall or any place) and put two long tables, all decorated with flowers and such, and the most sumptuous spread you can imagine— they had fried chicken, ham in three different ways, fried pork chops, brandied peaches, a salad of oranges, fresh bread, hot rolls, hot biscuits, fresh butter, ti-ti honey brought up from Milton, Florida—"

"No, no! don't tell about the food. Not now!" wailed Ada.

"I'm about to get hungry all over again," buzzed Kosta. His voice woke Miss Lulie, who began tussling about for peppermints.

"—and they had borrowed the big coffee urns from the hotel at Palaprat Springs: that's all for the menu, you can rest easy. I *had* to tell you, so you'd see what a feast it was. So they had the tables laid out—oh, I forgot the liquor, they had the drinks in the back hall; they'd set up a bar. So it was mighty gay there for such an early hour of the morning, I declare. I helped Biddie with her costume—it was a blue habit, beautiful really, but for the operatic stage, not for the muddy fields of central Alabama. Then I went outside, bundled up in a black cape, to see the carnival in the front yard. They had given the pore dogs short rations two days previously, and starved them the night before: this was supposed to encourage them to seek the quarry. They were flailing around, those dogs, setting up a mournful racket, held by their master. The horses were all tethered to the front fence, and all the guests—quite a covey of rare birds and beasts in themselves, you know those mid-Alabama families!—were stalking about, drinking and hooting, on the front porch and all over the front yard, stomping down whatever semblage of shrubbery or grass remained in that season.

"Then this marvelous thing happened that I'll never forget even if I live to be two hundred and am photographed for the newsreel. *Vanity* was the trigger fired it off. Biddie Sayres came down to inspect the buffets, saw that all was ready, then she stepped to the mirror in the front of the double-parlor to have a long look at who else but Biddie Sayres. To have a good long look before calling in the hungry guests. Only she called in the *other* guests."

"Ghosts," said Kosta hopefully.

"Well, see, she wanted more light on the subject (and the subject don't forget is Biddie in pale blue with feathers) so she could see herself clearly in that mirror, so she just threw open the French windows on to the porch without a thought, and the smell of that sumptuous repast came right out *bump!* into the noses of those pore starving houndawgs and if they didn't just break loose. Yessir, break loose! Oh, if you could have seen it! In a lifetime, you can only see one or two things as wonderful, and if you have sweet anarchy in your soul, as I do, it takes on triple pleasure. Those hungry animals just served themselves breakfast while the world looked on, bigeyed. It really *was* buffet style. They went over the porch rail and through the window right onto those tables like a cloud of locusts, like a wave breaking over a big rock, like a grass fire in a dry season: I mean, they *whooshed!* I can close my eyes still and see Biddie as she appeared for one instant inside that window: eyes and mouth making three perfect O's.

"Well, by time anybody came to their senses—'cause it happened in a flash; those dogs were in charge, completely in charge. They swept onto those tables, and ate for themselves what can only be described as a *hearty breakfast*. Why they ate the chrysanthemums out the silver bowls—anyway they bit them and threw them on the floor. The chrysanthemums. But the sight of all those alert tails like the pennants of knights streaming to the fray! And the sounds! Biddie screaming bloody murder, then crying out, 'Nasty brutes, nasty brutes, get out of here!' and the sound of glasses falling, and pork chops being amiably ripped asunder!

"Course they did round them up, but only after they'd demolished the place. But I personally loved them for it, and would have gladly taken my clean handkerchief and seen to their greasy snouts, if they'd wanted, but I don't think they cared. The master of the hounds didn't beat them, but he cussed them out for sure. And they sat there, those houndawgs, not saying a word all the time he lectured at them, with their eyes fixed on distant points of the horizon, but not a bit sad, in fact quite pleased with themselves. But, omigod, *Biddie!* She was tears and honey from one end to the other (Miss Mickey Stickey herself) and hysterical; she was carried upstairs with her blond hair trailing, while the guests sort of stood around looking at the wreckage, one or two of them would sort of lean over and pick up a spoon or something and put it back on the table sadly, then they all went away mumbling, and *there's* the hunt for you.

"Well, Biddie couldn't pretend to get up any hunting parties after that, 'cause Mrs. Sayres came to her senses and took a stand; she said flatly that one dogfight in the parlor was one too many for her, and she'd always disliked the idea of riding anything bolder than a Shetland pony anyway. But the affair did a lot to sweeten Biddie's character: she changed, for the better, after that. But from then on, when she'd fix her hat or something by that particular mirror, she'd often give a sudden wildeyed glance toward that window (nailed tight by then) like as if it kept always the possibility of giving entrance to a cry of flop-eared demons hell-bent for some fancy victuals. But even to this very instant, Biddie has never seen anything funny in the episode. I reckon she *never* will."

Fiffy's story pleased us all greatly. Especially I was taken by the picture of those houndawgs just sitting there, saying nothing, looking off in space while being scolded.

"Now it's my turn," said Acis. "I've remembered a good one. Did any of you know Miss Cora Pearl Mackey?"

"Everybody knew her," said Fiffy.

"But not everybody knew what her job was."

"She didn't work," Fiffy insisted.

"Yes, she did too," said Acis. "Everything to do with pearls, because of her name. But chiefly she was employed by Goldstein's Jewelry Store as a pearl-feeder."

"How's that again?" exclaimed Allan.

"She went once a week to Goldstein's and they'd give her a different string of pearls from their storage vaults each time. And she'd wear them a week, to restore the luster to them. 'Cause everybody knew she had the best skin for feeding pearls."

"I don't get it," said Allan.

"Of course you do," explained Fiffy. "Pearls fade out when they're not worn. There was an opera singer at the old Chicago Opera used to wind her pearls around her white cat at night. In fact, always had a white cat for that purpose."

"Now, behave and listen," said Acis. "Anyway, as time went on, she began to believe she had magic powers. . . ."

Just then, with a creak, Miss Lulie stirred in her sleep— she was dead asleep in her chair—and woke and began to cough furiously. Ada jumped up to give her a glass of water.

"The delegate from Bark-shire will speak now," said Fiffy.

"Poor Aunt Lulie, we've kept you up long past your bedtime," soothed Ada.

"It certainly is." Lulie yawned.

"Come on, Snookems, I'll help you upstairs," offered Kosta, gallantly proferring his arm.

"None of your tricks," she waved him off, and took Allan's arm instead, and tottered off. Acis never finished his tale, for we all caught a fit of yawning from Miss Lulie and couldn't stop.

"You'll have to finish your story tomorrow," said Ada. "I'll tell you mine right now. There was this lovely girl named Ada who spent all day fixing for a supper, which was a great success. Then she went to another—went upstairs to Miss Lily White's party! And though they put a handful of pearls, and some sparkplugs, and some chewed-up chrysanthemums, and I don't know what-all else under her mattress, she slept for seven days and nights, without noticing them."

"She deserved the pearls and the sleep, too," said Acis. "It was a fine party, hon."

"Hit the hay." Kosta yawned, and after clearing the table, we did.

"Lizzie will never have Brother John's character," I heard Fiffy saying when I came down for breakfast. She and Kosta were dallying over coffee, and telling each other the stories of their animals. I listened while they rambled on, unable to speak, until I'd had my coffee.

I don't have to tell you who Kosta was describing. "Baudauer had an enormous vocabulary," he said, "finally I used to talk French so he wouldn't understand. But I discovered he knew French, too, and why not? he was a French poodle, so I had to resort to spelling things out, you can see what kind of bore that was. But like some French people, he had a terrible *snobisme pour toutes choses anglaises.* He used to go with me to my tailor, and he'd sit and watch the fittings —I could see he had a powerful desire to wear pants, and English tailoring at that. We used to go along to Marylebone High Street to my favorite bookshop, Edwards, then stroll over to Regent's Park. This was his greatest pleasure in all the world, 'cause in a little stream there in the Park there were eighteen kinds of swans, three hundred kinds of ducks, millions of unidentified waterfowl, and God in His wisdom knows how many sparrows and pigeons—all fussing about right at one spot where the English come with bags of crumbs and goodies to feed them (the British have a *thing* about birds, you know) and there was certainly plenty happening at once, with beating of wings, and clucking and squawking and carrying-on, to say nothing whatsoever of the British being British as far as the eye could see in every direction. Baudauer wouldn't even *try* to chase anything or anybody: he'd stand there grinning and cocking his head first one side then another, as if to say, 'My, my, my, my, my, what a splendid spectacle!' I was not, myself, unmoved, I may tell you."

"England is heavenly," said Fiff. "When Brother John was young, *he* adored tricks and surprises, he'd often hide inside a summer slipcover in the parlor, pretending to be a part of the arm of the chair—sometimes waiting for hours on end to catch the unwary. But when he was grown, it was his exquisite dignity and snowy beard that endeared him so to me. He'd sit with me when I read, and put out his paw to help when I turned the pages."

"I keep a special hate-file," whispered Kosta, "of people who never see the difference between a pet and a beast-companion. Baudauer was never a pet in their sense."

"I'll subscribe!" cried Fiffy; they exchanged conspiratorial smiles.

They had all been up for hours, save Uncle Acis, staying in bed with his summer cold now in full bloom. He didn't come down till Allan had started arranging Miss Lulie in the back seat of the jalopy amidst her magnificent assemblage of ratty cushions, wrong-refolded roadmaps, and sand left from beach expeditions. She had put on her green eyeshade with the button smack on top of her noggin, and was receiving the attentions of Kosta, whose hands she kept patting, where he had them on the window of the car. Her old mummy face was one big smile, and I believe she had lifted her droopy old eyelids enough to see out from under them. I chatted with Allan, then we shook hands; Ada exchanged kisses with her kinfolk, and they prepared to set out.

"Bye, see you soon, bye-bye, drive carefully, say hello to everybody, bye!" Everybody shouted at once.

"Bye, toots, see you in the funny papers!" was Kosta's loving goodbye to Miss Lulie. She beamed.

"Pesky meddler!" she chortled, waving her clever paw admonishingly. Then Allan stepped on the gas and the car lurched forward and shot out the gate. Miss Lulie, incapable of resisting this impact, toppled back, still smiling, into her cushions, and was totally lost to view save for her little gaily waving hand, that was somewhat stiff but tireless—it was still fluttering, a distant dot of action, when the car roared toward the highway. She was greeting, one supposes, the ragged sky and all green growth in view.

"That Lulie! she'll outlive us all," said Acis, shaking his head.

The rain began again that afternoon, and fell in steady monotonous tattoo; we knew the dog days were with us, and occupied ourselves with a dozen different projects. Ada was sewing, Miss Fiffy embarked on a letter-writing marathon; Kosta was buried in detective novels—I spent most of this time with Uncle Acis. He was suffering a really first-rate summer cold, and had moved downstairs to the room with the piano, where he had access to most of his books. An impossible invalid, he read all night, wouldn't take medicine, wouldn't rest, got up and pattered about barefoot, wouldn't behave—Ada and I would swear we were dealing with the original problem child.

Outside the Bayou was high and muddy, the gardens soggy, the vivid greens of trees and plants almost electrical in the gray world. The alyssum was beaten to earth, the flower-heads of zinnias and asters leaned drenched and tousled, in every-which direction. The cosmos, poppies and other fragilities were shattered and spent for good and all—gone till next summer; while the lilies which might have waltzed but didn't, where they had trumpeted white and waxen were now seen only green pods swelling. The sun was in hiding.

"Where *is* that fool sun?" said Fiffy at the window constantly.

We settled into a gentle condition of revery; no one talked more than necessary, and when we sat to table, all eyes gazed out on the wet world. Ada played the piano for hours on end, and I'd sit in the corner of the room, watching and listening. Uncle Acis, in his book-littered bed, watched her every move. I tried often to leave them alone, but they'd both beg me to stay. The music, fanciful and high-flying, would chase the grayness and dare the rain.

After two weeks of this you can see what a ringtailed joy it was to wake up one morning and find the sunlight blazing, the Bayou sparkling, and the entire world steaming. Everybody exploded from the house, Uncle Acis insisting on going down to the pier to sit in the sun, and Fiffy appearing suddenly in her famous tattered sunhat, wild as her unkempt hair. Modena and Tony were in the kitchen garden, repairing the ravages of the rainy spell. Fern did up the piles of linen, covering all available lines, so that the back yard seemed a nervous white tent-city.

Me, I was going to work on laying-out the herringbone path of bricks I had commenced. I thought I'd better do it while the ground was soft. I was using some old flat bricks that came from a chimney standing on the property since Acis' folks had bought it: sole reminder of a cottage that had burned. They were stacked under a cedar tree in a clearing not very far from the house, beyond the clump of mimosas that framed "Pan Grieving." Since the route from where I worked to my brickpile led over a fence and through a tiny stream, a wheelbarrow was useless. I carried my bricks in a carton, a dozen or so each trip. It made slow work, but I was content to dig in the rich dirt, and place each brick just so, the sun hot on my naked back. I was attracted by this occupation, and I found a need for perfect execution, in spite of an impatience to see the walk, and an area around the statue, completed and ready for the first promenader. In my mind, I made a fantasy while I worked, of how I'd put a string or a ribbon between two sticks at the house end of the path, and invite Ada to cut this and stroll with me ceremoniously to inaugurate the paving.

By the end of the day I had completed a good distance of herringbone bricking; when I closed my eyes I could see inside my lids the zigzag pattern in green, bordered by pink grass—the optical opposite (the eye's repose) of the rosy bricks set in the bright lawn. It was Kosta, who'd been sketching by Flycatcher Creek, who came to fetch me for supper, leaning over me where I squatted on the ground, and writing in pastel chalks on my back.

"I wrote *W.P.A.*," he said. "It's what came into my mind."

I woke with the sun next day and went tiptoeing downstairs. I could hear the murmurs of sleep in the house, not snores, but the lull of sleep that's audible. The air was perfectly clear, and over the Bayou, still and shining, the yellow ball was blazing, already bearing down though not in full possession of the sky.

I stopped to study Pan's face an instant, and to pull away some mimosa puffs that had fallen into the crook of his arm, then ducking under the low branches I traipsed off toward the clearing. Over the fence, avoiding the barbed wire, I picked my way deliberately through the blackberry clumps, waded the cool streamlet, and climbed the other bank. Once in the clearing I filled my box with bricks and started back to the yard. After about forty-five minutes I had finished, in my demonic activity, the rest of the walk, and guessed that a morning's work would complete the promenade around the statue: Ada could inaugurate it at the hour when four-o'clocks bloom. I was in my fantasy again, when—

"Hello."

I looked up, then stood up. From squatting on my haunches, the sudden movement upward made my head swim, and the saw-tooth lines of the path seemed to run back and forth: at the end of the path stood Perrin, all in white, holding an overnight bag, and smiling an insolent "charming" smile. I found myself suddenly gooseflesh.

"No, no, no!" I heard myself shouting, forbidding him to trespass on my handiwork. "It's not finished, don't walk on it!"

"Looks finished to me," he said, coming heedlessly on. He put the bag down and came up to me. "What in hell happened to you? You lose a screw? We didn't know you had left town until you'd been gone for weeks."

"I can't imagine you'd be especially concerned at my not announcing my travel plans. I mean, in view of the way you seem to just pick up and go. That's what I did, I just picked up and left." I spoke without looking at him. "What are you doing here, now, if I might just inquire?"

"I've come to put a bird in your room, for a surprise. A very special bird."

Hardly conscious of what I did, I threw a brick just past his head, as naturally as one might wave a fly from the face. It was so unprepared a gesture that he didn't even wince or step aside. He kept right on grinning, but finally he glanced at the brick, then at me, shaking his head as if scolding a child. Naturally I don't think I intended to hit him. My aim is pretty accurate.

"Well, Cousin," he said, "you *are* a passionate imp."

But it was as though the act of tossing that brick had released me from all propriety. I was suddenly reckless, lightheaded, full of high spirits. I picked up my box and fled to the brick pile. Perrin, undaunted, followed me, talking all the while, but I didn't hear one word he said.

All the time I was filling my box his shadow covered me as he stood beside me in the grove. I began to gather a fury inside myself. He didn't realize my exalted anger at his detested presence until I stood and looked into his eyes.

"What's the matter with you?" he asked.

It seemed I had waited for his recognition of my mood,

for at his question something exploded inside my ribcage like a light bulb dropped from a second-story window, and I just socked him as hard as I could in the face. I suppose no one has ever seen an expression on his face equal to the recoil of surprise and growing anger as blood came from his nose. But he didn't disappear in a puff of smoke, as I rather expected. Perrin was solid after all: he hit back. I ducked and caught the blow on my shoulder, leaving me bruised for weeks afterwards. Then we tangled, and over and over we rolled, midst brick rubble, pine needles and grass—scuffling, clawing, panting, saying not a word, but fighting shamefully, tussling like two swamp cats.

I felt, in finally seeing Perrin grimed and bloody, a kind of fierce pride of destruction—I wanted to crush him utterly. Though I should like to partly blame the luxury and fury of that hot sun, though I should like to scold the scents and languors of that landscape, yet already before the fight was done I sensed that the truth was the truth of Perrin being Perrin and me being me—with the world still and green around us, we were the inevitable zone of fury at the center. At last he pushed my face, and broke away and ran to the other side of the brick pile, stood there sobbing with rage, wiping the blood from his nose: I had brought blood to the too-perfect face, and satisfied of this, was suddenly weary and desolated.

"God, how I hate you for your stupidity," he said scornfully.

Then Uncle Acis, the early riser, appeared—perhaps an Uncle Acis we neither really knew, solemn of countenance. He walked slowly into the clearing and over to us, looking from one to the other.

"It is over now?" he asked. If we had said *No* he'd have retired.

I nodded, Perrin shuddered and became silent.

"Then maybe you'll wash up a little on the back porch and think of coming in out the jungle." He was ironical, but sadly, unsmilingly so. He went to Perrin and put out his hand.

"Perrin," he said, by way of observing my cousin's totally unexplained presence there. He gave Perrin his handkerchief and herded us to the house.

I began to tremble in the manner of one after a fight, and my momentary sense of desolation was giving way to an extraordinary exhilaration, a lightheartedness wholly unexpected. But march in the house to parade my sweaty, matted-hair wildness before the ladies I would not: I felt suddenly naked, reasonably, for my trousers were split up one side. As we rounded the house, and started up the back steps, Modena and Fern staring at our apparition, I quietly slipped out and ran away, down to the wharf. I threw myself face down on the boards in the hot sun. My little neat morning had exploded. The after-effect, however, was certainly not confusion. I tried with all my might to find in my heart some sense of guilt, yet found only logic; after that a kind of pride that was rough and Priapean.

But this exultancy expired and I was sad to have inflicted pain, for seemingly with each jab of my fists Perrin had diminished in stature, I saw him now as small, the incorrigible Monkey of the World—and I had drawn his blood. Well, it had happened, that was all: we two had skipped together round the hot equatorial belt of anger, and rushed as eagerly to the cold opposing poles of hate. What was left for us but a rich and gentle indifference?

I lowered myself into the green water, and struck out in a straight line, swimming with my head submerged save for the breath on each fourth stroke. When I pulled spluttering to a stop I was a far reach out in the Bayou, seeing, as I looked back while treading water, the boathouse, the pavilion, the house itself among the trees, all in miniature, brightly lit by the blazing sun. I saw Miss Fifield in her shaggy hat, with arms book-laden, strolling slowly and vaguely toward the pier.

Snorting, thrashing, sporting like a dolphin, I plunged my

[180]

head into the salty Bayou and swam back: I was exhausted when I reached the pier and, gasping for breath, pulled myself up onto the boards. Fiffy was above me, cool and upright in a corner of the pavilion. She smiled and threw me a huge towel.

"Here," she said. I buried my head, puffing too much to say a word. When I caught my breath, I cast a glance at her: she ignored the world, she was deep in one of her "gilt-edged securities." Finally I wrapped myself in the towel and joined her.

"I don't guess you could spare a cig," I inquired shyly.

"Of course," she said, and gave me the package, and the matches. I offered her one, she took it, we both lit up.

"Thanks," she said, and then she put her book down and intoned whimsically, "So you began the day by smashing at least one classic façade?"

I grinned in spite of myself, then looked quickly down.

"I . . . guess . . . so. . . ."

"Well," she replied, as though in having my acknowledgment that was the end of it. Then she looked up and added, "I daresay you had your reasons. No, don't tell me!"

"Is . . . Perrin . . . ?"

"He won't die," she broke in. "He may have marks, but he won't die. Your consolation must be that battle wounds often give prestige." She studied me. "Aside from these interesting scratches—" she pointed, "—you seem to have sustained an interesting eye and no more." Curiously I had felt no pain, but now realized that my left eye was closing, and that I had a multitude of minor bruises.

"Yes'm," I said.

"Don't you want to have a brandy, or something?" she asked solicitously.

"No, I'll sit here a minute with you," I replied.

"As you like. We're going to send Perrin up in the car; Acis is telephoning the doctor but hasn't gotten him yet."

"Doctor?" I gasped.

"Well, yes, I think his nose has to be attended: they generally do when they're busted."

"Oh!"

"I left the house rather than be just another spear-carrier to the scene—or damp-cloth carrier, that is. I like Perrin's verse to an extraordinary degree, but I begin to have *your* reservations as to his perfections as a person. If only he were more crude—or more delicate! If only at this moment he would roar out oaths and say 'Ouch', else die in extempore Alexandrines."

"What does he say?"

"Oh, that you are hot-headed, even hysterical, things like that."

"Perhaps I am," I said sadly.

"I wouldn't know," said Fiffy gaily, then began to scuffle in her books. "I carry *Bygone Days in Ponsett-Haddam* for the title alone: I shall probably never read it. I'm midway in *The Semi-detached Villa*, but it's really the weather to read sweet Robin, now isn't it?"

Flipping the pages of those same two fat little leather volumes I knew from before *(Herrick,* they said on the spines), she passed, smiling, mumbling individual lines or phrases she liked, to almost the end of Volume I, said, "Corinna," closed the book and took up Volume II, said, "Dianeme" at one point, then gave an "Oh!" of discovering what she sought, and read aloud,

> *"Tell me, said I, in deep distress,*
> *Where I may find my Shepherdess.*
> *Thou fool, said Love, know'st thou not this?*
> *In every thing that's sweet, she is.*
> *In yond Carnation go and seek,*
> *There thou shalt find her lip and cheek:*
> *In that ennamel'd Pansie by,*
> *There thou shalt have her curious eye.*
> *In bloom of Peach, and Rose's bud,*
> *There waves the streamer of her blood."*

[182]

Then she looked at me, those two lively sunken eyes the color of sherry under the ragged hatbrim. She seemed to wait for an observation on my part, but I sat tranced, watching the tattered raggle-taggles of her hair dancing at the edges of the hat. My adventures of the day had worn me out: I was suddenly completely exhausted.

"We better go up to the house," she said gently.

Inside, drama was the order of the day. Outside, the car waited at the gate. When Fiffy and I set foot on the porch, the crowd in the parlor turned to stare through the open windows.

"Here's the wild one," said Ada, pouring me a brandy.

Kosta gave me a baleful look, but Perrin, pale, stretched on the sofa with a bloody handkerchief to his nose, simply gave me a blank one. Uncle Acis made me sit down. Tony, surprisingly, gave me a great big grin. He brought the brandy to me where I sat on the porch outside the room.

"He can't go like that," Ada was saying. "Modena, get one of Mr. Acis' old blue shirts." Putting down my glass I pulled the towel about me, and went in to Perrin. The others as if by signal withdrew.

"Perrin . . ." I began.

"What?" he said wearily, averting his eyes.

"I'm sorry for what happened. I'm sorry."

"Why not just be relieved? Besides, you're not sorry."

"I *am* sorry; I lost my temper."

"So did I," he said, opening his eyes, and glaring at me. Then he sighed. "You lost your temper, kiddo," he added thickly, "and I'm just afraid you'll never find it."

"And while I'm looking for it, maybe I'll just find the truth of why I can't like Perrin Moreland," I said slowly, and had the satisfaction of seeing his face cloud. It was my voice that spoke, but I scarcely recognized it. He looked at me intently, then grinned a sickly grin.

"Oh?" he asked.

"Come, Perrin, slip into this, and you're ready." So his dirty bloodstained shirt was replaced by a fresh faded blue

[183]

one, and supported by Kosta and Tony he got into the car. His face at the back window was pale and bitter, but annoyingly sure of itself: he knew I was talking without knowing of what I talked. He slowly shook his head at me as the car pulled out the gate.

I went up and showered, and tended my wounds, then dressed and came down to lunch. I was, as you may well imagine, ravenously hungry after the events of the morning, and besides lunch was late. Nobody mentioned the fracas; either by common consent they turned its face to the wall as too full of enigmas, perhaps explainable as culmination of something gone before—else they had agreed simply to dismiss it. But I was conscious of a kind of exaggerated respect paid me, as to one who revealed unexpected qualities. There were a few jests about my black eye, which didn't bother me, though I was in pain. After lunch I fell into bed and slept soundly almost till suppertime.

Kosta and Tony returned close to seven o'clock with the bulletin that the doctor had fixed Perrin up, but that Perrin's nose might not ever be the same. Cousin Annie, they said, had flown straight into the screaming meamies, with feathers falling on all four sides.

"Mr. Moreland didn't say much," Tony told me.

I went after supper to sit alone on the pier, watching the last stain of day melt from the sky. The Bayou was full of gentle ripples, as a dozen contrary breezes played on its apple-green surface, while the first stars pricked the apple-green sky. The bats came out and flickered over the water, making faint clicks and squeaks, barely audible against the competing music of bullfrogs and katydids.

I was perfectly at peace with the world and myself. Other than a regret for my blow which struck the nose of my too-beautiful cousin; and a faint chagrin for having set off Cousin Annie's fuse, I couldn't be bothered. If truth were told, I had enjoyed the day. In spite of my aching eye and innumerable smarting scratches and bruises, I found the evening beautiful and found my soul peaceful. I told myself, not as arguments to assuage the hoped-for conscience, but as simple observations, that it was quite likely that an irregularity of the nose would improve Perrin's appearance; and that since Cousin Annie might be said to live for woe, complaint and genealogical weavings and unravelings—any of which she could find in today's hubbub if she applied powers of concentration—undoubtedly she would derive pleasure at last. You're a dreadful creature, I told myself, and myself answered *I ain't complaining.* So we smiled together, me and me, taking each other for granted. I had begun to think about finishing my paving project; wondered where I'd find a bit of ribbon for Ada to cut for the inauguration; then I recollected that the path had already been trod upon, by Perrin.

I was enjoying this solitude and lackadaisical meditation when Uncle Acis appeared, calling my name. By then it was pitch black dark.

"Hey," he said softly, spotting my cigarette in the corner of the pavilion.

"H'lo," I loftily replied.

"Are you hiding or something?"

"No, course not."

"Well," he chuckled, sitting beside me, "it's just like old time to have you and Perrin here raising hell."

"Hmmm," I answered, "though you notice he didn't stay long."

"No, bulldog, he didn't. I'm gonna have the legislature pass a law saying there has to always be at least ten miles between you and your Cousin Perrin. Think that'd help?"

"Search me. Though I think we took care of unfinished business today."

"Doubtless! Oh, doubtless! He only has one nose."

I looked up at the summer stars, gold cockleburrs caught on night's serge. I said sarcastically but lightly, "From now on, you better learn to stay out that grove. If you'd 'a' waited a minute longer, I'd 'a' killed him." Acis laughed.

"I declare, that clearing must have something about it, I dunno. Maybe it's 'cause we put that statue of Pan in the garden! Though, even when I was young . . ."

But I wouldn't hear his confidence, didn't want to.

"I know," he said, "I know. Or at least I *understand* everything."

"If you know everything, tell me everything!" I shouted.

"Ssssh," he answered softly. "Who can tell anybody anything? Oh, maybe two brothers close in age, walking down a country road on a moonless night . . . about a week after both their parents have drowned by falling down a dry well . . . but just about nobody else."

"Huh!"

"What you're looking for in this world is a confidante, not a punching-bag," said Acis, moonily gazing at the sky. "But it's all up to *you*, it's not my affair."

A few days passed quietly. Once, Uncle Acis coughing in the night woke me up. I heard Ada moving about the house, then Fern in the kitchen rattling pans. There was a chill off the Bayou, and you could feel that summer wouldn't go on forever. The incessant insects were loud in the dark. I imagined I smelt Ada's perfume, and drifted off to sleep in my fantasy. I wakened to hear Tony's voice singing, as he swept leaves off the porch downstairs. The day was brilliantly sunny, with a breeze; when you looked across the Bayou, or through the trees, you could see the first smudge of blueness, a smokiness that comes into the autumn landscape. 'Though soon as the sun reached zenith, the faint mist vanished, all was hot as ever.

Ada called the doctor to come down have a look at Uncle Acis, whose chest cold seemed rather complicated. Acis protested but Ada quietly went ahead and telephoned. Acis insisted on getting up, dressing, and all, to show he was quite all right. Just before lunch, when we were all on the porch (Kosta still cool toward me) Ada decided to dig out her big old Brownie and take snapshots of the entire household. So

[186]

nothing would do but Modena must turn down the fire under lunch cooking on the stove, Fern must leave ironing,
Tony leave fishing, Miss Fiffy leave letter-writing—we must
all arrange ourselves on the front steps, to be immortalized.

"Make us all look just perfectly beautiful, Ada," said
Kosta.

"I know," cried Modena, "as how we'll all look famished
unto the death. You shoulda waited till after dinnertime,
Miss Ada."

"You can't wear that sunhat, Miss Fiffy, 'cause I want your
eyes to show," Ada insisted in her soft voice, as she peered
busily into the camera, moving about to find the best vantage
point. Acis and Kosta were sitting on the top steps, Miss
Fiffy just below, with Modena and Tony below her. Fern
stood smiling at the bottom of the steps, by the hydrangeas.

"Oh, then I'll have to slap my hair down I reckon," said
Miss Fiffy. "I shouldn't at all care to be permanently de-
picted as the Witch of Endor. Or Floating Island, either."

"No you look fine. Just take off that hat."

"All right." So she did and Kosta snatched it up and put
it on the back of his head, like a smart-alecky child.

"Just my style," he bragged. He looked a perfect ape.

"No, you sit here," Miss Fiffy insisted, patting a spot on
the steps next to her. So I did.

"Move a little toward Kosta," Ada directed Acis, then
while we held our breath for a moment, she clicked the trigger of the black box. "No, no, stay there. I want to get a
couple more."

Ada kept on, clicking away, capturing forever in the strange
graphs of reality which are snapshots a kind of brash essence
of that summer day that blazed and disappeared. Now, later,
while I am telling you all this, I have those pictures on my
desk. I often study them, and from my mind I supply the
twinkle for Miss Fiffy's eye which is naught but shadowed
eye-socket in the picture. On Uncle Acis' tentative expression I superimpose the mercurial glance I well know; for
Tony and Modena, stiffly formal and "posing" on the bottom

step, I supply the wonted animation. Only Kosta, silly in the sunhat, and Fern, marvelously straight and smiling, are captured in flight, themselves in sharp black and white. In the pictures the sunlight is dazzling white on the steps, on Kosta's white shoes, Miss Fiffy's collar—all these things, in the snapshots, seem to give off a luminous glare, a kind of aureole. The shadows back of Acis and Kosta are jetty black, and on the steps alongside Fern at the side of the picture, is cast a sharp shadow-garland of hydrangea leaves; the shrub itself is outside the picture. And who is the stranger resting his head in his hands, elbows on kneecaps? That, friends, is me. Try though I may, with magnifying glass and contemplation, I cannot recognize myself. It *is* me: black hair with one cowlick over the forehead, the almost-smile of the eyes hidden by stern black brows, the almost-sensuous mouth in repose, but not me at all, unless in that one moment I appeared so. The locust leaving his shell must surely turn toward the transparent armor to say, "Gracious, was that thing me?"; I say to myself, "If this was me, who was I?"

In one view Lizzie has appeared, and Miss Fifield, exasperated but amused by the animal's flirty refusal to pose, is captured forever and a day with one hand stretched toward the cat, her eyebrows raised in an ironical smile, her eyes creased with amusement. Lizzie looks at her, having two ghostly tails where she moved at the moment Ada snapped the shutter. Ada refused to sit save for one, where she seems almost to hide, sitting on the floor next to Uncle Acis, and looking down. One of the snaps is meaningful to me now in a way it wasn't when it was first printed.

"Lizzie, you impossible animal!" Miss Fiffy had cried.

"Come here, Lizzie, puss, puss, pusssssssssst," Kosta said, leaning over and clicking his fingernails to attract the cat. Lizzie glared at him, then went toward him. I put out my hand to catch her, but she glided under it, making for Kosta.

"Oughta drown that little fleabag," remarked Acis dryly. Only in the picture Ada snapped just as he said it, he has the smile of a saint, and is looking down benignly at Kosta, who is bent way over, just in the act of lifting the cat with both hands. Kosta has a crafty smile, or it may be the strain of reaching down so far. Miss F., though, is the star of this tableau. She looks up toward Kosta earnestly, profile toward the camera, one bony hand raised in an undefined, time-disdaining, and very eye-pulling gesture: does that hand say, "Careful with my Lizzie?" or "Make her pose," or what? What sets it off is the expression of Fern who stands with hands clasped, watching Fiffy closely, seeming to echo that lady's mysterious unease like a dark affectionate mirror.

A minute afterwards Fern said, "I better help Modena with dinner," and went in. Modena and Tony had already vanished into the house, crazy Lizzie hightailing after them, toward the kitchen. Ada, after going into the hall to take the film out the camera, came back and perched on the arm of Uncle Acis' chair.

"How you doing, skeezicks?" she asked, pushing his hair back from his forehead.

"Fine!" he boomed, turning a mischievous smile.

"Then how come your head is so hot?" asked she.

" 'Cause I reckon I just have a touch of fever," sassed Acis, taking her hand playfully and patting it between his own.

"Like I thought," observed Ada, and disentangled herself. "You're going straight to bed."

He obeyed, thoroughly content with her bossiness. He did indeed look flushed and pink. After they left Kosta and me alone, we began conversation.

"Did you finish the one of Flycatcher Creek?" I asked politely, referring to a large canvas he had commenced.

"No." He stared toward the water.

"I certainly liked the sketch for it." I had, too: a big watercolor of the clearing, with two crepe myrtles in flower at one side.

"Thank you," he answered, somewhat less sharply. "Yes, I want to finish it, but—" he looked at me "—looks like so much happens diverting me from my planned projects. So much to amuse, so much to interest, so much to simply cope

[189]

with." He smiled a little, relenting, though he still hadn't forgiven me for the episode concerning Perrin.

"What news," he asked suddenly, "of Mistress Lola?"

"She's invaded Paris, according to Miss Fiffy's latest news. She doesn't write anybody but her folks and Miss Fiffy, I guess. Though I hope to hear a word."

"She'll like Paris. Everybody likes it, except morons and missionaries. Morons don't like it 'cause they're morons; missionaries 'cause anybody who had invented the revolting Mother Hubbard garment to stifle the naked beauty of Africa would naturally not like a place like Paris where the breast, the waist and the ankle have all been deified since time began. To say nothing at all of that old Ligurian butt, so round, so firm, so fully-packed—the artist's delight. America, I fear, is breeding for flat buttocks: it really seems a great mistake. Yes, really very sad."

I hadn't really contemplated this problem, so I didn't have anything special to offer as comment.

"Yes, Lola will love Paris," he went on. "It'll be hard to get that child home."

"They say she's turned out pretty bright in speaking French."

"Naturally—Lola's no simpleton."

"I can't imagine that crazy girl parley-vooing." I laughed. "It must be a treat to their ears in Paris."

"I hope she has a chance to get loose some, and roam around off leash."

"She's under the auspices of some woman who chaperons nice girls in France," I replied.

"Oh, Lola's not a nice girl," cried Kosta. "At least not in that sense. She's an angel child."

Well, the doctor came, and took temperature and looked at tongue and all those things they do, and said Acis had a touch of something or other—some wretched microbe. We were all pretty surprised 'cause it certainly had started as a summer cold, and Acis hadn't been sick since the Year One.

[190]

But it gave the household a chance to make a fuss over Uncle Acis, who generally was so independent about such.

He was installed now in what had been my room upstairs and I was removed to the library. Poor Uncle Acis: he was waited on hand and foot, read to, told stories, had flowers brought to him, and save for his naps, had a veritable Court churning about him always. Me, I'd have locked that door so quick! But I guess he liked it a little, once he'd gotten used to the idea. He *was* sick, not painfully, but that kind of slightly feverish state where everything tastes like tin, and water tastes funny. I guess everybody's been through that. Only with him, it seemed to hold on.

It was during that period that I most had the opportunity to talk to Acis. It was my duty to take him a cup of tea after his nap, not that Fern or Modena or Tony couldn't or wouldn't, but it just worked out that I'd wake sooner than the others around two o'clock in the afternoon.

I came very soon to realize that the Uncle Acis I remembered from my childhood was a creature so glamorous, so endowed with unbelievable powers, that nobody in the world could stand next to the image I cherished of him from that lost time. In sensing this, I came to be aware of the even more admirable nature of Acis newly seen. But I never *owned* him as once I had. His unruliness, his secret jokes, they were only for Ada now. I began to see how profound a feeling they had for each other. In catching an exchange of glances between them, in seeing Ada's way of touching his cheek, or taking his hand: small, quiet, undemonstrative but meaningful gestures—I found myself obsessed with the mystery of those aspects of loved individuals which are seen only in glints and flashes: the other loves existing in those departments of their lives or characters that have no relation to one's own connection with them. How, one asks constantly of one's self, can sound exist where my voice is not, how can music exist where my ear is not?

But just as the plainsman holding to his ear the conch hears the curious falsification of the sea's roar which will take the shock away from his first glimpse of the sea, I found in studying Acis and Ada a dozen metaphors for not only the dozen façades of their natures unknown to me, but for the kinds and colors of love, simple affection, and plain being-togetherness that I had yet to encounter.

These quiet discoveries, hunts and levitations of the spirit, altered Ada's position somewhat, though. She became again *my* contemporary, less that of Acis. More and more adorable I found her, more and more I longed to take her in my arms.

On those occasions when only we three were in Acis' bedroom, we played the oldest and most amazing triangular comedy of all: the gentleman, the lady, and the gentleman's long-time friend. That's the plot, but you can see already how this trio refused, even so, to fulfill the requirements. Because it wouldn't work out as young girl married to old man and presence of third party in form of unattached young man—we were all exactly the same age in spirit. Nor could it be overlooked that Acis was my uncle, nor that Ada and I were lifelong acquaintances.

How we flirted, we three, and loved one another for it. All playfully, all conversationally—who can say how much we knew of what we did and said? I didn't, Ada certainly didn't, Acis perhaps; certainly now I blush for certain moments. Sometimes it was Acis and me against Ada: this is primitive, deals with male pride. But Ada, the anything but primitive coquette, would soon overthrow that. Sometimes it was Ada and me teasing Acis: this is the League of Youth—much more serious, much more rash. Often Ada and Acis twitting me: Mr. and Mrs. Domestic versus Mr. Fly-by-Night. Often as not, simply the Three Fools loose in the world. It was all banter, all utter foolishness to pass the time, but now, looking back, I see a world of meaning. More and more I am convinced that when the sun is burnt out, they'll find on its cold cindery surface this motto worked out in soda-water caps and nicked pearl buttons: *If Only We'd Known* . . .

Having a need to explain by word or sign to Acis how much I remembered of the long-gone summers of the past,

I began one day to speak of it, but he wouldn't let me, for he remembered summers of his own.

"When I was little," he reminisced, "I stayed one summer with your folks in Choctaw County, it was when your grandfather and grandmother had been only a short time in that house. It's been a long time. I remember how many deer there were in Choctaw County at that time. Unbelievable. Their house was near the Tombigbee, and every evening, say at six or seven o'clock, there was this one particular big buck crossing the road, going up into the hills for the night. Early, early, every morning, he'd come strolling down to the banks to graze, proud and leisurely as you please."

"Did y'all go hunting for possum-grapes?"

"Lord, possum-grapes, I haven't even thought of them for a hundred years!"

"Little black ones *way* up in the tops of trees—they's oodles and oodles of 'em in Sophia County."

"Don't I know it! We don't have them this close to the Gulf; plenty of bullises and scuppernongs, though."

"And chufers!" I cried.

"Omigod, *chufers!*" bellowed Acis and we both near fell out laughing. I don't why, the sound of "chufers" I guess.

"Y'all must be getting real hungry," came Ada's voice as she sidled into the room. "Anybody so concerned over chufers. Well, supper will be tereckly."

"Is that old house still standing by the River?" asked Acis, wiping his eyes and sounding a magnificent fanfarade into his handkerchief.

"Far as I know, Grampa sold it during the Depression."

"You figuring on leaving Bayou Clair?" demanded Ada, sitting on the bed next to him.

"No, just talking. Reason I asked is 'cause they used to be two peach trees in the front yard—one each side the front walk—and I don't know what I wouldn't give to have either peachpits or else cuttings from those trees."

"I don'r'member 'em," I said.

"Sure you do," insisted Acis, pulling himself up a little.

[193]

"Your granny used to call them Indian Peaches. One had kind of red-and-white mottled flesh and the other was all rosy-red. When you peeled ones off the red-and-white tree the juice would ooze out red as blood, while the other, the red one that you *expected* to have red juice only had ole juice-colored juice. I never seen or heard tell o' any like them. I often wonder what happens to all those old-stock fruit trees."

"Way I remember," I said, wrinkling my forehead in concentration, "the house is still there, but the garden and all is hid from the road by two big signboards."

"Oh, Sainted Aunts," cried Ada, "don't tell him that: you know how he is. First thing he'll draft Aunt Lulie and they'll form a posse of two to go storming up to Choctaw County. Go chop 'em down, those signboards!"

"And not at all a bad idea." Acis scowled. Then he brightened. "Anyway, when I'm well, we'll go up there some day and find us some Indian Peaches, a cowcumber magnolia, too."

Although we were having fine weather, those perfect days of late summer when the nights begin to cool a little and there's a smell that comes from the earth itself, like potpourri, the household stayed indoors, arranged itself in graded circles around Acis' bed; instead of finding the wharf and the garden and such its habitat.

One night I came down from telling him goodnight, and got into pajamas, and began to scour the room for something to read: on the piano were piles of *Southern Home Gardening*, *Sewanee Review* (I don't understand this, Acis reads it faithfully, but it seems to be mostly discussions of things other people have written. I did read it though, and enjoyed it without understanding what it *meant*) and lots of funny foreign magazines. I saw lots of detective novels: Acis is a fool for English mysteries, his favorite is called *The Nine Tailors* which is mostly about bell-ringing and snow. Then I found Dr. Kane's *Arctic Explorations*. That *is* a book! Or

[194]

rather two, it's in two dingy volumes—don't be fooled by the covers of no-color, and the fact that the titles are worn away. It's really good: it begins with Dr. Kane right in Mobile (that's why everybody here has copies), and he tells how happy he is here reading books, drinking Madeira wine, eating French cooking, and stuffing alligators. I concede this is a reasonably happy life providing he caught the alligators first himself. Anyway the U.S. Federal Government gets in touch with him, and says Elisha, there's this real nice English explorer man that is lost up in Arcticland and we figure you can find him, so Dr. Kane grumbles but he goes off to the North Pole, and two thick volumes are the result, besides a book of his letters and a life of him by somebody else. Later he goes to Egypt. There's a fine part in *Arctic Explorations* that always gets me wrought-up. See, he's in this igloo, and it's cold as hell, so cold that his pistol begins to glow with a kind of cold phosphorescence and shines blue in the pitch-black dark. Course your first temptation is to say, Oh, pisha, Elisha! but I have since read about such things in *Natural History Magazine,* and I'm here to tell you it can happen just that way; they also have vegetable fire as well. Nasturtiums in the jungles of Brazil spit sparks of yellow fire at each other: think about *that* for a while!

So I looked at Dr. Kane, but I practically knew it by heart, so I stuck it back, and went on past *The Montessori Method* and *The English Mystics,* took a quick glance at *Diseases of the Horse* and *Bog-Trotting for Orchids* and a few others, arrived at *Minutes of the Park Board for 1887:* only it wasn't. Wasn't *Minutes* at all, but a box, not a book hollowed out (not in Acis' house, he'd have a fit) but simply a box with a hinged lid and one side made like a book binding. It didn't say *Hands off* or *Go way* so naturally I opened it right up: if it was private it should have been locked up somewhere instead of sitting on the bottom shelf where I found it. It was full of snapshots and postcards and one thing and another. So I dragged it up, blew the dust off the top, and took it over to the big armchair next the light. Curled up there, I opened my find.

Nothing sensational at first: old brown views of Bayou Clair and picnic parties. Lots of them taken in the old pavilion on the wharf that was blown away in the 1926 hurricane. There was always Kosta and Acis, both of them surprisingly young and devilish-looking—the time gap between them scarce apparent. There were girls in twenties' hats that hid their eyes, all posing and giggly-looking; one with a skullcap down to her nose, and a great big bow-ribbon smack over her privates. One girl in a white dress with a big flat hat looked so familiar to me, reminded me of Lola, and with a start I found myself seeing Cousin Annie at a tender age.

Postcards of the Chicago World's Fair of 1933, a calling-card of John Masefield, then—if you please, a fairly recent and quite unfaded snapshot of Acis, Kosta, and the Tiger Woman (Ione of happy memory, from the Bluebird), then more, the three in various attitudes taken on the front porch and on the front steps. With them was the celebrated, the canonized Baudauer: Acis, Kosta and Ione are baring their pearlies for the Kodak, but Baudauer, in every snap, looking offstage with an impressive, dark, and curly ennui. Modena grins in the side of one picture, and Tommy Cotten appears in one in his faded coveralls. Obviously Acis had called him from the tung grove to take the rest of the pictures.

Finally, the No. 8, we have Kosta sitting on his haunches, holding Baudauer up in front of him, forcing him to regard the camera. Baudauer, the famous clown, seems to scowl, under his great shags of eyebrow his eyes are flatly polite. He doesn't want to be photographed; he prefers being painted. What are you, his expression says to the camera, but a box that clicks? What good, pray, is that? Well, good enough to show me the wise woolly creature as chaperon for a somewhat unholy three. I couldn't put the pictures down, devoured them with my eyes. Ione here at Bayou Clair! My head whirled with questions.

[196]

But firecrackers come in packets: my next explosion was a very old, very elegant wedding invitation, rather large, rather florid, and a little grimy at the edge next to the open side of the envelope. Do you know what it said? This: *Colonel and Mrs. Francis Constant Fifield request the honour of your presence at the marriage of their daughter, Ninetta Susan, to Mr. Anthony Kosta Reynolds . . ."* Date 1898, place Mobile. Thereby, obviously, hung a tale. Or more likely a forest of them.

The snapshots, intriguing in themselves, were as nothing to this. Quickly shuffling through the summer, I could remember but one conversation between Fiffy and Kosta: at breakfast after the party. How carefully on that occasion, they had stuck to the subject of their pets, or rather, as they insisted, beasts. I sat pondering who knows how long, finally seeking my pillow to dream of summer picnic tableaux, Bayou Clair in the remote 1920's, an ineffable image of another time, of Fiffy young arm-in-arm with Kosta young, strolling through an infinite summertime that could never exist, save in a fool's dream.

Next morning, I dragged the box from hiding to study my treasure trove another time, to reassure myself in broad daylight of what I'd learned. Nothing had changed overnight. I sought out Modena in the pantry to ask about the snapshots.

"Ha, ha, this is me right chere grinning like a chessy," she said in great delight after studying the pictures.

"Who is this?" I asked, indicating Ione.

"Oh, that's Miss Ione Cawtuh," she said firmly, and I realized "Carter" after a second. "She is Miz Cotten's own sister, who visited here in the summertime."

"Which summer?"

Modena smiled craftily before she answered. "Oh, last summer, I reckon. I don'r'member." Then she took flight, busying herself in the kitchen and refusing to answer me. But I knew what I needed to know. Her very guile affirmed my thought, and I remembered what Lola had said the summer before. "Uncle Acis has taken up with some barefooted farm girl down there" is what Lola had said. For "barefooted" read "ankle-strap sandaled" and for "taken up" read the obvious, and there it is. But for the other puzzle, the wedding invitation, I didn't know who I might run ask about that. For that matter, on whom had John Masefield called?

"I'm worried about Acis," Ada confided. "He'd die before he'd say something hurt him. I wish he'd say he felt bad. He hasn't yet expressed himself about this damn old microbe. Last night after supper, I feel sure he felt lousy, but he wouldn't say anything. What can you do?"

"He's always been like that, I wouldn't worry—takes more'n a bug to kill Uncle Acis."

"I spose so."

But she began quietly to cry, with a spoonful of grapefruit half-raised to her lips. Biting her lips and batting her eyelids but the tears would come. Omigod, I thought, here's Weary Weeper after all! With a shudder she took control of herself, found her handkerchief, so I pretended to be too busy with my grapefruit to notice.

"It's only," she began falteringly, "that I love him so much. I want to be part of everything he does. You don't know how much I love him."

"Oh . . ." I searched for answer, but she went on.

"I must say I'm glad you and Miss Fiffy and Kosta are here, 'cause it'd be too much to ask to have to keep him in bed all by myself. He has to be entertained. Even so, if this lasts another week, we'll just have to telegraph the Ringling Brothers to hurry up bring their circus right to this house." She had recovered now, wiped her eyes and resumed eating.

"Incidentally," she said casually, a moment later, "what did happen in the woods the other day? Did Perrin just drop from the sky?"

I told her I had been annoyed at Perrin for walking on my paving, and how I'd planned that she inaugurate it, at which she clapped her hands like a child, liked especially cutting the ribbon. She was happy to discuss something other than Acis' illness.

"Why it's not finished yet!" she insisted. "You still have the part around the terror-Kosta; we can still inaugurate. I'll wear white, and carry two dozen long-stemmed something or others. The first day Acis can go out, we'll do it. Wonderful! But I still don't see why you bopped Perrin on the nose."

"It's really hard to explain. Perrin is my private devil, don't you see."

"He's not exactly an angel in pink-and-blue plaster, from what I hear, but even so he has only one nose, you know."

"Which he has stuck into my business once too often."

"I had my first kiss of Perrin—" mused Ada, stirring coffee, and I fell downstairs from heaven, bumping my foolish head on every step.

"—at a birthday party, in a game of forfeits. At Doodley Philipses'. Perrin had Tiger Lotion on his hair—how he stank! We all called him Stink-Pretty Moreland. We neither one wanted to kiss, but in the game we had to." She sighed.

Then I ran up again, somewhat relieved but determined to make an encyclopaedic diagram of lines of connection between everybody I knew in the world, and everybody they knew and back again.

"Well, let me see how my patient is doing," she murmured, putting her cup in the saucer.

The patient wasn't doing so well, he had fever again, so Ada, now even more worried, slipped downstairs to call the doctor. Her pale face and determined self-control put Fiffy and Kosta into fits, and they wandered around the house, not knowing what to do or say. Fern and Modena were whispering together on the back porch where they shelled the beans and put the eggplant slices to soak. Kosta was riffling through the magazines on the piano, and kept eying the instrument as though he'd play his highly limited repertoire if he dared. Fiffy had brought her writing-folder down and established herself at Acis' big desk, as though preferring

[199]

even the distracting presence of Kosta on this day of distress and tension.

The doctor came and spent some time in Acis' room, and afterwards took Ada aside and talked with her. The word *nurse* was much a part of his conversation, when Ada walked with him to his car.

"He says Acis must have a nurse, and is sending Mrs. Lantier out this afternoon. Says he's sure she's free. Acis is . . . very sick."

She went upstairs again. During that day Fiffy, Kosta and I were slowly possessed by a fear which none of us put into words. We avoided each other's eyes, afraid to read the thought that had come to all of us. The next day, too, was a terrible vigil where the world stood still. The sun shone, then it was dark, and then the sun shone again, but inside the house time was arrested; whispers replaced the usual gabblehiss that reigned there. The thing was, Uncle Acis was a very sick person, and none of us could really do a thing. Of course I knew the crisis would ease off and he'd be all right again, would trip down the stairs hale as oak, to set out fishing, or maybe to just sit on the pier and look at the Bayou, but during those still hours I could hardly contain myself. When I looked at Miss Fiffy and a rather owlish Kosta I sensed a double set of violin strings tuned much too tightly and just ready to pop with a *ping!* if the wrong word were said.

We finally set about, Miss Fiffy and I, to play checkers. Now I hadn't played checkers since I was a child, and neither had that lady played for years; it took us half an hour to decide how one played before we could begin. Finally Kosta moseyed over and helped us to find the rules again.

Mrs. Lantier, the nurse, was a pouter pigeon type, all bosom and no neck, with rusty tight curls, and a really scary cheerfulness. Every time she'd boom in, Fiffy would give a start, and glance nervously at me, her eyes demanding, "Bad news?" Modena cried silently as she worked in the kitchen, undone by the mystery of Acis sick, and finding Mrs. Lantier a completely novel experience. Fern, true to form, found refuge in her duties, scornful of Modena.

The first night we all went to bed late, and rose early the next day, all having rested poorly, all sullen and yawning. On the second day, the doctor was there the greater part of the time, though he made the trip to town once during the day. He was back in the late afternoon, and ate supper with us. We were all ravenous, not having done more than nibble during the day, so we were ready to attack with genuine gusto the fine meal Fern set before us. In the foolish way of all human creatures, we began to be very optimistic about Acis after supper, because we were well filled and happy ourselves. Besides, wasn't the doctor there, and the redoubtable Mrs. Lantier to boot? Surely flanked by such sturdy guardians, Acis could only zoom back to a rosy restoration.

Ada even managed a smile after supper, though only a faint one. She was pale and busy. Oh, how busy. I think her way of preventing herself from being thoughtful and upset was to make a thousand trips up and down stairs. She carried trays, pitchers, no one else must wait on Acis but her. Both Fern and Modena, who usually would have refused to let her do all this flying about, who would have demanded their *rights* (not their duties) stood by and permitted Ada her constant activity, understanding in their feminine hearts what governed her need for this.

The second night we played out a veritable checker tournament, playing quick and wild, and scarcely seeing anything but the board, or hearing aught else but the click of the checkers. Kosta sketched us in a pocket notebook; Mrs. Lantier came down once for a cigarette with us.

"How is he?" I asked her.

"He's sleeping like a baby. Just like a baby."

"And his fever?"

"A little less. Not much, but a little."

"If we can do anything—" I began, realizing as I said it that Mrs. Lantier must have the words engraved on her eardrums, after a lifetime of nursing.

"Don't worry," she said a little offhandedly, puffing a big ring of smoke. "He's a persnickety patient but not a bad one—I could tell you stories—though he won't do a thing unless his madam assures him he has to. I'm glad she's decided to stick by, though ordinarily I'd say she oughta sleep."

We all laughed at this: it seemed a very small omen of good that Acis would be true to form even in the hot world of fever he'd been inhabiting. The doctor had gone back to town saying there was little reason for him to stay, that he'd be back first thing in the morning, and we must all sleep. But we didn't. We sat there in the living-room, and sometime in the small hours saw through the front windows the moon sliding down the sky over the Bayou, sometimes white, and sometimes smoky when the clouds veiled her.

How we talked, of nothing. Talked ourselves right out, and finally with a start I heard a surprising buzz from Kosta: he had dropped off and was producing a faint snore that sounded like a wasp. Miss Fiffy nudged me and grinned.

We whispered together a bit, then fell silent. I don't know which of us dropped off first, but we certainly both slept.

I don't know what time it was that I woke suddenly. There had been no noise, unless Kosta had made an extra-loud buzz. I glanced at him, where he was sprawled on the sofa under the glow of the table lamp. His cockatoo crest was gleaming silver in the light, and his hands fidgeted a little in sleep. Miss Fiffy, sunk into an armchair, was like an old child hugging herself in sleep. Her face seen in repose, however, sans the liveliness of her eyes, revealed her age: she was a wrinkled old number indeed. Only her wild mop and familiar chip-diamond earbobs made her recognizable. I might otherwise have asked who is this little old woman who has made herself so at home here. Studying the two creatures I had suddenly an inkling of what parents feel in watching the sleep of children—being awake and knowing, possessor of the most vulnerable, viewer of the uninhabited face. Well,

Grampa, I told myself, how old you are, if these are your children. But those two wild ones *were* like children, and I loved them infinitely as I watched the trepidant entrance and departure of each breath they took. Something pulled me up from my chair: my leg was asleep and I had to wait a moment; then I tiptoed into the hall. There was a light breeze, and the house was so still that although I was in the corridor running the middle of the structure I could hear the rustling of leaves outside.

I sought the back stairs, and in passing the butler's pantry looked in on Fern asleep in a canvas deck chair she'd set there. On the table sat the brown earthernware teapot, the sickroom familiar, staunch and squat, probably unbreakable if it had survived the years since my own acquaintance with it. Fern's face was turned away from the door, and for a moment I waited to see if maybe she was only "resting," but no she was fast asleep.

Up the stairs I creaked, in spite of placing my foot just so; it was the snapping of the stairs that woke me up the rest of the way, pulled me out of the semi-drugged dream in which I wandered. Hurry to Acis, to Ada, that was my thought.

Outside his door I paused, puzzled at why I'd come. Terrible if I should wake him. . . . But the door opened a crack and one sliver of Ada's face, enough to contain an eye, looked out. Then the door opened and she whispered to me, "He's asleep." It seemed a logical thing to say, since I'd seemingly come calling. I nodded, saying in gesture, "Oh, yes."

"So's Mrs. Lantier," Ada whispered. She was woefully pale. "I sent her to have a couple hours, then she'll relieve me."

"Let me sit for a minute with you. I won't make a racket."

For a moment she hesitated, then she studied my face, and after waved me into the room, and shut the door. A tiny night-light was burning on the bedside table, beside a pile of books. On the other side of the bed was an extra table, dead white, with bottles and glasses, etc. The room had a terrible smell of several commingled elements: medicines, sickness, antiseptics. Most of all the sickly sweet alcohol odor. The bright crazy quilt had been replaced by a "sensible" coverlet, and Mrs. Lantier's depressing sense of order was everywhere in evidence. If I had swimming in the head from fever, I'd sure much rather intoxicate myself with eying those voluptuously-colored zigzags than have a modest white cotton spread stare glumly back at me.

Ada, by her presence, her inscrutable calm, was very much in charge here now. *Her* putting things in order had consisted of sending Mrs. Lantier off to bed. Surely Acis would sleep easier without all that starch in the room. I put my arm about her shoulders and gave her the smallest squeeze in greeting. She answered with a small sigh, and pointed to the other chair, on the other side of the room.

When I seated myself, I dared to look at Acis. His face was almost as yellow as the cheap paper for carbon copies, the skin was drawn, his cheekbones visible in a manner unknown to his visage. My expression must have betrayed my alarm, for she looked back and forth between his sleeping face and me. I smiled a lying smile, to reassure her, but my heart was crumbling away inside me. Death sat on Uncle Acis, as plain to see as the flag over the jailhouse. But Ada knew. She had her eyes glued to his face, and with a kind of chill, I realized that she had her breathing perfectly synchronized with his.

We sat. I learned by rote the tight little bunch of flowers that was repeated a million times in the wallpaper. I memorized the grooves of the boards beneath my feet. Strangely I had ceased to be sleepy.

It was when the sky over the Bayou commenced to take a bluish cast (the moon had long since disappeared and left black night) that Acis, sighing, turned his head, put his hand up to the pillow, and woke up, squinting at the light. He turned his head slowly, till he saw Ada, who was holding her breath.

"Ada," came a tiny voice from the pillow.

"Yes, hon? What is it?" She leaped to the side of the bed.
"Oh, Ada, I hate being sick."

"I know, hon, I hate having you sick. But you'll be all right soon. You'll be well tereckly."

But he just smiled at her, and squeezed her hand, then closed his eyes and sighed gently. The words they had exchanged meant nothing they seemed to say: it had been a polite leave-taking I'd overheard, for he sighed a third time, and began to tremble all over. When after a terrible minute he stopped trembling he was dead, and no mistake. We both stood petrified, till Ada turned on me a look of such frenzy and pallor that for a second I thought she was out of her mind. But with a terrible sternness she began to feel his pulse; finally put her hand to his heart. Then she said in a very cold tone, without looking at me, "Please go downstairs." Moving in a trance, I did manage to drag out of the room.

As I stood in the hall outside the door I heard that roaring in my ears that means the blood is rushing. I had a terrible tugging sense of unreality, like in dreams when you can't escape danger. Acis? But no, it wasn't possible. I went downstairs.

In the living-room the light of the table lamp seemed very yellow because of the first bluish light outside over the black shadowed trees. Miss Fiffy was awake, looked chilly and dazed, and Kosta snorted a couple of times and opened his eyes when I came into the room. They both looked at me questioningly. Kosta stretched and stood up, already wide awake, like a cat. But Fiff was one of your morning draggers: she wouldn't wake completely until noon.

"Uncle Acis is dead," I said, surprised at the childishness of my own voice. "Just now."

At this they exchanged a look, then they both came all over nervous. Miss Fiffy made several tossing movements with her hands, like she had great need to speak but couldn't. Kosta, too, clasped his hands together when I said it, then like a bolt he ran out on the porch. The truth was that their

[205]

first reaction to this news was one of profound embarrassment. To the depths of their curious, indefinable and unique souls they were embarrassed. Why Acis, so much younger than us? was their first thought. How difficult for us, so old, to face Ada so young, with Acis so early and so unexpectedly gone.

Finally Fiffy spoke, croaked a single word. "Ada?" I indicated with a toss of my head that Ada was upstairs.

"Should I . . . should I go up to her?"

"Not quite yet."

"How terrible, how . . . bitter."

Then I noticed Fern in the door, biting her lip.

"I don't want Miss Fiffy to be upset," said Fern seriously.

"I'll be quite all right, Fern. Really. But you better fix coffee for this young man. Oh, and you better go tell poor Modena. Or do you want me to? I will."

"No, I'll tell her, Miss Fiffy, you go to Miss Ada. I have coffee already on the stove. . . ." And Fern hurried out. Miss Fiffy turned to me, her eyes large and luminous in her fatigued face.

"We're in charge now. We have to be. There's so much to do that's so sickening. Most of it is up to you. The doctor first, I guess, though he's already coming. Anyway." She was kneading my arm fiercely. "I'll go up to Ada, and you . . ." She almost smiled, when she turned to look toward the door. Outside Kosta was sobbing brokenly and dryly, a repeated sound terrible to hear. ". . . you look after that problem child out there." You'd think that a humorous remark to make, and strange at such a time, but she said it so simply, looking into my eyes, and clutching my arm, that I didn't question it. When she released my arm I went out to him. In comforting him, I forgot to cry myself.

Save for drinking some coffee, and making Kosta drink some (while upstairs Fiffy tried to persuade Ada to unlock the door of Acis' room and let her in), I have little recollection of the rest of the day, what with the doctor, Mrs. Lantier, trying to get through two local exchanges to my folks in Persepolis, telephoning the relatives in town (Cousin Annie went to pieces right on the telephone), the arrival of the undertakers, and a thousand other things. But I'll never rid myself of the image of Miss Fifield's face when she came suddenly down the stairs and saw the men with the straw basket: one might think they'd come for her.

"Poor Mistah Acis," mourned Modena, at the stove. "There's a fine boy gone."

"Poor Ada," said Fern succinctly.

"Poor *everybody*," sighed Fiffy from inside her handkerchief. She was rubbing her face with *eau de Floride*.

Kosta, an unsteady vessel ready at any instant to pour forth a new Niagara, turned abruptly and pressed his face to the window. Outside the sun was brilliant. We were eating soup and sandwiches at about two-thirty in the afternoon. The doctor had given Ada a sedative and plopped her into bed. They had all asked a thousand times for the recountal of Acis' last moments, and I'd told them until I was blue in the face, and still they wanted details.

I had before me the unpleasantest task of all: to go and find the clothes for Acis to be buried in. All agreed that it was my task and Ada should not be consulted. So I bowed to the consensus of opinion. But the task was doubly noxious to me, in that I'd have to invade the room where Ada slept. Being drugged she couldn't wake for sure, but the thought made me uncomfortable.

"I'll come up with you, help you tote," Fern said.

"All right," I replied. "Let's get it over with."

"Just lemme finish these dishes."

In the shadowed room, Ada had her hair loosened. It was the first time I'd seen the length of it. It was much longer than you'd think, seeing that chignon at the nape. It made a dark night on the bed, and amidst this darkness her waxen face a round moon. She had one arm up on the pillow, near her head, like a child, and was really lost to this world.

[207]

Her cheeks were colorless and only a faint color showed in her usually rosy lips. On the bedside table was a half-eaten chocolate bar. Fern regarded her with cocked head, then shook her head, sympathetically.

"The suits are in there," whispered Fern. I lifted out the blue serge without a moment's pause. As I did, Acis' ghost danced out of the closet too: his *smell* suddenly distinct and frightening. It was a faint whiff compounded of many elements: Acis' very own personal smell. I closed the closet door quickly. I was beginning to consider the terrible unjustness of his death. My numbness was wearing away, though I wouldn't let it, not yet.

"No, no, no, take this here shirt with buttons. If you take that one, you'll have to bury them pretty cuff-links with it. You know them cuff-links are for you. Think what Mr. Acis would want."

"He'd wanta be living," I murmured.

"Mr. Acis is gone to peace," said Fern gently. "Can't none of us reach him, no matter how we try. But judging by what I know of that gent-mun, I know sure's my name's Fern, he'd say take the one with the buttons."

"He certainly had more than one set of cuff-links," I answered testily.

So we scuffled through drawers, and chifforobes, and got together Acis' last dress-up. Save his drawers. The idea of underdrawers in conjunction with death and the yellow lights and organ music was almost too much for me: I almost broke down, whether laughing or crying who can say because I contained myself.

Through all our racketing, Ada slept deeply, with her dark hair fanned out on the pillow and coverlet; the green cloth shade, pulled halfway down, rattled at the window, where the sun gleamed fitfully through the screen of branches outside. When we weren't pulling open drawers or whispering or tiptoeing, you could hear a cicada singing somewhere outdoors.

Finally Fern, heavily laden, started downstairs, while I

went into the bedroom where Acis had died, looking for his fresh wash which had been brought there after the last wash day. Fern had been ahead of me, or Modena, or both. The bed was stripped, the medicines had vanished. Only the permanent aspects of the room remained, all that smacked of sickroom had vanished, and the windows were wide open.

I found what I was looking for right away, but lingered a moment in the room. I gazed across the top of bushes to the Bayou. I heard a motorboat and the Reverend Macklin putted into view, hugging the opposite shore—I could almost believe he knew the reaper had been to our house. I thought of Acis' dance of disgust on viewing the preacher-man, and pondered the crazy design of life: that a dung-beetle plodder like the Reverend Macklin should go on busybodying through the world, and that an Olympian flyer like my uncle should vanish. Then, on turning from the window, my eye snarled on the pile of books on the bedside table. The last texts Acis had viewed. I went over to look at them: two mysteries, *Robert E. Lee,* Volume II, some sketches by Kate Chopin, *The Robber Bridegroom* by Eudora Welty, and a bunch of literary magazines. *Sewanee,* some English things, and a big thick foreign one printed in several languages. This last was on top, and I picked it up and flipped through it, finding what can only be called a message from the dead, for no other phrase will do. I had long known of Acis' habit of making a dent with his fingernail in the margin, to indicate something which gave him particular pleasure (go look at Dr. Kane or Rabelais) and found almost immediately in this volume these lines:

> . . . . *our wondering psalms*
> *Bearing up day to its summits day long!*
> *Which now in its dustfall time*
> *Sifts. The attraction*
> *Of stone to stone pulls at the road.*
> *Clouds thin and tear into nothing.*

Patience and faith, my heart!
All urns are gathered in dark
With leaves that sang in the sun
Of some rapt mind burning long
In its visions, which vanishéd.

There, deeply and decisively incised in the margin, the little groove of Uncle Acis' fingernail. Silently I locked the door. Silently I fell upon the striped mattress, and silently, silently the denied tears began to flow. Acis gone.

The Roman summer's rout

A s FAR AS FUNERALS GO it was a great success. It was clear
sunny weather, with a cool breeze, and when you passed
among the mobs in the funeral parlor you could get that
whiff of mothballs and camphor and cedar that showed how
recently all the sober mourning clothes had been dragged out
into the light of day.

My parents and my brother Tobey arrived, my father was
considerately upset at Acis' death; my mother was so interested in seeing me that I think she more or less overlooked
the event that had pulled them down to Mobile. My brother
Tobey had never really known Acis, he came along as chauf-
feur.

Everybody was saying "So terrible, so unexpected!" and
straining their necks in every direction to have a glimpse
of Ada. People who hadn't seen each other in half a century
were encountering one another at every turn. There was a
great crowd, of course, and people spilled out onto the front
gallery of the funeral home, and gathered in knots under
the oaks on Government Street.

Mr. Charlie Moreland, and Perrin, and even old snuffy-
stink Cousin Lakeland made up the wake, along with some
other cousins and miscellaneous hangers-on. Perrin was
wearing a big padded bandage over his nose, and what his
eyes said to me over his patch wouldn't be fit for decent ears
to hear. Mr. Charlie was abstracted, and Cousin Lakeland
was talkative to the point of lunacy; he hadn't had so many
unimpeded ears thrown open to his chatter since the century
was young.

On the morning of the burying day, my folks came to the

[213]

funeral home at about 8 A.M. (they were staying at the Admiral Semmes down the street) and I went over to their room at the hotel to have a few hours' sleep. I woke up, showered, ate a bite of breakfast, and strolled back on up to the funeral parlor.

Perrin, always indefatigable, was there, laying out quite a line for Allan Stewart, who had brought Miss Lulie. Miss Lulie was being made-over by a bunch of silly old women, all saying "Poor poor Ada, how long in all were they married?" and "Acis was really very young," and all hugging and patting Miss Lulie, who scowled distastefully at them all. After she'd gone in and had a squint at the body, Miss Lulie came back out and sat on the front gallery, pulling off her black gloves.

"They got pore Acis painted up like a dog's dinner," she said in a loud clear voice, which brought a great silence and round eyes in her vicinity. She just sat there studying Kosta's face, and he perked up a little at being sought out by so noteworthy an item as Miss Lulie.

I went over to speak to Allan, who was fascinated by the bandaged Perrin. They were apart from the crowd, on the sidewalk. Perrin, thoroughly conscious of the effect of his bandage, was being charming in spite of it, maybe *through* it, like X-ray, I don't know. I put a comradely arm around Allan, and looking sharp at Perrin, I said: "Don't let him trick you, Allan, he's a great one for doing that."

"Aw," said Allan, six feet of embarrassment, "he was just telling me about this Mercedes they going to sell in N'Orleans."

"Our lamented uncle not in his grave yet," sang Perrin, "and you begin again to persecute me. But for our uncle I might be dead today." He turned to Allan, and said, indicating me, "This member of the family is given to fits, you know. Ever since childhood." He sighed. "It's many the time my uncle has saved me from his hands. Now, alas, I have no protector." Poor Allan, not comprehending this

[214]

melodrama which Perrin had spoken with a perfectly straight face, looked from one to other of us.

"You see what I mean?" I said to Allan. "He just can't talk straight." Allan laughed faintly.

"Ask him," I said very meanly, and I admit it was mean, "how he got that ca-knocker on the snout."

Perrin was about to deliver himself of some words outlined in fire, but Mr. Charlie came up just then.

"Cig?"

"Thank you, sir, think I will."

"Allan?"

"Yes sir, thanks."

"Perrin can't smoke just now. Incidentally—" Mr. Charlie turned to me, "I have some mail for you." And from inside his serge coat he produced a fat envelope liberally splattered with bright-colored stamps. Postmark: *Paris, France.* The curly all-over-the-joint hand conjured with a flash the saucy face of Lola, though I noted she was attempting to imitate the penmanship of Fiffy.

"Oh, thanks a lot," I said with alacrity, snatching it right out his hand and stuffing it inside my own inner pocket.

"Oo-ee," said Mr. Charlie, withdrawing his hand and shaking it, pretending he'd been burnt. Allan sniggered.

"Must be his sugar-ration," drawled Allan.

"Don't know what 'tis." Mr. Charlie laughed. Perrin sniffed.

"Look what's been let out for the day," Mr. Charlie observed, and we turned to see the Mapey sisters—Miss Tavie and Miss Mary Cross—trundling up Government Street; I knew them at once from the tales about them, but it was a real shock seeing them in broad daylight. They were tiny, decrepit, hunched creatures, with enormous eyes, and busy hands. They were attired in fantasies of their own invention, all black, including monkey-fur capes (what else?).

But Ada and Fiffy had yet to make their appearance, though Cousin Annie was relishing grief on the gallery near Miss Lulie. Ada had upset all branches of both families by

[215]

wanting to bury Acis at Bayou Clair, in the side yard, same as Baudauer. She had insisted greatly, and had been broken down only by tears and recriminations on the part of all, in the front parlor at Miss Fiffy's. For it was to the Fifield house that Ada had flown on coming to town, refusing the hospitality of Cousin Annie. Cousin Annie, already distraught at Ada's refusal to be served chicken broth and dark flowing sympathy at her house, had called on Family Pride and Blood Strains as only she can call, in order to organize resistance to Ada's choice of burying-ground.

I'm sure Mr. Charlie didn't give a merry old moss-covered damn where Acis was put to rest; Mr. Charlie's attitude was that one bit of real estate is the same as another for such a purpose, Access and Exposure counting for naught. My father would have agreed to Ada's ideas, I think, but my mother had been brought round by Cousin Annie. That poor bobbly-head was speechless at Ada's choosing Miss Fiffy's house in preference to being "made over" at the Morelands'. Not that there was any rivalry or dislike between Fiffy and Cousin Annie, but hadn't Perrin's last stopping point in Mobile been Miss Fiffy's when he flew to New York; hadn't Miss Fiffy been on hand when Son's too-perfect nose was bashed?—now here was Ada seeking asylum with Fiff, and talking of dumping Acis in the side yard at Bayou Clair, for all the world like so much leaf-rakings. More than Cousin Annie could tolerate. How much movement, constant and expressive, her thin neck upheld!

So, for everybody, the real star of the day was Ada, who had yet to appear at the funeral parlor, and here they were 'most ready to set out for Pine Crest, for the burying. We stood there, our little group of four, puffing our cigarettes (save Perrin) and watching the little Mapey sisters being attacked by Miss Elissa Moylan as they started up the walk toward the building.

"Isn't it a shame—?" began Elissa with real enthusiasm, when she was abreast the two old sisters.

They burst into cries, all commingled, their little mouths

and hands all going at once, turning to each other for confirmation.

"Oh, we couldn't believe it—since he was a child—our papa and his papa—Point Clear—summertime—ever since—poor—wasn't old—Ada—terrible, terrible—we saw him at Dog River bridge buying shrimps—no, sister, crabs—Oh, well—such a fine boy—why, Ada, I declare—he was fifteen—such a pretty girl, even—he was the best—if she is just a little—horseman you can think of—how would you say, well-rounded—and then, when his—yes, well-rounded—papa died—course styles in beauty change—he went right into—where is Ada?—and worked so hard didn't he, sister? Oh, it's terrible—I couldn't believe it—we learned by accident. Mary Cross and I have given up reading the papers 'cause they print such unhappy things."

"How," Miss Moylan interrupted the twin torrent, "did you hear of Acis' death?"

"Why," said Miss Mary Cross, "in the paper that was wrapped around our country butter when the woman brought it in. She comes every Friday. Country butter and buttermilk: it's what keeps us alive."

"It's very good indeed," said Miss Tavie seriously, eying the crowd. "She brings us corn in season, too."

"Where is Ada? the poor child, I do want to see her. She's had such an unhappy life."

"She hasn't come yet. In fact she may not," put in Miss Moylan knowingly. "They refused to bury Acis at Bayou Clair like she wanted. Like he wanted to, they say."

"Why, who refused?" demanded Miss Tavie.

"*Everybody,*" said Miss Moylan, indicating the hopeless wickedness and folly of the world, and her intense dislike of it, by the word.

"Jesus, Joseph and Mary!" murmured Miss Tavie, genuinely frightened, and the two sisters, clutching one another, hurried into the funeral parlor.

"God, that Miss Moylan," groaned Mr. Charlie. "Why don't she go home? If she's not careful she's gonna miss that

[217]

four o'clock broom to Spring Hill. Heaven help her relatives."

"Aren't you going to read your letter?" Perrin was asking me. "There may be word for me in it."

"Let him read his letter when he wants to," said Mr. Charlie, then he went to Kosta who had beckoned for him. Kosta had been lassoed by the Mapey girls to escort them in for a glimpse of the remains: he called Mr. Charlie to attend Miss Lulie Stewart. A line of Stewart cousins had appeared though, two or three pretty girls in their teens, and a boy of about ten, all scared and proud of the old lady, who by now was conscious of being noticed and was taking advantage of it.

Seeing that Perrin really wanted to get rid of me, so he could go on impressing Allan, and in view of the fact that Ada had still not appeared, and that I loathe funerals—well, taking all this into consideration, I began to walk slowly around the corner of the funeral home, past the side entrance and out of view of the festive crowd in front. Behind the funeral parlor on the side street are old brick stables giving on a little court, now weedy and empty. I turned in there, and sighing a deep sigh of relief at being alone, pulled out Lola's letter and looked at it, scowling in the bright sunshine. In the corner was scrawled *42 rue de Tournon, Paris, 6eme,* and this looked more familiar to me than the line above: *Laura Moreland.* Laura Moreland! But no, only Lola, and evermore to be so! I tore it open impatiently, and pulled out the letter, spilling some snapshots onto the sandy cobbles. I retrieved them hastily, wiping them carefully with my handkerchief. Oh, Lola, the silliest of all—there she was, her hair in ducktail curls all over her head, perched on a stone balustrade in some kind of a park. She was in a dark coat, her legs delicious in nylon stockings. It was a fine sight to see her grinning her sassy smile for the Brownie. Lola doesn't care if it's a shoebox with a roll of film in it, or Cecil B. with cameras on wheels—either way she gives her all. Moistens her lips and turns her good profile. I smiled to myself, studying those snaps of Miss Personality. The others were of Lola and some foreign-looking boy, and a washed-out blond girl.

My dear country cousin, is how she began, that flip thing. *I guess it's too much to ask to ever expect a letter from U. U are the world's worst correspondent. Where are U now? I am in Paris as any fool knows that keeps up with the world. I finished school in Switzerland, or as much as I wanted. One sight of Paris was eeeeeeeenough for me. Daddy is easy, but I have my doubts about Mother. See if you can't build up the beauties and virtues of Paris if and when you see her. I'm writing to Miss Fiffy to do what she can. And I'm working on a pip of a letter designed to reduce Mother to tears. When I read it, I almost cry myself. The theme is why every young girl should have a year in Paris. Every young girl, that is, named Laura Moreland! Honest, its just indescribable! I mean, it really is! It's like Mobile and New Orleans only very much more so. I live near the Luxembourg Garden, that's where we snapped these. The others are Angus and Betty Bergeron from Baton Rouge, they're a perfectly precious couple and we go around together. Met them in Lucerne, and they got me my hotel room in Paris. When will you write the real dirt on what happened to U and Perrin and Philine, that bitch, in New York? Well, like say in the army, up your gigi, haw, haw, haw. Scarcely yours, The Lady Laura Moreland.*

P.S. Do you know that I went in the Sainte-Chapelle and sat down in all those lovely colors and thought about you for one solid hour. I don't want to give anybody a turn, but you know I think I may turn out to have a soul. A Soul. Anyway, meanness, I thought about you for an hour. And you're so impossible. You do make me so mad! Anyway, please, write me. Love, Lola.

After that I just stood there smiling a double-barreled smile: one smile on my lips and one inside me. Then I carefully refolded the letter and put it away. The snapshots I put in a little compartment of my wallet. I stood there a second longer, and then the present crashed in on me, and I didn't know how long I'd been away from the crowd in front, so I hurried back. But everybody was in the same position, so I supposed I'd been away only a minute or two.

"Soon as Uncle Acis is lowered into the loam, I'll make a bee-line to the Bluebird, for I intend to get thoroughly plastered. It's a kind of obligation to Uncle Acis. Why don't you come, too?" That was Perrin, speaking to Allan, who was flattered at such an invitation from an elder, especially one who bore battle wounds and the enigmatically veiled visage. Allan smiled broadly.

"Oh, gosh, I'd like to, Perrin, but I reckon I may have to drive Aunt Lulie home. I dunno, though. The folks are all in town: I may be free. Could I let you know?"

"Hell, just come on the Bluebird."

"Okay, swell."

"Am I not invited to this binge?" I inquired very pleasantly.

"Why not?" said Perrin offhandedly, meaning *not under any circumstances.*

"Oh, I can't anyway, but wish I could. I'm ready for a real twister."

He studied me carefully. "Was it such a good letter, to restore your spirits so?"

"Yes, a real good letter. I'm glad to hear from that girl."

"Hmmm," said Perrin. "Let me read it!"

"Hell no, it's personal."

"Even to me?" Perrin smiled insinuatingly. I ignored this.

"You kids have a good time tonight," I said to them. Then I tugged at Allan's arm, and pointed at Perrin's left foot. "Watch out for that, Allan."

Puzzled, he looked down, then back at me. "What, what?"

"That left foot there," I said in mock surprise. "You haven't noticed it's cleft?"

"That's nothing, Cousin." Perrin smiled, amused at

[220]

Allan's confusion. "They're both cleft, and if you like I'll show you my little pointed tail." We grinned at each other, or rather bared our teeth, and who knows where this conversation might have led if just then Miss Fiffy's old car hadn't pulled up, and out came in succession Fern, who opened the back door to help out Fiffy, most unfamiliar in black with a white necklet, then Ada pale and expressionless, her face shadowed by a wide-brimmed black hat.

The crowd that had waited outside for the spectacle was not disappointed. The sense of theatre was stronger than ever when the new arrivals pushed toward the door. In studying the faces of the people watching Ada's entrance (watchers watched) I drew a sudden breath to see towering above the crowd Ione the Tiger Woman, all in black save for a purple beret nestling in her impressive curls, like an emu egg half-buried in desert sands. Her eyes were red from weeping. The older pig-faced woman I remembered from the Bluebird was with Ione and looked rather ill at ease.

"Look!" I cried to Perrin. "It's the Tiger Woman."

"Yes," mused he. "She who was almost our Aunt Ione. Oh, I don't think Uncle Acis would have married her, but you can't tell."

"Why what do you mean?" I glared at him, knowing perfectly well what he meant and remembering those snapshots at Bayou Clair.

"She was Uncle Acis' mistress longer time than Ada Mary was his wife."

Ione, Acis, and Kosta, I saw them sitting on the wharf together, a vision that flashed through my mind and vanished. I was about to say something to Perrin, but Cousin Annie came took his arm and yanked him away.

Miss Elissa Moylan was darting right toward Ada, planning to take the arm not guided by Miss Fiffy, to "assist" "poor" Ada up the stairs and catch a little glory from the star of the show. Happily Mr. Charlie stopped Miss Moylan by getting there first and mumbling something to Ada. Miss Lulie had gotten herself to the door, and when Ada stopped

[221]

to kiss the old mummy, the old mummy said something to Ada, patting her cheek. Ada nodded affirmatively in reply, and the rest of the mob began to pour into the funeral parlor. The organ was droning away; I began to have a terrible ache and hollowness.

Inside, I was just sliding into a row of chairs about three or four back from the front, where Kosta had piloted Miss Lulie, when Miss Fiffy cast a sharp glance about, saw me, and signaled in her almost unnoticeable wigwag that I must come instantly to Ada. A flick of the eyebrow, a droop of the lid, and I knew what she meant and joined them. Ada turned nervously and saw me. "Stay by me," she pleaded. She implored with her eyes, saying wordlessly, "All this. Oh my God, all this!" I patted her arm as we turned to see the minister come into the yellow-lit room. The smell of tuberoses was so strong I could have vomited. For me, the smell of death is the smell of tuberoses.

After all the dreary ceremony and the silent drive back from Pine Crest we took ourselves to Miss Fiffy's house where after sherry in the parlor we went back and sat down to a fine supper: Fern, Tony, and the tearful Modena (unaccustomed to town, and to death) had created marvels to perk up all the moody personages. There were, besides Ada, Miss Fiffy and me, my folks, and Kosta. After her coffee Ada excused herself and went to her room, Kosta left shortly after. Miss Fiffy and my folks and I visited together for a while. They made me promise to come home for Thanksgiving which was then only a matter of weeks away. My father said it was my part to help Ada with any problems over the estate.

"There shouldn't be too many problems, actually," said my mother. "Acis was fond of doing things in his own way, heaven knows, but I'm sure he put all his papers in order. Who was his lawyer?"

"Bobby Craven, of course," replied my father. "It was Acis got this boy his job."

"That he left so soon thereafter," sighed my mother. "And what are your plans now, pray?"

[222]

"Oh," put in Fiffy airily, "we'll need him here for a while you know: Ada certainly for the farm as well as red tape: me, for legal and extra-legal advice of all sorts."

"Oh?" said my mother; I think she was impressed.

Way it turned out, Ada insisted that Kosta and Fiffy and I should stay on at Bayou Clair for a while longer. There was a world of papers and petty complications, more than anyone had anticipated, to be cleared up, and the requests and demands of unnumbered cousins to consider: everyone must have a "reminder" of Acis. We agreed that Ada couldn't be down there alone, so all agreed to take up our stay at the Bayou.

The ghost of Acis came tumbling everywhere out of desk and dresser drawers, dancing out of closets, popping up in unexpected places. A pocket mystery with a hairpin for bookmark discovered all waterstained on the end of the porch between two night-blooming cerei. His fishing tackle in disorder in a pantry drawer. Magazines and seed catalogues arriving by mail, all bearing neat typed labels addressed to Acis. Old Man Something-or-Other coming from Cedar Point to beg cuttings from Acis of certain camellias, unaware of his death.

The grim ache in my chest whenever I thought of him persisted and deepened: I felt a great failure in not having made him know, at some point, at some moment, by the smallest of gestures or a single word, the extent of my affection for him. Sometimes I think the regrets for *mights* and *ifs* are stronger feelings than passion at its fieriest. For passion has one direction, whereas those regrets are double-edged, and swing like pendulums between the regretful moving forward in time and the regretted disappearing into time past, but changing form and dimension constantly.

Kosta was busy doing some paintings of the house for Ada. She wanted a view of the front of the house looking up from the pavilion on the pier, another of the house seen from the

[223]

gate, with a gleam of water in one corner of the picture. So Kosta set himself busily to work. He had produced a great dingy canvas sketching-umbrella, and sat under it on the lawn, with his palette on an apple crate, other equipment scattered about him on the grass. Modena was fascinated by this activity, and before she departed to visit her relatives at Grand Bay, spent all morning running down with Cokes, or observations, or beguiling smiles, to view him working away.

"Oh, Mr. Kosta paints grand" was her summing-up.

Fiff, unexpectedly, was out of sorts. She was having some kind of imbroglio by mail with her relatives in New Orleans over a family problem, and was profoundly affected by Acis' death besides. For a week she scarcely left her room, save for meals.

Ada—well, Ada disappeared. She was up early like always, before anyone else. She'd work with me on sorting out this or that of Acis' papers, very uninterestedly, leaving all decisions to me, for about an hour every day. Then she'd put on her sunhat, and taking up her little straw basket from the back porch, she'd disappear. She had remained in a kind of private daze ever since Acis' death. She conversed, she ate, she listened politely, but she was far away. Her color had not returned to her face. So my only conversational companion was Kosta, the horny old devil. I'd go and sit with him while he painted.

"That's the bluest cedar I ever saw," he said.

"Blue?" I questioned, staring at it.

"Yes, blue. Look how blue it is."

"But it's not a real *blue* blue," I replied knowingly, thinking of Miss Fiffy's cornflowers. He laughed.

"Blue enough. Like me. God only knows how blue I am."

"Are you blue?" I inquired, finding it unbelievable.

"Wouldn't you be?" he asked, dabbing on strokes of dark green. "Everybody I love is dying off round here."

"Everybody?"

[224]

"First Baudauer . . . then Acis."

"Well," I crowed, "you still got me and Ada and Miss Fiffy."

He looked at me. "Hmmm," he said. "And a tasty morsel you are, too. But I don't have you. Nor Ada nor Netta."

"What'd'ye want," I teased. "Egg in your beer?"

He sighed. "I guess what I need is a trip to Europe. I haven't been there since 'fore the war. I'm 'bout ready to go over and recharge my batteries. I speak artistically, of course."

"Maybe you'll see Lola," I mused, smiling at the thought of that flippant individual.

"I'll see more than that," he muttered, his tongue in one corner of his mouth as he concentrated on a precise stroke or two. "You know what I wanta do? I want to buy a barge and travel down the Seine and those other rivers till I come out in the Mediterranean. I'll take Modena along for cook, provided she'll wear the costumes I design for her. I'll have Lulie for mascot, and I'll take Netta along to sit in the prow in a kind of picture hat, scattering flowers on the water. Then let's see, oh yes, I'll have a kind of throne for me, very Roman donchuknow (naturally I'll wear loosely-draped specially-woven white wool, like Raymond Duncan) and sitting on the floor either side of me I'll have two specially selected Princeton boys to fan me with fans like Cleopatra and the Pope always have. I say Princeton boys, 'cause they have the best crew cuts. There I'll sit, leaning back in my throne, rubbing their fubsy heads while the Loire valley slides past. Have you ever rubbed a really good Princeton crew cut?"

"No!"

"Try it sometime; it's a sensational pleasure. Let's see, well, I'll have Ada making the music, naturally. Then . . . you . . ."

"What about me?" I asked, fearing to know. "What'll I be doing?"

"You'll be dancing before me, dressed only in one well-placed pearl, I mean the navel. A baroque pearl."

"Gosh," I cried blushing in spite of myself at the idea of me flopping about publicly like that. "It'd take years of lessons 'fore I could do that."

"Oh, I don't know," he said, plying the paint again. The cedars were taking shape on the canvas. Then he turned his other grin, the shy one, toward me. "Wanta see something cute?" he asked.

"Sure," I answered dubiously.

"Look right there," he said, pointing to a clump of shrubbery in the painting. I looked. I thought it was fine, but neither better nor worse than the rest. I was just about to say so, when I saw the point: one half of the closest bush in the view, if you squinted a certain way, was painted as a green poodle sitting on its haunches regarding the spectator. *Baudauer!* Two dots of shadow made his eyes, and a frond of spiraea made his tail extending beyond the edge of the bush. Carefully looking over the rest of the finished portions of the picture, I found another green poodle neatly balancing the first, over in the other half of the picture. Baudauer again! While in the puffy clouds painted on a china-blue sky (here come more Baudauers) I found two white poodles turning somersaults. They were marvelously done. I'm sure you could have looked at the painting many a year and not seen if they weren't drawn to your attention. It was a simple case of *How many poodle dogs can you find in this picture?* I laughed.

"Kosta, Kosta!" I cried. "You are sure enough one obsessed fellow: two things, and they both start with P!"

He laughed too, the silly, and went on painting.

For about a fortnight, we had a strange situation. Ada became Acis' ghost. Yes. Slowly she began to read the seed catalogues he read, which never before had concerned her. She even took to writing at that big rolltop desk that she'd always claimed to hate so. She took up all of Acis' private fads, like insisting on the plate with a partridge painted on it for her toast and honey in the morning; utilizing expressions and phrases typical of him; aping his reactions to things. It seemed, for that space of time, as if in understanding him exactly and recreating him faithfully she might conjure him back from the other world. But in reading his beloved Rabelais she fell to earth again: it was beyond her. She couldn't really burst into bellylaughs over the book as Acis had done all his life. Though even when she finished this curious period, she never gave up wearing his old shirts. She wore his shirts as one would a coat, over her dresses, tails flying, and her sunhat perched on her head. On Fridays, when she and Fiffy went crabbing off the pier, it was a sight to see the two of them, throwing out the bait, and plying the net.

But where Ada was taking herself the major part of the day, no one seemed to know. Fiffy, as the days passed, became more and more curious. To say nothing of me. I, however, feeling the need for the last warm sunshine of the year, had decided to finish the project of herringbone pavement around "Pan Grieving." Fiffy, finding the house empty, what with Ada vanished and Kosta busy painting, came with a deck chair to sit and watch, sometimes reading to me from whatever she was currently enthusiastic over. Even Lizzie, foolish and frolicsome, found the house oppressive, and would be on constant safari in the hedge or flower beds, busy at some game of make-believe tiger that she played.

"What are your plans?" Fiffy asked idly.

"Don't have any, what are yours?"

"Oh, I have lots I guess. Acis' passing made me realize that the bird is on the wing, so to speak. My bird. Incidentally, I had a letter from Philine. She asked for news of you."

"What's she up to?"

"That child makes me impatient," snorted Fiff. "She's studying at the Art Students League a little I guess, but not seriously. Her folks are fed up with her gallivantings, want

[227]

her to come home for once and for all. Do you know she's never really written me a why or a wherefore for her skipping off with Perrin. What do you think of that?"

"Well, that's not very pretty," I said thoughtfully.

"And then some," said Fiffy, nodding adamantly.

"What else she say? beside studying at the Art Students League?"

"Nothing, really. What makes me mad is that she's very careful to write in such a way that you can't read between the lines. That's the worst of all!"

"I agree," I told that lady.

"I begin to get really annoyed at the girl. But then you know I could never really care for most female creatures. I prefer males of all ages."

"A lady like you," I framed compliment, "wouldn't ever have to worry for lack of male company." Then I went to get more bricks.

"You're a flatterer and a born gallant," she told me when I returned. "But how will you finish your days: the witty bachelor or the father of a family?"

"Search me, lady," I said.

"Your vagueness is refreshing. I'm worn out with these cutters and dryers who already have their lives mapped out when they're six years old. It's unnatural and *should* be illegal. *Eclatez* with the fireworks and blossom with the rose, that's *my* message to the numbered and cubbyholed. Take Elissa Moylan—if you could see her engagement calendar and neat monthly budget book, you'd die in your tracks. *Die!* Elissa always knows exactly where she is. She knows what date it is, the correct time, she knows where she was an hour ago and where she will be in another hour. She knows who came to see her yesterday and who's coming tomorrow; what bills are due the end of the month, and how much she spent for birdseed in the past year. She knows all but two things: who Elissa Moylan is, and why Elissa Moylan is. Just to show you how much it's against nature: look at her yard! Grass won't grow there."

[228]

"From what I know of Elissa," I remarked, "she prefers things dead or dying, so as to furnish topics of conversation."

"Don't you see, that's why she's such a terrifying gossip. She hates things that are not strictly on schedule and arranged in advance and that's just what life never never is. She hates *life,* but she's avid for news of its movements, 'cause she has that hope in her heart to gain control of it somehow. Lop its ears and tie it to a tree! Oh, she's a case."

"Go way, Lizzie," I growled. She was trying to help.

"Give me my idiot child," said Fiffy, emptying her lap of books. "Just pass her to me."

So with much exposition of opinion by Fiffy and many an impudent sortie by Lizzie, I came finally to finish the paving, and we walked about and admired it.

"Needs some kind of edging; something very dark green," observed Fiff.

"Beer bottles," I suggested. "We could empty them first."

One morning I decided I'd just follow along after Miss Ada when she went moseying out of the house, switching through the shrubbery to her own private Smuggler's Den she'd established somewhere out of reach. When I saw Ada's hat amongst the leaves, moving slyly toward the Bayou, I followed. The house and gardens are built on a little rise of land which slopes gently and almost imperceptibly toward the Bayou; on your right hand as you face the water, the front yard, beyond the edging of satsuma and bamboo, sharply declines for a few yards then flattens out like a lower terrace which after a while gives on to a marshy patch and the little meandering stream, too small to be honored with the name of creek, but which Acis' mother had christened Flycatcher Creek because of the multitudes of sarracenias which grow along its marshy shores—both the reds and the yellows. All this portion of the property is rather open, having only a few cypresses and green bay trees, yet it is hidden, by the shrubberies edging the yard, from the house.

In years past there had been a footpath threading this

[229]

section to a *passerelle* across the narrow dark water. Once across, one followed a well-trod path through woods and fenced fields, finally strolled along the Bayou to Revenue Point. When we were children, the little stream itself had been the end and object of the expedition, for who would venture on through unknown ways to the rather forbidding grove of oaks that was Revenue Point when this miniature river and its banks supplied minnows, water moccasins, road runners, marsh hens, and an occasional green turtle? But now, it all remained unvisited, for the *passerelle* had disappeared completely in a hurricane. There had been a rustic gazebo dreamed up by Acis and Jenkins the gardener, built of driftwood and odds and ends of old signboards, long the haunt of Acis' mother in the summers of the past. It had given up the ghost in that same hurricane, falling in a crumpled heap. "My gazebo just went back to being raw materials," Acis' mother is supposed to have said sadly, on first viewing the wreckage. It was still there, a pile of rotting wood totally hidden by blackberry briars, making a hummock of greenery in that low open spot.

Ada seemed heading toward that point when I began trailing her, but when I reached the clump of bushes through which she'd disappeared she might as well have flown straight up into the sky. She was certainly nowhere in sight. I studied the fringy grasses, knee high, now turning a light coppery brown, hoping to see some sign of her passage. But nothing was there. I looked in every direction, puzzled. I could command a wide view, and nowhere—either along the Bayou (illogical, there was no foothold in those rushes and oozy mud) nor Flycatcher Creek—could I see the slightest sign of life.

Suddenly a distant movement caught my eye. I turned my face, and saw Ada a considerable distance beyond the stream, picking her way delicately through thickets of elderberry and willow oak. Only her sunhat and blue cotton sleeve were visible as she slowly made her path. How had she crossed the stream? It was too deep to wade, too wide to jump.

[230]

"Hey, Ada!" I reared and she turned, startled. But then she only nodded very gravely, ducked back of the branch she was holding out of her way, and vanished again, leaving me feeling pretty stupid.

"I think she must take the little rowboat," I said to Fiffy, as we finished breakfast one morning.

"Well, between you and me and the gatepost," confided Fiff, "all that moping around by herself makes me nervous. It's a little too Lady of Shalott for me."

"I tried to follow her, but she's just too sly."

"Humph!" said Fiffy.

"But she'll be all right. She just has to get a-holt of herself in her own way, that's all."

"I guess so. Anyway, I'm just as glad she's out of reach for this particular moment. Same goes for Kosta. Because I want you to take a walk and a talk with me."

She announced this flatly and simply, but I knew by then that when Fiffy is flat and simple, there's a sting coming in a minute. Knowing her tricks, I didn't argue, though I wondered what she might have on her mind. But she was making her old business-as-usual face. So we pulled ourselves together and set out for a stroll. Puffing happily at our cigarettes we ambled out the gate and up the road in the direction of Terriel. When we reached the old bridge we branched off across the open fields on an auto trail, Fiffy walking in one rut, and I in the other. We stopped to pick a few Turk's cap lilies and a purplet or two; finally stopped to sit on a log for a minute. Fiffy was humming to herself, then broke off abruptly and said, "I want you to be my confessor."

"What?" I demanded, wondering what she might spring.

"You heard me very distinctly indeed. *Confessor.*"

"Anything you say."

"You think I'm joking, but I promise you faithfully I am not. It's not that I'm going to tell you about a very serious flaw in me."

[231]

"I think you must be flawless; you are as far as I'm concerned."

"Ah," intoned the old lady ironically. "But there you have it; what I'm going to tell you about is something where you were not at all concerned. You hadn't yet shown yourself on the scene."

For an instant I thought she meant she was going to tell me something that had happened before I was born, and began to think about the old wedding invitation that I'd seen in that cache in the library. She was silent for a few seconds, studying her nosegay. Then she lifted her tously head, and smiled a little sadly. Fixing me with a glance, she said:

"Did you know that I am a murderess?"

I came within an ace of making some inane joke, but her face showed me she was perfectly serious. It was no gag; I sat speechless.

"*Did* you?" she insisted.

"No, ma'am, I certainly didn't."

"Come on, let's walk, I can tell you better moving." She was already standing, I jumped up, she turned and started across the field again. I followed. When I came abreast, she looked shyly toward me, and said: "Just shows you can't ever tell, doesn't it? Well, I am indeed a murderess. The death of Baudauer is heavy on my conscience."

"Baudauer!"

"Yes, Baudauer—the lamented, the sainted, the eternal."

"But how—?"

"By omission, not by commission. I love him, too, though not so much as Kosta did—does. I could have saved him, I think."

My head was reeling by then, as you can imagine, and each of Fiff's comments qualified so quickly what she'd said before that I scarce knew where I was.

"Lady, you sure know how to keep people jostled up." I grinned. "I'm waiting to hear that you've invented an invisible can-opener, and solved the problem of perpetual motion."

"Can't you be serious?" she said. "You're usually too serious, now when I want you to be, you're all frivolity. But perpetual motion is no problem: it's *stopping* perpetual motion that's a problem, that's what nobody has invented. As for the invisible can-opener I don't know. But enough of gaff, you're not a very serious confessor, I must say."

"I'm sorry," I said gently. "I'll behave. Go ahead."

"I've told you—I'm responsible for Baudauer's death. It's the only cruel thing I've ever done. I except humans, 'cause I've never felt it incumbent on me to be anything *but* cruel to hypocrites and morons."

"You said . . ."

"Do you remember when you first came to my house, when you were looking for a place to stay?"

"Yes?"

"I told you then my house was haunted, and it *was*. Only all that snapping and creaking I heard at night was not human: I thought I heard Baudauer's toenails clicking on the floor of the halls, and running up and downstairs all night. I'd have taken any living creature into the household at that point—you can imagine my joy when you appeared: of known origins as well as quite imperturbable. You were my agent of exorcism, and without knowing it, gained my undying gratitude as well as my affection."

"I must say, Miss Fiffy," I told her honestly, "that I never met a less haunted-looking lady than you, when I first came that day at noontime."

"*Haunted-looking?* In more ways than you could guess, young man. No matter my appearance, I'm the most haunted lady in Mobile County. There's not one thing about me not haunted. Sometimes I go in my parlor and over each chair see the thousand ghosts of the people who sat in it, and I'm here to tell you that the ghosts of their remarks heard concurrently make a pretty squeak and splutter in my poor tired ears. Oh, yes, I'm *really* haunted, and mighty proud of

[233]

it, thank you. After all, it took a lifetime of ceaseless activity, let alone constant expression of opinion, to *achieve* such a retinue of phantoms. Every time I look down at the floor, I see I'm followed by the ghosts of every pair of dancing slippers I ever wore thin, and every time I comb my hair I think of how many tortoise-shell combs have lost their teeth over me. It's a humbling thought, though complimentary, too. Think if the spirits of all the lemons who gave up the ghost in my tea could be assembled! Imagine Dauphin Street paved with lemons from the River to Termite Hall!"

Well the idea of Dauphin Street paved with lemons sounded pretty bumpy to me, even if brightly-colored, and I could see Miss Fiffy was so relieved to have admitted some vague guilt over Baudauer (whatever it was) that she was capable of becoming giddy in two minutes flat, so I tried to steer our talk back to its main track.

"About Baudauer . . ." I began, but she dropped from the sky right away, and sighed.

"Besides, I'm a ghost myself. We're all ghosts of our loves, that's rewarding—of our hates, too, that's where Baudauer was the victim.

"Yes, I was responsible. Kosta was in Atlanta, and I was here with Acis and some other people, and I wouldn't go fishing with them, but stayed on the pier reading, and minding Baudauer. He was supposed to be kept away from the garbage, especially the compost heap. But Modena or somebody had left the gate back there open, and I saw Baudauer very cleverly stealing along the hedge to go back in that direction. And I let him. I knew he'd already been deathly ill over something he'd eaten there, but I let him go. That night he was sick and I didn't do a thing. I could have given him an emetic of some kind. I was paralyzed by an old anger which I thought had died years ago. But it cropped up—the spiritual equivalent of a summer boil on the rump, one might say. Something too profound to explain to anyone. Something too ingrown, too old . . . how I can explain I don't know . . . I don't really hold grudges . . . but something came over me, some meanness hidden in the bottom of my soul . . . I just stood by, and let Baudauer eat filth, let him be sick, then when Kosta came to get him the evening after, I . . . well, when I saw Kosta's face, I came out of my trance, and realized for the first time that *I'd* been *in* one. It was a gesture against Kosta, of course, not against Baudauer, who was an angel, but who was so close to human that I forgot he was an animal and had no defenses. Kosta and I were once engaged to be married, you know . . . we weren't, of course, we quarreled; we both thought we were the sun at midday. Everybody knows you can't make marry two suns or two moons: you have to have one of each otherwise you achieve a *committee,* not a marriage."

Full of pity for Fiffy and Kosta, and Baudauer as well, I said, "But, Miss Fiffy, Baudauer was *old,* maybe he really did die just from that. From being old."

"So Kosta reported. The vet is supposed to have said so. But that doesn't matter, my intention was there: Baudauer may have died of my intention alone. Animals are very sensitive to vibrations."

"Whichever way, I wouldn't worry about it now. I mean, it's past. It can't be undone."

"*It* can't," she cried succinctly, "but *I* can."

"Does Kosta know this?" I asked.

"Course not. For a terrible while, I thought all his references to the poor poodle were just a means to weave a noose around my neck, but no, he loved the beast, he grieves daily for him. And the noose is already there: *Time.*"

"First time I met Kosta, he was speaking of Baudauer," I observed.

"Does he ever speak of anything else?"

"Well, right now he speaks a great deal of Europe, and wants to go traveling."

She sighed. "It's what he needs. Then, too, he might find another poodle, though I doubt he'll ever keep an animal again."

"He is certainly busy painting poodles into every land-scape." I smiled.

"And so am I . . ." she murmured rather wistfully, but then she looked up and smiled herself, very brightly. "Oh, Kosta," she said, "he'll do anything."

Kosta finished the view of the house from the front. Ada was pleased and everybody naturally got a big kick out of the concealed poodles in the clouds and foliage. Especially Modena. Time and again she'd be studying the picture, and saying, "Sassy dawgs."

So Kosta began painting a real fantasy. Installing himself and his accoutrements on the lawn near the summerhouse, he commenced a view of the side yard. A simple picture of mimosa trees, pine trees and shrubberies. But every bush was a poodle, every point of black indicating a twig became suddenly an eye or a nose of a poodle. All the trees were swarms of poodles, the clouds were dancing poodles, and right near the fencepost in the painting, what was at first glance a little sweet olive tree, was really Baudauer himself in a plumed hat, looking right *at* the spectator. You could look at the picture as a landscape and find it rather curious, but if you looked at it searching for poodles, it was silly and a treat for sure.

Ada, regaining a little of her lost color and finding light conversation a little easier, spent a little more time with us, but the greater part of the day still found her lost to sight. I was more and more determined to know where she was hiding herself, so I hit upon the idea of going down to that wrecked gazebo and hiding there before she came sidling through the trees, hoping to see how she crossed Flycatcher Creek, and to trail her. So one morning, when I'd announced I'd walk to Terriel, I instead slipped out the gate, followed the road, came back over the fence and by detours and a million twiggy exasperations reached the mound of green, down by the water.

I had a quiet hour to myself during which I turned over all of Fiffy's scandal of Baudauer, and reached absolutely no conclusion. Then just as I'd lit a cig, I saw something blue and white trailing along at its own unconcerned gait, and here came Ada popping through the leaves. She was whistling between her teeth, some old popular jukebox ballad from a year or so before, and looking precious little like a fresh widow with a complicated grief. She looked to me like nothing in the world but plump Ada Mary Stewart in a beat-up sunhat out having a stroll for herself on a sunny day. She was carrying a digging fork and a net bag.

She traipsed along, scowling at branches she had to bend aside for her passage. Finally she stopped dead still, ceased her barely audible whistling, and turned and looked back toward the house attentively. I came all over grins, 'cause I knew she was looking to see if I was following her like before, and I got a big bang out of sitting there knowing that for the moment she was following me.

She stayed motionless a long moment, looking back and listening, then she crossed the clearing—I lay low in grasses then—and reached the streamside. Well, she'll have to fly or swim now, I told myself. But no, unhurriedly moving on the footpath, she started back upstream. Fascinated, I saw her gingerly tread a single pine trunk that lay across the stream, her adorable feet tapping and sliding along the rough bark of the pine, her shoes held fastidiously high in her hand. I found the spectacle irresistible: here she was, lately widowed, object of great curiosity to the world, regarded by many as Miss Enigma herself, and what doing? Why, dancing a dignified monkey sarabande in midair over Flycatcher Creek. But now I knew her destination and let her get ahead. She was bound surely for Revenue Point.

When she'd long since disappeared, I crossed myself, went through the piney woods, then strolled leisurely across Tommy Cotten's vegetable patches, past his house, then into an open grove that gave on to the sandy shore. I could hear the cries of children and dogs somewhere in the trees.

Revenue Point is a high spit of land, not quite an island—sometimes, in a rainy spring, it becomes a genuine island. The Bayou winds along one side of it in a gentle curve, receiving the waters of Temboury Creek which edges the north side. In other directions the Point is surrounded by stretches of marsh grass, dotted with occasional willow oaks. Along the Bayou itself is a kind of sandy causeway stretching from where Cotten's acreage ends just to the low clay bluffs of the Point.

When I reached these bluffs, I decided to follow the water edge around as far as I could, and come up from the Bayou side. I did so with some difficulty, but at last, puffing, I reached the top, and immediately saw at a distance Ada's blue and white. So I stood behind an oak until I caught my breath.

The Point is like a large natural pavilion, with a nice view of Bayou Clair in both directions, and of Temboury Creek inland for about a mile. There are eight magnificent live oaks, lots of pine, two or three magnolias, a scattering of persimmons, hollies and sweet-gum saplings. All of these trees have their share of Spanish moss hanging in wisps and supple banners. In some lights it seems mauve, in others a faded green; if you ask anybody its color, he'll say gray. It catches light and refuses to give it back—even in the most dazzling sun this moss is muted, soft, of indefinable edges. If you lie under an oak and look straight up into these soft tatters and see them moving very subtly, some in counter-motion to others, borne on the elfin shifts of air, you begin to think after a moment you are bending over a clear pool and watching the drowsy sway of sea grasses.

This grove is haunted. So high, so open, so grand, so utterly silent, and somehow so disturbing. They used to say that the ghosts of Spanish sailors and men-at-arms ambushed by the Indians could be seen sitting in a circle here on moonlight nights. Old Man Cotten (Tommy's father) claimed to have seen their armor shining in the winter moonlight.

Ada, if she knew these stories of bloody deeds and blood-less night-wanderers, certainly didn't show it. You know what she was doing? She was straightening up the grove; playing house, with Revenue Point for her house. She had found all the tincans, bottles, rags, etc., left from how many hundred years of picnics; she'd made a neat pile of the burn-ables and was busy pattering around in the pine needles, whistling happily and scrabbling in the dirt. She was plant-ing something. I began to worry my way through the bushes to get a little closer. I was following along the bank, and suddenly slipped, sending a little avalanche of dirt and leaves racketing down to the water below. Ada straightened up, hearing the noise, and came a little toward me, so I stepped out of the bushes, grinning and a little embarrassed.

"Oh," she said, not a bit surprised, "I thought it was an alligator."

"How in the world could an alligator get up here?"

"Oh, *alligators*," she said vaguely. "They'll do anything." At this I burst out laughing, remembering the remark Fiffy had made about Kosta.

"And who pressed your funny-button?" she inquired. She thought I was making mock of her.

"I was thinking of something Miss Fiffy said."

"Oh."

"Whatta you planting?"

"If you must know, I'm planting jonquils. I'm making a fairy circle, and damn you to perdition if you laugh at me."

"I wouldn't laugh for anything at you planting a fairy circle. Hasn't been too many years back my Aunt Lily was taking me into the woods near Persepolis to point out such to me. I might even help you." She relented at that.

"How did you know I was up here?" she asked.

"I followed you."

"I just didn't want to talk to anybody, you know. I knew Acis so short a time, really, and I was afraid people talking might jar him out of my head. I wanted to jell that darling while I could. I loved him so much—don't say anything! I

[239]

wanted to explain to you, but don't say anything. Here, plant these."

"Well, I tell you, Ada," I joked, "you'll probably get the Good Grovekeeping award for this year, after all this." From my position in the center of the grove I could see now the extent of her labors. The clearing had been rid of fallen branches and assorted garbage, but more, several scrawny saplings had been cut down and lay to one side drying.

"My picture," she said without smiling, "is going to appear in the *Druid's Home Companion.*"

As we rested later, lazily blowing smoke into the air, we fell silent, and in that time of quiet we both became terribly conscious of each other's presence. I mean, at the same moment we both came under the spell of being alone in that haunted grove, of both being young and not to be called indifferent, so we quickly went back to work, not looking into one another's eyes. Neither said anything, neither did anything, but I know what I sensed, and I sensed that Ada's thoughts were identical. I knew, too, that I had chosen the right day to follow her. It was the day she crossed the equator between the northern hemisphere of grief and the southern—I had helped ferry her across the line. When I ushered her into the house neither Fiffy nor Kosta nor yet Fern nor Modena found it strange that I should have found her out in her hiding-place and shared a morning there with her. All noticed that Ada was "better."

The next mail brought a letter from none other than the Lady Laura Moreland of happy memory. Though for the life of me I could no longer remember some of her expressions exactly. The silly child, I found myself desiring greatly to see her.

I couldn't believe Mother's letter when I got it, she said. *I guess I never will believe it. Uncle Acis was so young! and there's no earthly reason why he should be dead. I'd just come back from Chartres with Angus and Betty Bergeron when I received the letter, then I had this beautiful letter from Miss Fifield giving some of the details. Oh, if I could write a letter like that! I have about a million questions to ask, but only one to ask you. Why don't you write me? I want so much to hear from you. Uncle Acis' death made me sad, I've been in a blue foozy ever since, and I've started thinking how many miles there are between me and Mobile County. Too many! Ever since, I've been real homesick. Besides, Paris is so beautiful this time of year, beautiful sad sunshine, summer tourists gone home, and I just sit outside and think for hours at a time. That's what sidewalk cafés are for, you know, to sit and think or else to have big arguments over nothing. That's why the French are all so smart, and all so opiniated—'cause they've had good training in their cafés. My favorite is two blocks from me, called Le Tournon from the name of the street. There are lots of people who sit at tables and play cards, and others who write. They have a pretty red Irish setter who chews tin cans. I sit there all morning loving Paris and being homesick for Mobile in a beautiful black wool shawl with silk fringe that Betty lends me. I guess if I were home I could be homesick for Paris, but I couldn't sit in a sidewalk café in a black shawl, there's the difference. But it's Uncle Acis I'm upset about, and not ever having word one from you. Dear impossible cousin, please write! Lots of love, Lola.*

Naturally no one could refuse a demand like that, so I sat right down and wrote her, added messages from Ada, Fern, Modena, and naturally a page from Fiffy was enclosed. She wanted Lola to find her a kind of bon-bon she'd suddenly remembered was made in Paris.

One morning, some days after, Fern packed a picnic lunch and Ada and I set out to spend all morning and early afternoon at Revenue Point. We had saved all the piles of litter for this day and had four bonfires to tend. Smoke curled richly and plumily up to meet the hanging moss, as Ada raked her fires with a stick, I mine with a burned-off broom.

Suddenly we stopped dead still, staring across the grove at one another: the sound of a familiar put-put came from the Bayou. We rushed to the bluff and parted the leaves: it was the Reverend Macklin going downstream. I realized with a start I'd never seen him save in that boat; he might well be grown to it.

Not having seen the preacher for some weeks, we found need to greet this familiar little figure that moved in our landscape—in unison though unpremeditated we began to bark. I barked deeply; Ada yapped. He couldn't hear us, for the wind was wrong and carried our noises upstream. But we barked furiously in greeting, elated with our foolishness. Even if he'd heard the sounds he couldn't know they were for him, and even divining that could never have comprehended our salutation. We barked joyously until he was a spot in the distance then we fell down exhausted on the needles and leaves.

"Why did Acis despise him so?" I asked her. "He's kinda sad."

"Acis said he was mean to children or animals, I forget which."

"Oh."

"Oh, my," laughed Ada. She was breathless. I took her in my arms fiercely and covered her face with kisses. She pushed me away, still laughing and puffing, and scrutinized me without saying a word. I feasted my eyes on her pink flushed cheeks as she lay amongst dry leaves.

"Ada," I said passionately.

"Hmmm?"

"Why don't we get married? I mean, after a while?"

She looked at me: it was one of her days when she was gray-eyed. Then she sat up.

"Are you serious?" she said.

"Yes."

She dropped her eyelids and during a moment's pause I

[242]

watched the sun shining in her lashes. "All right," she said, looking up again. "I think it would be a very nice idea."

"I love you," I said. "I never reckoned how much till this instant."

"I love you," she said meditatively, as one might say *Today is Tuesday,* quietly and seriously in a tone of discovery. She sighed a frivolous sigh, ending in a treble note. "Isn't life silly sometimes, I mean really silly?"

"Yes," I answered, taking her tightly in my arms.

"I never intend to sleep alone in a single bed again as long as I live," she said mockingly. I kissed her sweetly and lingeringly. After that we didn't talk a great deal. But we certainly giggled a lot about nothing. That grove was neater than a paradise garden when we finished with it, and we were so tired we didn't have energy to do more than throw rocks in the water and not talk.

"I guess I've been intending to marry you," mused Ada later, as we ate our picnic, "but I didn't know it till you said it."

"I didn't know till I said it."

"Then ha-ha," she said, "we're only victims of circumstance."

I mumbled through a mouthful, and she went on.

"People—" she nodded—"that found something to talk about in my marrying Acis will have matter to talk over for years to come now. But I don't care. We'll have to wait a while, though. At least ten months, if not a year."

"I'm game," I said.

"I just wonder what your folks will say?"

"Oh, we can handle them," I replied. "What I wonder is where we'll live."

"Here," said Ada unperturbedly. "Here on the Point, in a tent."

"Hmmm," Fiffy said, studying us as though she were Miss X-Ray as we entered the house. She cocked her head, and said, "Hmmm. Tum-te-tum. I declare." In the pantry she

[243]

plucked my sleeve and pulled me into the nook of the stairs.

"What," demanded she whimsically, "is the story? Only love, likker, or fever can light up folkses' eyes like that Come you must tell me. Good news from nowhere, I presume?"

After I told her, she'd only say, "Wonderful, wonderful!" and nod her head, but she advised that it be kept secret a bit longer. Only Fern was behind the pantry door, and heard, 'cause afterward, she and Tony and Modena were full of sly smiles, mysterious references and all like that.

Kosta alone missed the undercurrent. He was so absorbed in his paintings that he'd hardly come to meals, unless somebody went out and dragged him in; so busy chattering about Europe he scarcely noticed anything or anybody. But Ada told him one day, and after ten minutes of excitement and kissing Ada and pinching her plump arms and cheeks affectionately, and teasing her scandalously, he went back to painting, and never thought more about it. Miss Fiffy, though, was as enchanted as Kosta was indifferent. Finally one day in a furious burst of enthusiasm, she said, "You know what I'm going to do?"

"Put on your best dress and your best hat, and fly to the moon, I reckon," was my sassy reply.

"Oh, rumbun, nothing like! No, I'm going to give you and Ada all my recipe books—*all* of them, including—"

"And we'll just take them," Ada said happily.

"—including my dissertation on the difference between two small onions and one large one."

At that I pretended to fall out in a dead faint on the sofa.

"I don't think Philine is real concerned to have them, you know, though I always intended she should."

"Maybe you should ask her," suggested Ada without the remotest suggestion of enthusiasm.

"No, I've decided!"

"It's a wonderful gift," said Ada, and gave Miss Fiffy a hug.

"Look, look-a-there," Fiff said pointing to me flat on the

[244]

sofa waiting to be noticed there. "Sir Hubert has dropped dead!"

Then, abruptly the last warm days were over, the callicarpas were leafless thrusts of bright berries along the fences, and chrysanthemums in riot and demonstration. The long summer, the green summer, had waned at last; nights brought a mist over the Bayou, and we all wished on a perfect silver sickle dangling over the cypress trees. Lizzie was found to be pregnant, her first, though the father's identity was a mystery.

"Don't know who might be her gent'mun fren'," joked Modena. "Mighta been a possum or mighta been a swamp cat."

"Tell me, missy," Fiffy demanded of the animal, "have you gone and played false with a polecat?"

"We haves to wait and see her babies," said Modena.

"I shouldn't be surprised," remarked Fiffy, "if that sly Pan in the garden hadn't come off his perch some moonlight night."

"Which sly Pan in the garden?" tittered Ada. "The one in terra-cotta, or the one in oils?"

"My," I said, mock-scandalized, "what you two don't think of!"

"You forget I've had the benefit of my father's rather remarkable collection of mythological works," explained Fiffy.

"Me, I'm a country girl," said Ada.

When the day came to close the house and go into town, preparatory to the Thanksgiving trip to Persepolis—Ada was going with me, to help spring our news on the family—I took a long walk around the grounds and all through the house. Scuffling along through the clearing of the brickpile, where Perrin and I had tangled, I found a single shirt button. I picked it up wonderingly, a relic of another time, another place. Perrin, no longer a nagging ghost at my elbow, had dwindled to a button in my hand. I kept the button in my hand till I reached the pavilion on the pier, then I threw it in, and watched it sink in the brownish-green Bayou. Maybe, I thought, an alligator will rise and swallow it, expecting a bon-bon.

I knew the shape and color of that summer was gone forever, and knew too that doors had opened into which I'd not looked; that I'd crossed bridges without knowing what streams I traversed. My grampa used to say the happiest people were those who *blunder* successfully through life. I had a feeling of anticipation for the events of the season now unveiling itself, comparable to the sharp hunger occasioned on a brisk wintry day. I relished the prospects of summers to come: I had reached a new plateau of experience, high, wild, and bracing. For the first time in my life I had an idea of the future, an image of time stretching before me like a field of snow awaiting the impress of my feet. Dear Ada, rosy Ada, inevitable Ada . . . her path alongside mine.

As I stood staring into the water, Kosta came strolling down to the pier, coat collar turned up, cigarette puffing.

"I'm very sad today," he said. "I see Acis everywhere, in the house, in the yard."

"With all those girls carrying on in there, I don't see how you could observe anything but a few blurred figures spinning by," I replied. He smiled wistfully.

"I don't know when I'll be *here* again," he mused. "I think I shall be sailing in December. I hope it's possible."

"Where-all will you go?"

"Italy first, naturally. Sunshine. Maybe Spain. I have friends in Malagà. But I won't go to Paris till spring: I want to arrive at the exact moment, you know."

"Sounds wonderful," I said.

"Soon, 'fore I go, you and Ada must sit for me."

That afternoon we loaded up the old Hispano with our assorted smaller luggage; the car would return for heavies. Ada and I planned to stay with Miss Fiffy in town, before starting upcountry. Our sole delay was Lizzie—she wouldn't be caught. Wouldn't answer when called, wouldn't be caught when pursued. No, would only whisk about under the trees, pretending she'd forgotten her name. Finally, Miss Fiffy threw down the animal case in disgust and told Modena to keep the pesky beast there at the Bayou. I glanced back as we drove off, and with a pang saw Modena settling the chain and padlock on the gate, between trees starting now to shed.

When, after a very pleasant trip home to Persepolis—Ada and my folks got on famously; they approved, unexpectedly, of the engagement—we returned to Mobile, we found Perrin very much the topic of conversation for one reason or another. First, when his bandages were removed, it had been immediately remarked that he was getting fat. His face had quite filled out. Cousin Annie's heavy-handed solicitude during his "convalescence" coupled with his evening beer-drinking tours of the city, had taken their toll. That was a blow for somebody who was a famous beauty (you can't say it any other way, the whole wide world knows he was *beautiful*, not just good-looking).

Miss Fiffy had the last word on that, too. When Ada and I went to have coffee with her one afternoon, we found her cleaning out old boxes in her tiny cluttered library, amongst her "gilt-edged securities." She had made a neat (if hefty) package, containing her recipe books and the celebrated dissertation, for us to lug away.

"Hasn't Perrin changed?" asked Ada.

"Oh, yes, indeed," nodded Fiffy. "Our high-flying Icarus has drowned not in the blue Aegean but in his very own fat. And after Saturday night's affair, I begin to think he may prove the town Wild Boy after all."

For Perrin had been carted off to jail, in a raid on a beer-joint brawl down near the shipyards. Everybody was a-buzz with this bit of news. It is extremely unlikely that he even had a chance to sniff the interior air of the jailhouse before Cousin Annie heard, and alerted the entire civilized world, but the fact remains he had put his foot inside the jailhouse. More, he had been *docketed*, as the saying goes.

"Philine is coming home," Fiffy went on. "I shall give her your greetings, shall I not?"

"Yes, certainly," I replied, thinking Philine was already a ghost as far as I was concerned.

Shortly after this, old Miss Lulie Stewart died, quite modestly, at home in her bed, to the general surprise, for a Brünnehilde-like immolation had long been predicted as her undoubted end. Anybody who liked to play with fire much as she did! We were all sad at her death, Ada was quiet and obviously upset, for though Miss Lulie had long been out of touch with the world in its momentary sense, she was a favorite sort of landmark.

So Ada and Allan Stewart and I made a rather muted trio as we strolled to Kosta's studio one afternoon, to tell him goodbye as he went off to the Mediterranean. It was a cold gray day, and between the weather and the climb up the stairs, we were all pink when Kosta yanked open the door and pulled us in. We had brought him a bag of chocolates from Three Georges, and he gobbled one down, and hugged us, and helped with coats, all at once. He had been bitten by the go-bug for sure, and was beside himself, ready to dance a tarantella and fly out the window.

He led us into the studio where bright fires were burning in the grates, and the tea-table was laid in the clearing. The place was exactly the same, and different, in the manner of artists' studios seen after the gap of a year. All the plaster divinities were rearranged, Baudauer in formal pose scoffed at humanity from a gold frame over the nearer mantel. There was a jug of pine boughs.

There was also, décor unexpected, Philine herself scuffling in a portfolio on the sofa, pretending not to know we'd entered. With a shock I realized she was not as beautiful as I remembered her, and that she might as well have been

[248]

another chair or mock-Turkish tabouret for all her presence meant to me.

She looked up finally, very quietly closed the portfolio, and smiled a great assassinating smile that swept over us all and came to rest on big Allan Stewart, who stood rooted.

"How do y'do?" she said to him, "I'm Philine."

She held out her hand, he took it and introduced himself. Only then did she turn to the rest of us. Inexhaustible Philine! But not for me . . .

"I don't believe you know my fiancée; Ada, this is—"

"Ada Mary and I met one Mardi Gras," quickly put in Philine.

"Hello, Philine," said Ada, very civil and proper.

"I think all manner of congratulations are in order," said Philine, looking at the two of us with the air of a school-teacher giving spelling prizes. But she as quickly subsided and placed herself on the sofa next to Allan, and turned a twenty-four-carat smile toward him. Kosta arrived just then with the tea-tray.

"Now,"—he grinned, bustling with things—"we're gonna have high tea poured from a considerable altitude."

"I invited myself," Philine murmured, "the minute Kosta told me y'all were all coming this afternoon."

"My astrologist," Kosta was saying through a cookie, "told me once that chocolate gave me coarse vibrations: I've eaten it regularly ever since."

So we munched, and stirred, and swigged, and chatted, everybody going at once. Philine, it turned out, was going to make a quick trip to New Orleans, then return to Mobile to take care of things for Kosta, and would live and paint in his studio while he was away. I don't have to tell you that Allan agreed to help her pack some paintings of Kosta's for the Atlanta show. Nor that she set a definite date and wrote it in a little notebook with a tiny gold pencil. Allan was definitely hooked. In the midst of this the bell jangled, and Kosta put down his cup, frowning slightly.

"Damn," he said, "those girls are early."

[249]

"What girls?" drawled Philine.

"From Gaspard's Landing," Kosta said quickly, as he started for the door. "The Council ladies . . . they're going to buy a painting for the new chapter house."

"The Reverend Macklin's new church," said Ada flatly, looking straight at me.

"Oh."

It was two well-rounded matrons, country ladies in impressive hats, who paraded in before tiny Kosta. There were introductions all around: they were Mrs. Madrid and Mrs. Schott. Mrs. Madrid was the older, with white hair and a face quite weatherbeaten indeed. Mrs. Schott was shy and soft-spoken. They agreed to a cup of tea, and proved cheerful company when they thawed out. But they never ceased to regard all of us with that delicately watchful air which the invincible reserves always for the mischievous. Finally Kosta led the party tactfully to the paintings stacked face against the wall.

"Hey, Lizabeth, look at this!" Mrs. Madrid cried, tumbling over a pile of Bayou la Batre scenes.

"No, you come here," rejoined Mrs. Schott, enthusiastic for one of the Balkan portraits.

"Just look at that landscape," I said very seriously to Philine, as we looked over the woman's shoulder. "Did you ever see such *chiaroscuro?*"

"Never in my life!" said Philine huskily. Mrs. Madrid studied the painting closely.

"Ooooh!" breathed Mrs. Schott, as Kosta dramatically revealed a Court portrait, whipping it around suddenly. A bejeweled brunette with great smoky eyes, circa 1910. We thought then that surely they'd buy a portrait. Her cry of alarm and pleasure was so great, we all instantly crowded around. I thought the face in the portrait familiar but couldn't place it.

"Who is she?" I asked Kosta.

"Yes, who is it?" repeated Mrs. Madrid.

"Oh, well . . ." mumbled Kosta, dusting the top of the

[250]

frame. "Don't you see . . . it's the Countess Hricky-Hruby . . . in Court dress."

"She's a good-looking character," observed Mrs. Madrid.

"Her life was very tragic," said Kosta simply.

"She's the one," questioned Philine, "that was killed by the stableboy?"

Kosta seemed to frown slightly, then looked tenderly into the eyes of the portrait. "Yes . . ."

Impressed, I followed Kosta's gaze. Talk about your rascally monkeyshines! You know who it was? Ione, the Tiger Woman, painted with black hair and no curls. I near flipped a ruby. I walked over to the landscapes, for fear I'd laugh out loud. When I had control of myself, and went back, I realized it was a long-standing joke between Kosta and Philine. Philine would ask a question, or point out a detail, and Kosta would every time affirm the unbelievable dramas that lay back of that serene sloe-eyed gaze. All those dramas were pretty damn unbelievable, too, I can tell you, but those ladies ate it up, and asked for more. It was certain they'd never buy a portrait by then, so Kosta didn't stint. There was a world of paintings of Ione—even one of Ione as a young hussar, sporting a little black moustache, and looking like racy doings on the Strüdelplatz. The eyes gave her away every time.

"The Countess' young brother Stefan," explained Kosta briefly. "He died, oh, about a year after this portrait was painted."

"By an over-dose of mascara," whispered Philine close to my ear, and I hiccuped. Ada frowned.

Those ladies dickered long, but finally chose a handsome view of Bayou Clair, all green and blue, to hang in their new chapter house. Hopefully I studied it for a poodle, but no, I couldn't find one. Moment they were gone, Ada demanded to know what there was about those portraits, and we all became a little embarrassed. After all, if she didn't know of Ione's existence . . .

[251]

"It's just that they're fakes, that's all," said Kosta, saving the day. "I painted them right here."

"And your real portraits?" asked Ada, at which Kosta turned sadly to the big one of Baudauer.

"There," he said.

"No, no, the things you did in Montenegro and all."

"Packed in neat cases; I don't want to sell them or any of Baudauer, never never never!"

Now Kosta is long gone, flown to his adored Mediterranean, from whence we've received several beautiful postcards with completely illegible messages, except we do get the fact that he's sending us an unusual present.

"I know what that will be," groaned Ada. "It'll be a violin case made from the you-know-what of an elephant. We'll just have to say it's what we've always wanted."

"Now that you describe such a thing," I mused, "I must say I'd like to see what it might be like."

"But we neither one play the violin," insisted Ada.

"We could keep something else in it," I ventured.

"Like what?"

"Well, the vases and junk we're bound to get for wedding presents."

"I wish," said Ada, "we didn't have to get married. I do wish we could just go on down to Bayou Clair and rip out the telephone, and live in sin with the gate locked. Wouldn't that be nice?"

"Then I wouldn't have given you my grandma's ring," I admonished, fondling her plump hand. She looked at it, a gold trinket set with four small sapphires.

"Oh," said she impishly, "then I guess we'll have to have the ceremony." I silenced her by covering her face with kisses.

So that's the Prologue, the story really begins now. The other day I stood in a field watching birds flying south and thinking of all that's happened since I've flown South, since I left cotton country and came down to the Gulf Coast. As I stood there in the fading light I saw Ada start across the field toward me, and I saw with a jolt that she was really almost a total stranger. I had fallen in love with Acis' Ada, with Fiffy's Ada, with summer's Ada; now I begin to find my own Ada. Perhaps love begins best as awe and curiosity then crystallizes: clumsy sand and intense heat produce the windowpane, there's your history of glassmaking.

But I know why I must be grateful, I know how I am beneficiary. I can see, for the first time clearly, how a little world took form before my eyes and played its little golden age then scattered forever. At this moment, as Ada and I make our plans for Bayou Clair, learning from Tommy Cotten how to be farmers, I often pause to smile and think of the wonder of the last year.

Could I be now so happy if I'd not been instructed and equipped by Ada, Fiffy, Kosta, Acis, Fern, Lola, even the shade of Baudauer—all these who are the visible Head Gardeners, Sweepers, Elevator Operators, the Careless Princelings and Sleepy Duennas of another and brightly plumed world that exists just out of sight on all sides? No, for they each own a bright splinter of truth, and sense its uses.

If all this had to be told in one line it'd be *How I commenced to be me,* but even if one line could *tell* it all, one line couldn't *fill in.* Besides, happily life's not that simple. Happily! Happily not that simple. So there you are, or rather . . . there I am, hand in hand with Ada.

THE END

[253]

SAM HODGES
B-4

HOWELL RAINES
Whiskey Man

JUDITH HILLMAN PATERSON
Sweet Mystery: A Book of Remembering

JAY LAMAR AND JEANIE THOMPSON, EDS.
The Remembered Gate: Memoirs by Alabama Writers

MARY WARD BROWN
Tongues of Flame

MARY WARD BROWN
It Wasn't All Dancing and Other Stories

EUGENE WALTER
The Untidy Pilgrim

Deep South Books

The University of Alabama Press

VICKI COVINGTON

Gathering Home

VICKI COVINGTON

The Last Hotel for Women

NANCI KINCAID

Crossing Blood

PAUL HEMPHILL

Leaving Birmingham: Notes of a Native Son

ROY HOFFMAN

Almost Family

HELEN NORRIS

One Day in the Life of a Born Again Loser and Other Stories

PATRICIA FOSTER

All the Lost Girls: Confessions of a Southern Daughter